# WHAT THE
# WAVES KNOW

## TAMARA
## VALENTINE

WILLIAM MORROW

*An Imprint of HarperCollinsPublishers*

WHAT THE WAVES KNOW. Copyright © 2016 by Tamara J. Valentine. All rights reserved. Printed in the United States of America. No part of this book may be used or reproduced in any manner whatsoever without written permission except in the case of brief quotations embodied in critical articles and reviews. For information address HarperCollins Publishers, 195 Broadway, New York, NY 10007.

HarperCollins books may be purchased for educational, business, or sales promotional use. For information please email the Special Markets Department at SPsales@harpercollins.com.

FIRST EDITION

*Designed by Diahann Sturge*

Library of Congress Cataloging-in-Publication Data has been applied for.

ISBN 978-0-06-241385-7

16 17 18 19 20  OV/RRD  10 9 8 7 6 5 4 3 2 1

*For all of the moon dancers among us who grace us with their ability to swim into the magic of the world—for sharing the songs we cannot hear, the fairies we cannot see, and the dream of taking flight . . . and for those who love them*

# WHAT THE

# WAVES KNOW

# CHAPTER ONE

Normal kids are afraid of the dark. Skittish, I suppose, of the way it stuffs the hollow corners of their rooms with nothingness and wraps around the day like a muzzle until the clamor of the world runs quiet. I fell in love with the night after I lost my father inside it, in love with the way it folds itself over our ugliest secrets in a black lacy veil, transforming the saddest moments of our lives into little more than broken bits of light flickering overhead. After my father disappeared, I came to imagine him floating in the velvet creases of the night, watching me move through the years. I came to embrace the utter blackness stretching its arms out, hushing the world to the scratchy *eet, deet, dee* of a cricket's song wisping through the breeze so softly you can hear the floorboards sigh.

But then, I am not normal, no matter how politely people try to argue the point. I last heard the sound of my voice eight years ago when it chased my father into the darkness. Then it was gone. And the moment that I was a kid, the real kind who skips Double-Dutch and neatly tucks teeth beneath their pillow waiting for fairies to arrive, vanished before it even fully materialized.

When I was born to Ansel and Zorrie Haywood on October 3, 1960, my parents named me Izabella Rae Haywood—Izabella for a dead grandmother I never knew; Rae for a string of light that was missing from their marriage. Put all together, I am breathing proof that for a single moment my parents were not cannibals snipping at each other's back, but one: one body wrapped around itself, one sigh let loose on the night, one author of their next chapter.

Their story began two years before my birth beneath a harvest moon, where they were dizzy with love. This according to my father. According to my mother, it was the third blood moon and food poisoning from a basket of bad clams. Given what followed, I believe her. What they did agree upon was it began in Tuckertown, Rhode Island, where seagulls outnumber people twenty to one. Really, Tuckertown isn't a town at all, just a broken-off spindle of land jutting clumsily out into the Atlantic Ocean. It does not have a market or even a school to call its own. What it does have, though, is a stall-sized post office once used as an honest-to-goodness rest stop for the pony express. And if you have your own post office, you get to call yourself a town. This is not to say the post office is the whole treasure trove of Tuckertown. There are also twenty or thirty ramshackle cottages, four docks where lobstermen haul in their traps each evening, filling the town with a marshy stink, and one billion crooked-winged osprey scavenging for carcasses. Not much, but it's where I was born and lived the first fourteen years of my life.

My parents spent the earliest of those years sorting out a nickname that fit, because there is the name God gives you and then there's the name the whole rest of the world calls you. Late in the foggy gray of October 1961, when my first birthday rolled around, Reverend Mitchell of the Talabahoo First Congregational Church poured holy water over my head, baptizing me "Izabella Rae in the name of our Father who art in heaven." But by then God was the only one still calling me that. My father who art on earth called me Belle, and my mother, Izzy.

Somewhere around my second birthday, sweetsy names gave way to ones of utility, and my full Christian name returned to me in a broken series of monosyllables, "Iz-a-bell-a Raaaaae!" flinging through the air with hatchet precision to chase me to my plate at dinnertime. This morphing continued until, finally, by my fifth birthday I answered simply to "Be" when my father caught me up in a hug, and "Iz" when my mother did not. In no less than five short years I had been whittled down to the weakest forms of "to be" in the English language. It is a fact I have spent a good amount of time considering.

Grandma Jo says, "Izabella Rae, every great story begins in its weakest form and builds upward from there."

She may be right or she may be wrong about that, but lately I have come to believe that, great or lousy, in the end we are all just the caboodle of stories we leave behind. The moment you die, all those stories tumble from their basket sticky-edged, and however they clump together, there you have it. Before you even wiggle one toe in the grave people come stand around your coffin to collect them. When I die, they will cluster beside my dead body whispering, "And that thing with her father . . . Poor soul never was quite right afterward." And that will be true.

On that day, those bunched-up stories are the only real thing left of any of us, and as fate would have it, most of mine began on October 3, as if God himself touched me on the forehead and said, "Izabella Rae Haywood, I give you life, and each year on your birthday that life will change forever."

And starting on my fifth birthday, that's exactly what happened. In truth, it began two months before, in the summer of 1965. It is one of the only moments with my father that remains whole in a bucket of bent and broken memories, and it was the day I came to know Yemaya.

That August was the kind of hot which leaves you chewing grit between your teeth, "turning us all into the devil's dust mop," Grandma Jo would say. And this particular Sunday was roasting everyone into a state of crankiness, especially my mother, who stood barefoot in the drive, hair pulled up into a loose twist with one hand wedged on the pointy tip of her hipbone. Small damp tendrils clung to her neck, making her wiltedness almost beautiful, as if the heat were melting all her sharp edges.

"I cannot believe the two of you are going to spend a day like this cooped up in a truck for three hundred miles just to go splash around in Potter's Creek. It's got to be a thousand degrees out here."

My father chuckled, throwing an extra reel of fishing line on the front seat of our old Jeep. "It's only five hundred degrees in the water. Come on, Zo!"

"She's going to miss church." My mother tilted her head at him. "And Sunday school."

"Sunday school." He chortled. "God's country is out there. He's too damn smart to waste a day like this with a bunch of stuffy old Bible-mongers! Go throw some shorts on and come splash with us. I know just where to find him!" When my father grinned dimples bore deep into his cheeks in a Robert Redford sort of way that melted the whole world into happiness, only he had darker hair and soft gray eyes that glimmered with mischief. My mother called it his get-out-of-jail-free card.

"You're impossible!" My mother dropped her hand from the crest of her hip, shaking her head with a smile. I thought, not for the first time, that my mother must be the most stunning woman in the world in my father's company.

"I try." He kissed her full on the lips until she pushed him away, clonking him gently on the head with the back of her hand.

Not knowing what to do, I busied myself with Malibu Barbie, whom I'd dressed in Ken's camouflage trousers and tall rubber boots. The ski pole I'd stolen from my Ski Queen Barbie and given her to use as a fishing rod was bent from where I'd tied a piece of thread to the tip, with a lipstick-red stiletto shoe as a hook. I sent it spinning around and around, watching the shoe fly in circles.

"Come on, Zo. Come with us."

"Ansel Jacob Haywood, you are stark raving mad if you think I am going to lock myself in that tin can in this heat." She glanced at Barbie's heel swinging in the air.

"All right, but if I do the catching, you do the cooking!" He laughed, plopping a floppy hat on my head. Two minutes later, we were spinning backward out of the drive with my mother frozen up like a statue on the pavement watching us go. Through the rear window, I could see her forehead pinch into a furrowed brow and for a second I thought she might run right after us, but she didn't and I watched her shrink to the size of a spring tick until the truck veered left down Route 95, the droopy rim of my straw hat bouncing along to "C.C. Rider" on the radio.

My father was one-eighth Narragansett Indian and seven-eighths mystery. The fact of the matter might not be important if it weren't for the Nikommo, which only descendants of the Wampanoag nation can hear. When I was little, with the wind whipping and whining at my windowpane, sending my quilt over my head until my knuckles ran white, my grandfather would dig me free from the folds of fabric with a chuckle. *It's just the Nikommo chattering to their mother, the moon.*

I had been raised with the Nikommo and knew the tiny woodland sprites of the Narragansett passed their evenings whispering to anyone who would listen, telling them where they needed to go—leading a famished hunter to a wild boar, a person lost among the fir trees back to his trail.

*It is the right of the Nikommo to guide the land; it is the right of the moon to control the tide. Close your eyes and eavesdrop. In the morning, you will tell me what they were rattling on about.*

It was no use. No matter how hard I listened, I could never make out what they were saying, where they wanted me to go. But my father heard them all the time, even if he never called them by name. The world was always chattering to him, calling to him from all four corners without notice or apology. And today, it had beckoned him three hundred miles from home to fish for salmon, although given the chance for a do-over I believe he might have thought better of it and pulled that floppy hat right off my head and sent me to the church ladies. Because I decided on our very first catch that I loved fish. I do not mean fried up with lemon rind over a campfire as he intended, but alive and swimming freely about my ankles, nipping and tickling my toes.

The epiphany struck while I was standing in Potter's Creek, sixty miles north of the New Hampshire border.

There we were, up to our underpants in water when—
*Boom!* It hit me and I understood straight down to my toes
why God spent his Sundays knee-deep in water instead of
inside some stuffy church toppling with women in dusty
hats stinky from mothballs and old Mr. Pontell snoring
from the back pew.

Dancing with the current, throngs of salmon leapt in
and out of the water like one hundred and one silver nee-
dles pulling trails of pink ribbon in their wake, stitching
a path up the rocks, shattering the surface into slivers of
mirror zipping through the water and reflecting all the
colors of the world on their backs.

"Be! Look!" My father's voice ratcheted up three deci-
bels in the way it always did when he was on a mission
nobody else in the universe understood but me. "My God,
they're beautiful. Have you ever seen anything so goddamn beautiful?" He flicked his finger across the rapids
until a thousand water pearls skittled over the face of the
creek. "Do you hear her?"

"Who, Daddy?" I reached for his hand, stumbling in
the current, but he was wading in deeper to listen and I
was afraid to follow. This was the story of us. My father
slipping away to the Nikommo and me tripping after
him—desperate not to be left behind.

"Yemaya. Do you hear her? She's calling them home."
Glancing over his right shoulder, he studied me for a
second. "You do, don't you? You hear her." The statement
bounced off the water as fact and I listened with all my

might, but just like with the Nikommo, the words he could hear were swept away in the wind and all I could hear was the *shush* of water and splash of salmon.

Giving him a nod, I teetered in the tide, trying to find solid ground as he turned back to stare at the creek. The water rushed over my toes, foamy whitecaps skating along top.

"My grandmother saw her once when she was about your age, said she was the most beautiful thing in the world. Mother of all mothers, protector of children. Long black hair, just like yours. Eyes the color of a perfect storm. Just like yours." He glanced at my face as if trying to force the pieces to fit, and for a moment I knew he didn't recognize the way they came together. It wasn't the first time I had witnessed the current at work in his eyes, tugging him one direction and then the other until he was left spinning like the foamy whitecaps at my ankles. "If you watch, really watch, just below the water where the sun sparkles off the rocks, you just may see her. And if she's in a good mood, she just might toss you one of her magic pebbles and it will bring you good luck forever." The wish pressing up against his words was hard to ignore.

He stretched a hand out to me, and I tried to go to him, I truly did, but the current swept me one direction while my father motioned me the other. Before I knew what was happening I was pulled down hard against the rock I'd been propped up on, sliding down the slippery edge. Down into the water. Sailing away with Yemaya and her million silver salmon.

I can't say how long I was under before I felt my father's hand cuff around my wrist and yank me back. "Don't let go, Be. Don't let go!" *Don't let go. Don't . . . let . . . go.*

And then we were on the stony edge of the creek bed, me hiccupping out water, my father holding my small hand in his like a robin's egg while he dabbed at the cut above my brow with his shirt.

At first I thought the blood had trickled into my eye, blurring up the world until it tottered upside down, but that wasn't it. An enormous salmon danced into the air, its chrome gills billowing out into tiny angel wings fluttering it toward the clouds in exactly the same way I imagined a person's spirit might break free of its body and soar toward heaven. Long as an arrow, it shot into the day and I swear the morning sun looped into a halo around it.

"Daddy, look!" I squealed, waving my free arm toward a ring of ripples ten feet in front of me and forgetting all about the gash over my eye. I jumped up and down, swaying to keep my balance in the absence of my father's hand. It's a sensation I have yet to grow used to.

The dimples poked in at his cheeks. He picked me up and tossed me into the air before splashing me back to the stream. Lifting his rod from its sheath, he let go a low whistle and cast it forward. The tiny yellow anchor at the tip of his line zipped through the morning and plopped into the water with a small splash. As though not a thing in the world had happened. As though I hadn't nearly died trying to bridge the distance into his world. I could not have known then that bridge may as well have been the River Styx, could not have understood that once you crossed, you could never come back alive.

"Woo-hoo! Would you have a gander at that?" My father yanked the line, reeling a large fish into the breeze so gracefully she might have still been swimming the waters of Potter's Creek.

The fish's body lurched, her eyes confused—betrayed. I realized the vision was not of an angel dancing through the day, but of a mother caught up by the jaw like a tangled marionette, and I imagined a beautiful woman with long black hair and eyes the color of a perfect storm hanging from my father's pole.

"She's stuck, Daddy. Let her go, let her go. Let go! Daddy, *help* her!" My screams did not stop until my father set the fish free, swearing at the crimson cut left by her razor scales, but it was too late. The fish swam several drunken circles before tottering to the surface on her side.

"She's just resting from the fight," my father said, sucking at the corner of his hand. Glancing at the tears wetting my face, he sighed, squatting low, and dug two chunks of amber from the mud before rinsing them in the creek. "Be, look! Yemaya Stones!" Cupping his hands, he shook the stones together before tucking one in my palm. "There. Now you are stuck with me forever." He grinned, tweaking my cheek.

Although there are plenty of others—*There is nothing scary in the night . . . If you wish a secret wish on a falling star . . . I'll never leave you . . .*—when I consider my childhood, this is the very first of my father's lies that I can uncover.

Determined not to return to my mother empty-handed—and having frightened my father off the idea of catching our own dinner entirely—we stood at Mr. Matteson's fish market that night with a hundred fish staring back at me with sad eyes. In that moment, I came to understand what it meant to be God. God was anyone strong enough to pull you straight out of your world with one good yank and powerful enough to decide whether or not to put you back in.

"Salmon?" Mr. Matteson asked.

"Haddock," my dad corrected, glancing down at me.

"You see the coverage of those protesters at the Dallas County Courthouse yesterday over those three guys indicted in that Reeb murder?" Mr. Matteson offered in the way of small talk as he wrapped the Haddock in waxed butcher paper. He was short and squat with dark hair that was retreating from his forehead with determination. "That Dr. King's started one hell of a mess down there in Selma." He shook his head slowly in the way that almost always meant *It's a damn shame*, sticking a strip of tape on the paper. "I swear, this country's falling apart under LBJ."

"Must've missed it," my father said dismissively.

"Voting rights," he sputtered. But if he felt one way or

the other about whatever he was going on about, he didn't say so.

"You want to stop at the A&W on the way home, Be?" I looked up at my father in time to catch his dimples taking shape as he threw me a wink. "You know, celebrate a great day?"

Shrugging, I let my eyes flick toward a billboard outside the window. A woman wearing a man's plaid button-down with the cuffs rolled to the elbow held up a small box that said: JELL-O—THE FIRST NO COOK EGG CUSTARD EVER! Normally, I loved the A&W stand, sitting in the car while waitresses in black tuxedo trousers with an orange stripe down the sides and matching hats hustled out to bring us root beer floats and hot dogs. My father brought me there for special celebrations, but I didn't feel like celebrating. I shook my head.

*Take not with* thy own hands that which thee has not begotten. It's written on the Sunday school wall and in the Bible, too.

"What does that mean?" I asked my mother once when she came to pick me up from the small classroom in the church loft. The distinct smell of old paper and holy dust wafted through the room.

"Don't take what isn't yours or God will punish you," she huffed, trying to stuff my mittened hand through the sleeve of my coat. I turned my eyes from the large coffee stain that had long ago bled over the blue carpet and studied Mary's sad amethyst eyes looking down from the wall—and I knew for sure she was looking at me.

Over the next several years that scripture stuck with me like a wad of stepped-on bubble gum, somehow making sense of the timbers falling away from our lives.

My father and I had stolen from God. We had snatched one of Yemaya's mothers, taken a life that wasn't ours to take, and the ghost of that fish followed me through my childhood. Sometimes it returns to me still. In a wayward dream, she stares at me with sad watery eyes tallying the details of her murder, mirrored gills searching for the cool rush of water. There is no telling what might set the memory flying into my head: a particular bounce of light in the water, the rickety old fish cart down on the docks, the recollection of what happened to my father. But the memory comes back to me clearest sitting in the stuffy pews of the Talabahoo First Congregational Church with Mary's mournful eyes looking down at me; I remember the fish and the moment Daddy and I were God.

That September my mother returned to school to finish her PhD in art history. A month later, my father decided if she was going to chase her dreams, so was he. He surrendered his position as an English professor at Brown University to become a freelance writer, and in one quick turn, our house became a series of misses: missed bedtime stories, missed jokes around the kitchen table, missed midnight strolls on the docks.

When Grandma Jo was not visiting to keep me entertained, I spent hours flopped on the floor of my father's office drawing pictures. You would think with all that time apart my parents might have a lot of catching up to do when they saw each other, but instead the space between them seemed stuffed with unspoken words and when they came back together, and those words were finally set free, it turned out there was not one single kind thing left to say.

Arguments began to crop up between them like weeds overtaking the path that connected their lives. When my father was not on his way to Columbia to find skulls of crystal, he disappeared into deep oceans of darkness and his writing.

"Where are you going?" I sat crisscross-applesauce on my parents' bed, picking at a scab on my knee.

"Manchu Picchu."

"Why?'

"To feel the ley lines." My father balled up a shirt and stuffed it into his backpack.

"Why?"

"To recharge my spirit."

"With who?"

"God."

"Can I come?" Glancing up, I cocked my head, waiting for an answer.

"Mommy won't let you." He winked at me. "Next time, okay?"

"Okay," I nodded, turning back to the television, where Lassie was leading Timmy into an abandoned mine to save a missing boy.

**Sometimes I went** with him when he won the battle over what type of outing was appropriate for a young girl, or when he didn't tell my mother. Like the time he woke me at three in the morning, sneaking me down the back staircase.

"Where are we going?"

"Shhh . . ." He tipped his finger to his lips.

"Where are we going?" I whispered, slipping out the door and reaching for his hand. I did not care if the Nikommo were friendly; the thought of tiny people in the woods gave me the heebie-jeebies.

"To swim with the moon."

"Why can't Mommy come?"

"It's just for us." He pulled something small and round from his pocket, turning it in the light of the stars, and it took me a full minute to recognize the stone from Potter's Creek. "Mommy can't hear her," he mumbled, more to the stone than me.

I wanted to go home. Staring at the inky ripples from Moonstone Beach, which my father believed poetic for the experience, with cold sand squishing between my toes, I knew I wanted to go home. Being sucked under the waves on our fishing expedition was so fresh in my mind that I could still feel the water burning up my lungs. But I didn't say so. I didn't want to ruin the magic for my father like my mother always did. I didn't want to be left behind. Just offshore, a fat moon danced on the sea, wavering with every breeze, while my father stripped down to his skivvies.

"What if there are sharks?"

"They wouldn't dare bother a moon dancer," he said, as though that were a real thing. "Come on." He laughed, running into the dark water and leaving me alone with the Nikommo.

I shook my head, willing him to come back, willing him to choose me over the tide pulling him away. But he couldn't see and I knew that my grandfather was right. The current was not his to command—that was the right of the moon.

"Come on, Be. Come dance with the moon!"

Slipping off my nightshirt, I remember this. . . . I remember thinking I would rather drown in the arms of the moon with my father than be left alone, would rather die chasing the light with him than live in the darkness as he swam away.

"This is our secret," he explained. "Secrets lose their magic if you give them away, so you can't tell Mommy, okay?" Hooking his little finger around mine, he gave it a squeeze and I squeezed back in a pinky promise. The truth is, I wouldn't have told anyways. She wouldn't have understood what it meant to waltz with the moon.

When the first fingers of dawn took hold of the horizon, we collapsed on the beach half naked and pulled a blanket around our shoulders, watching as the morning light snuffed out the stars. And that is where a woman hunting sea glass found us asleep several hours later.

I don't recall my mother yelling. In fact, I don't recall her uttering a single word. She just looked at him with eyes bloodshot and puffed up like marshmallows over the campfire, wrapped me tight in a fresh blanket, and marched me upstairs to dress in dry clothes.

Sometimes I didn't get to go when my mother won, or caught us. Sometimes he vanished for weeks at a time into the wind. I didn't know where he was, but I knew where he was going: God's country. And I knew why: the Nikommo were calling.

When he was home, he would disappear into silence at his desk for days then fox-trot into the living room and dance my mother around like a soldier on leave, as if he'd been right there spinning her dizzy all along. In his defense, with his eyes buried deep in his typewriter and his back to the outside world, he could not possibly have seen me plopped on the floor with my crayons by his study door. He could not count the times my mother hesitated at the landing, letting her eyes linger on his turned back over a basket of laundry or a stack of files. He could not see the question forming on her lips, wondering how to shatter the space between them, or realized how the tapping of his typewriter so thoroughly drowned out the soft brush of her fingertips running over their wedding photo as she climbed the stairs to an empty bedroom. He was either intoxicated by the light or bogged deep in the darkness—that's what she would say—sunk into a story that promised to sail him away from his own.

I don't like to say so, but the truth is, I blamed her—for keeping me from him, for not breaking down and crossing the threshold, for not calling him back like she meant it. And the more he wrote, the more that darkness began to swallow us all, until by the time my sixth birthday rolled around, that emptiness had taken us over with tumor-like persistence.

# CHAPTER TWO

This is what the *Oxford Dictionary* says about departures. "*Departure:* (1) the act or an instance of departing; (2) death; (3) setting out on a new course; (4) divergence. *To depart:* (1) a starting point."

This is what I say. Departing is when all the tiny pieces that make you whole spring away from you like a big fat touch-me-not and get lost in the grass beyond any hope of coming back together. It is the very moment when all your stories tumble from you, and you are reduced again to the weakest form of "to be" in the universe, leaving nothing to do but begin again.

There is nothing left of the evening of October 3, 1966, except a cluster of broken bits of memory. I try to gather them up and put them together like puzzle pieces, but they are lacking glue for the edges to hold and too many pieces have gone missing.

Determined to spend my birthday together as a family

and leave work behind, my mother had raced daylight to herd us onto the last ferry across the bay to Tillings Island, sending the three of us puffing and laughing up the ramp. For one solid second, my father's eyes had sparkled when he snatched our hands up in his, the dimples tweaking the centers of his cheeks, just the way they do in my memory. I wedged myself between their hips like a bulletproof shield so my mother couldn't spoil it and took my first real breath when we got to my grandma Haywood's cottage before dusk—but that is where things start to get fuzzy.

Here are the things I do remember:

One. Fall roses tumbling over the cottages of Tillings Island, where the streets do not have names, but the houses do.

Two. Fireflies skittling through the evening in golden slivers flickering on, off, on. . . .

Three. Praying. With my parents spending all their time quarreling over everything from money to the proper direction for toilet tissue to unroll, I was wasting all my time rendering up prayers to make them stop and receiving not a single morsel in the form of an answer, leading me to wonder about all those hours spent in Sunday school. My teacher had described hell with its fiery mountains as a place tucked deep in the bowels of the universe. During these last months, I came to know for a fact that she was wrong. Hell was right here—smack-dab in your living room, or backyard, or any other place where your parents chewed each other's face off three times a day right in front of you.

Four. Stairs. I know there were stairs, because sometime around sunset a thick fog of silence began slinking up them in the way it did every time my parents went to war. This was my birthday night and their anger was floating up to me like a swirl of smoke, welling up inside me until it threatened to pop me into a million tiny bits. I tried to hold it back; I truly did, spending a good hour pacing back and forth between the door and my bed, trying to drain the fury out of me. But, as it turns out, anger is more like a water balloon than a drain.

Five—and this is the big one. The stupid candles and *I hate you, hate you, hate you* bouncing out the door and into the night.

Somewhere between my father unpacking his work and slipping onto the sofa with a packet of papers, the smile had run out of my mother and she was snapping at him to light the birthday candles before I came down from my bedroom. I happen to know this part to be fact, because I was already stomping into the kitchen pissed as a white-faced hornet that they were arguing on my special day.

"Forget it," my mother hissed in Daddy's direction. "I guess I can just do it myself, along with the cooking, cleaning, and decorating, while you chase your fairy tales." She stormed out of the kitchen into the dining room, match in hand. "Come on, Iz. Come make your birthday wish."

She might as well have placed the flame from that match squarely under the seat of my father's pants, because something snapped so soundly inside him I still swear I heard a *poink!* slap through the air as he turned to scream after her, "Jesus fucking Christ! I cannot do one goddamn thing right with you, can I?"

The fight was back in motion. I tried one more time to lob a quick prayer God's way, offering him back my birthday wish—and it was a doozy, a candy-apple-red bike with trainers I'd been waiting all year to wish for—trying to stop it. But it was Sunday and I can only assume he was busy watching the fish fly in Potter's Creek. The anger I had not been able to rid myself of popped right out of my mouth in the shape of words.

"*Stop it!*" The words spun me right around until I was facing my father. "Stop it, stop it! I hate you! I wish you would just go away!"

And there it was; I had given up my perfectly planned birthday wish, letting it loose with no way to get it back, before I realized what had happened. The truth was, I was screaming at the air, but my father was the only one left in the room to hear it, and at the time I'd believed that was good because he was the one I knew for sure would scoop me up with a heartfelt "I'm sorry, Be" instead of delivering a sharp slap to the side of my cheek for mouthing off. I cannot recall a single time before, or since, when I have been more mistaken.

Dazed by the force of my anger, I almost missed my father whispering, "Fine," as he climbed the steps, leaving me standing alone, unscooped and unapologized to. Fifteen minutes later, my birthday wish came to life as my father marched out the door with my voice tucked in his pocket and both were swallowed up by darkness.

A thousand times my father had chased shadows from my room, promising nothing evil lurked in the night. In that very moment, deep in my gut, I knew he was wrong. Knew it but could not warn him before it was too late, because that was the very moment my words ran dry.

And that's it.

What began as the clearest memory of my life petered into a cloud of noise until there was nothing but staggering emptiness and the gnawing sensation of a memory that belonged there and might be the key to unlocking my voice. The truth is, I tried a thousand times to find the courage to pull the memory free, to reach right into the hole and yank my voice back out. But each time my mind brushed against the jagged corner of it, the feeling of falling from a cloud brought me to my knees. And when the dizziness steadied and my stomach stopped flip-flopping all over the place, the memory was gone again.

# CHAPTER THREE

Word of what had happened reached Tuckertown before we did, and the year that followed is less a memory than a residual feeling of walking through the world with that same sensation I'd felt at Potter's Creek—alone and off balance without my father's hand.

If there were whispers or rumors, I was too young to realize. Periodically, sympathetic neighbors would stop by with a pie or fresh-cut flowers from their garden and tilt a curious glance in my direction with a wave as though my being mute meant they were, too. Not a single word had crept through my lips since my sixth birthday and my mother devoted much of her time trying to wriggle them free.

"Just say something, anything," she pleaded. Every tinge of hope and panic in her voice said she didn't want to believe I couldn't, didn't understand that the secrets buried in my memory had me by the throat so tightly that the words were strangled. That I could never ever give them wings. "You know the bad words you aren't allowed to use? You can even say those. Go ahead, let one fly."

There was no way for her to know that I'd already said the worst words in the whole world. I'd breathed life into them, let them loose into the universe, and they had destroyed us all. I was the only one who understood . . . who knew Yemaya and listened to the Nikommo, who had spent a whole lifetime clinging to my father so he wouldn't go and, in a fit of anger, had wished him into nothingness, a nothingness so pure and powerful he never came back. I walked through the days with the Yemaya Stone in my pocket, silently wishing him back, not saying a word for fear the magic would spill out and I would accidentally wish her away, too.

I'm sure we ate, because neither my mother nor I starved to death during that time, even if my mother had shrunk to the width of a withered-up strand of linguini. And we must have shopped and left our house for necessities, because I do not remember being without toilet paper or Kleenex. What I do recall being fresh out of were answers. Had he found God's country? It always seemed to be moving from one place to another. When was he coming home? Did he still wake up in the middle of the night to dance with the moon?

Still, I cannot pull any one moment into clear view. The closest I ever get are the times when Grandma Jo came to stay, and even those are blurry snapshots of my mother switching from diet cola to Canadian whiskey and the soft pressure of my grandmother's hand stroking my back to get me to sleep.

Although I didn't see it then, I was coming to understand the true nature of my parents' quarrels, that they were all the same fight—the money, the candles, the toilet tissue. My father had turned the roll of Charmin around so that my mother could no longer reach into thin air with confidence and know it was there, know he was there. He had shifted the direction of our lives with it, in ways that we could not turn back.

My father was gone, but the truth of the matter is a person never really leaves you all at once. He slips away from you inch by inch until he has left you a thousand times. First, he marches right out of your life, leaving you only with memories. Then, one by one, those memories march out on you, too, and they take pieces of you with them as they go.

When I started kindergarten in the fall of 1966, I began to appreciate the bits of myself that had gone missing. I spent the morning slunk low in a corner desk at the back of the class wishing myself invisible in a room thick with the smell of pencil shavings and Elmer's glue. It hadn't taken long for the other children to figure out I couldn't speak.

"What's wrong with her?" a blond-haired boy with a face oval as a peach pit whispered.

"I think she's a retard," sniggered the squat redhead beside him.

"Robert!" The pretty young teacher, Miss Weatherall, visibly paled. "We do not use that word." I noted the fact that she had not added, *"No, she isn't."*

"Yeah, you big stupid goober head." A small girl in a tattered pink shirt leaned forward from the back row, pushing back a tangle of mousy brown curls. "She's just quiet."

"And we do not call our friends 'big stupid goober heads.'" Miss Weatherall flicked her eyes from the red-haired boy to the girl.

"I didn't call my friend a big stupid goober head; I called Robert one." Her name was Libby Frederickson, and I found out later that her mother had died of leukemia when she was three, which explained the array of mismatched outfits she wore to school and the explosion of curls left untamed by a mother's hand. She became the first and only friend I would know before leaving school for good.

The next month passed with all the speed of honey in a hive in February until one afternoon when Libby and I were crouched low catching ants beside a puddle, placing them one by one beside the moat we had carved along the edge. I set my ant, a big fat black creature with long front legs, down on the edge just as a pudgy black boot stomped up beside me.

"Hey, look, everyone! Silent Sam plays with *ants* because nobody else *w-ants* to play with her!" The words crooned down around me in a little jingle, crunching up my stomach until I could barely breathe.

"Shut up, goober head!" Libby pounced to her feet.

"Silent Sam, Silent Sam, mouth stuck shut with a jar of jam!"

I stared down at the ant chewing my lip, a habit I'd acquired to remind myself my mouth was there, even if for no other reason than to chew my own skin off.

"I said, shut up!" Libby stepped forward just as Robert brought his boot squarely down on the ant I'd been playing with. Its front legs began pedaling pathetically in the air while it died and I mopped mud from the corner of one eye.

"Ooooohhhh," sang Robert. "Look, Silent Sam's a crybaby!"

I had just cleared the dirt from my eyeball when I saw Libby go airborne. "She is not!" she screamed, shoving Robert back.

"Is, too!" Robert snapped, shoving Libby so hard she sailed backward into the middle of the moat with a loud *splat*.

I am not at all sure where the anger inside of me came from; it seemed to bubble through a tiny opening in my gut and exploded out of me with volcanic force. For one singular moment I was Electra, grabbing two fistfuls of mud, chucking one after the other at Robert until there was nothing left standing before me but a muddy brown blob, which did indeed make him look every bit like a big fat goober head. In my altered state, there was no way of knowing a small rock had been embedded in the last mud bomb. It had hit Robert flatly on the cheek with sufficient force to draw a trickle of blood below his eye.

Sitting in a plastic chair in the principal's office later, I tried to stitch together the lopped-off sentences slithering through the crack at the bottom of the door.

"Specialized programming . . . children with unique needs . . . If she could learn sign language, even . . . "

Digging the sharp corners of my nails into the pads of my fingers, I squeezed my eyes closed, willing the world away. A faint tickle shivered at the bottom of my throat. I pressed my lips together and swallowed three times until the urge to scream had passed.

"You are sorely mistaken if you think for one minute I'm going to let you place my daughter in a classroom full of retarded children!"

"We do not use that word, Mrs. Haywood," I heard Miss Weatherall say softly. The funny thing is, it would have stung less if she'd said it with force rather than pity.

"I'm sorry, but this whole conversation is *retarded*. Iz is not delayed." My mother stormed through the door, latching on to my hand, and dragged me bouncing like a tin can on a string beside her to the car.

"Izabella Rae. You do not need specialized education and we both damn well know it. You're too smart for your own fucking good. I'm not going to let them stick you in a class full of . . . " *Retards*. She didn't say it, but the word slipped into the car between us like a letter whisked through the crack of a locked door. " . . . people who need it." She sighed, looking at me sidelong. "Although maybe I should after that shenanigan today." I could see her weighing her options and coming up a fistful short. "What am I going to do with you? You know Daddy wouldn't want this."

I shrugged, staring hard at the trees flipping past my window. Why she thought I cared what my father wanted was a mystery to me. In the time since my father left, my sadness had turned to guilt, and my guilt had landed flatly on anger. I didn't give two soft hoots what either of them wanted. They could both pack all their wants and ship them to Timbuktu for all I cared.

"Look at me." Turning my head further toward the window, I started counting the trees. "I said, look at me!" She grabbed my chin, wrenching it toward her so hard I bit the inside of my lip. "Goddamn it, Iz. What is going on inside that head of yours?"

What would I have said if I could have answered? She could never know what it meant to hear the whispers of teachers who think you're stupid slipping through the one-inch gap beneath the door. Or to have to sit at a desk with an idiotic support teacher while all the other kids go off to play. What did she know about having only one measly friend in the whole wide world? One friend who doesn't care that you're a freak, because she is, too. Who doesn't care if you talk, because she can talk enough for both of you. Who knows what it feels like to have a parent spin off the face of the world and leave you sitting there with your feet stuck to the ground. What did she know about being yanked out of school just when you were getting to be best friends?

I shrugged, turning back to the passenger window. *Five . . . six . . . seven . . .* A sharp sting settled in my throat, making it so hard to breathe, my eyes began to water. I swiped the corner of my lashes with my shoulder and counted harder until she gave up.

That night, I lay in bed for hours watching the shadows creep along my walls like spirits who'd wriggled free of their forests, wondering if this was the Nikommo. I had been trailing one for a good ten minutes, trying to find its source, when my mother pushed open my door, causing me to close my eyes and lose sight of it altogether. The bed barely shifted when she sat on it. I can't say how long she stared at me before I felt her fingers run across the scabs on my lips with a sigh that caught like a cobweb in the air between us.

"Jesus, Iz. Don't do it. Just once, don't follow him." I clenched my eyes and rolled over with a sleepy snort, waiting for her to leave. "I miss him, too, you know."

That, I knew, was a lie. She didn't love him, not like I did. I couldn't remember the last time she'd really acted like she cared. Then, when I was just on the shirttails of sleep, it came back to me.

I had been watching *The Flinstones,* fixated on Fred

sneaking into Barney's house wearing a burglar's mask, when there was a loud crash from the upstairs bathroom. On the television, Betty grabbed Fred by the wrist and judo chopped him from side to side with a *bam, bam, bam*. Then the banging of Fred's head against the stone floor turned to pounding at the top of the steps. Betty's voice melted into my mother's, yelling for my father to open the door. A moment later, she came tripping down the stairs and grabbed the phone, tugging the cord until she'd pulled the coil straight and it threatened to zing her into space like a slingshot. Balancing the receiver between her shoulder and ear, she dumped the junk drawer, fishing a key out of the mess before dropping the phone to the floor and disappearing back upstairs. I knew she'd gotten the door open by the squeal of the hinges my father had been forgetting to oil for the past three years. There was a sharp muffled scream. The pulsing screech of sirens. Men in blue uniforms with a gurney. When she came back down-stairs, my mother was wrapped around my father like a cocoon, leading him down the steps. Two white towels looped around his wrists and I could just make out the blooms of crimson unfurling across the terry cloth like petals reaching for the sun. She laid him on the gurney and tucked the sheets around him, nuzzling his head. I could see she was crying. That's when it happened. When they tried to wheel my father out, she would not let go of his hand, had held on so tight one of the medics was forced to pry her fingers free.

"Come on, Iz." She'd tugged me to the car so quickly I never did find out what happened to Fred and Betty.

"What's wrong with Daddy?"

"He got hurt." She choked, swiping at her cheeks. "But it's okay now. He's going to be okay." Even then, I'd known she didn't believe it, but she was wrong. He came home two weeks later, bandaged like a mummy and carting a bag of brown bottles. When he saw me, he scooped me into a bear hug.

"Are you better now?"

"All better." He kissed my cheek, then walked to the garbage pail. "See? I don't even need medicine anymore." And he threw the bottles away.

That was the last time. The last time I could recall my mother really acting like she cared.

**Two weeks after** I crowned Robert with a loaded mud bomb, my mother delivered me to my first session with Dr. Miller, a young psychiatry graduate from the Rhode Island Mental Health Association, in an office painted in bright greens and purples with Winnie the Pooh sketched on the walls. A year later, there was Dr. Nichols, and then Miss Lincoln, a pediatric play therapist who spoke to me through puppets. There was an art therapist, a slew of medical doctors, audiologists, neurologists, and internists.

The first year of my silence was blamed on post-traumatic stress disorder. The second year on acquired behavioral deficit. This went on until the seventh year, when it was blamed on sheer stubbornness and my mother plopped me into a chair in Dr. Boni's office. Dr. Boni was a fossil of a therapist—old enough to have met Sigmund Freud in person. The thing that set Dr. Boni apart was he never pretended to understand what it was like to have your voice box come up empty as a tin of cookies on Christmas Day.

"What is it like to never speak?"

It may sound strange, but I was thrown by the question. Nobody had ever had the balls to ask me that before, and the look on his face said he really wanted to know.

Even if I had agreed to answer the question for him, I could not. You don't really know what it's like until you are six years old on Santa's lap at JCPenney's and all you ever wanted was a cotton-candy-pink dollhouse with green shutters, but you have no words to ask, so you get another stupid paint by numbers. Seven years old and shaken awake by a nightmare you are left holding in your heart because you have no voice to give it wings. Eight years old and folded neatly in your Sunday best, unable to save your soul by confessing that you chased your father straight out of existence. Nine years old and pelted with snowballs by strangers screaming, "Silent Sam," until you are sure you have breathed your last because you cannot yell for help. Ten years old when a girl tells the whole world you were born without a tongue and with no way to call her a bitch. Eleven years old and you know every single chapter of

*Treasure Island,* but can't talk about it with anyone. Twelve years old when the cutest boy in the world says "hi" at the ice cream shop, but you can't answer, so he walks away. Thirteen years old and given a child's menu because you can't explain you're a grown-up now.

Then, three weeks before your fourteenth birthday, you look down at the bright red slash on your clean white panties unable to tell anyone, and even if you could speak, it doesn't matter because there is nobody to tell anyway. Only then does the situation *really* start to take shape in a way Dr. Boni would never understand.

To exist without a voice is to forever live in your weakest form. You are forced to boil a universe of feelings, fears, and dreams down to a half-inch margin in a tiny flip-top notebook.

*Quiet,* I scribbled, which was an outright lie because when you don't speak you are stuck inside yourself with a gazillion unspoken thoughts clamoring inside their cage rattling to be freed. You can hear a duck crinkle to the grass across four fields during hunting season, hear your mother sigh a thousand dead dreams two rooms away.

Dr. Boni looked deflated.

The monologues commenced each Wednesday at four o'clock, when Dr. Boni pinched the crease of his trousers between his fingers, hiking them over two twiggy ankles, and sat down. The session ended when he punched his arm clear of his jacket cuff to glance at his watch. He would ask me questions I hadn't one spit of an inkling how to answer: *Why won't you speak? What are you afraid of? What did your mother do to make you so angry with her?*

*Nothing*, I scribbled. Out the window, a pear tree bowled over in the wind. For a full minute, I watched to see if it would snap in two, trying to sort out how anything fragile survives under the weight of the world.

At first I refused to tell him anything. I'd just sit in the chair and doodle while he asked questions. Sometimes he just talked. Then I started writing him things I knew he couldn't tell my mother just to see if it would drive him crazy holding on to my secrets for me, or if he'd tell her when I was out of the room. I told him that I snuck my mother's cigarettes every now and then and that Libby and I had tried drinking once. I even told him that sometimes I snuck out after my mother fell asleep and slipped down to the docks to watch the moon dance in the ocean.

I knew the rules and my mother had agreed to them: he would not disclose anything that did not put my life in danger or hurt anyone else. Anything else was fair game. To his credit, he never did tell and after a while he kind of grew on me because of it. Once, he asked me why I felt I couldn't tell my mother my secrets, what was I afraid would happen? I grabbed a piece of paper from his desk and gave him an honest answer.

*They would lose their magic.*

The questions continued for six months until on my final visit it was laid clear there would be no going forward without first going back.

"Listen, you're paying for my professional opinion, so here it is."

I was spinning myself dizzy in Dr. Boni's desk chair—which let out a high-pitched squeal on every turn while he spoke with my mother—staring at a fly somebody had seen fit to smash, but not remove, from the ceiling fan.

"Izabella is not trying to hurt herself by doing this, and she certainly isn't trying to hurt you."

The chair spun faster, squealed louder.

"She's trying to protect herself the only way she knows how. She has blocked everything about the incident with her father out of her conscious mind: the police, the night, all of it."

*Faster, faster, faster. Louder, louder, louder* . . . until I thought I might throw up right there from spinning his words away. Vaguely, I felt his eyes flick in my direction, heard him pause, and veer away from the details of that night.

"She has shut the door on the whole affair so tightly," he continued cautiously, "her voice is caught on the other side. She's scared—scared of what she'll find if she opens it. Ultimately, the only way to get beyond a fear that overpowering is to show her the monsters in the closet are not going to destroy her. She has to stand face-to-face with that day and survive the moment."

"You want me to take her back?" A tinge of panic laced my mother's question.

"That's my recommendation."

"I can't."

"You can't protect her from her own memory."

"What if . . . " She glanced at me and let the question die in the air.

"She is not like her father." Dr. Boni looked squarely at my mother. "It isn't the same thing. This is not," he paused, glancing my way, "organic in nature."

I had no idea what the statement meant, unless he was implying I was free of pesticides, but my stomach knotted into a ball just the same. Besides, I *was* like my father, just like him. I had his dimples, and his nose, and his freckles. I danced with the moon and understood the tides, and even if I could not hear the Nikommo, I knew that they were real.

My mother stared at him quietly for a drawn-out moment then grabbed her bag and held the door for me before following me out to the parking lot.

"Iz." My mother shook her head, marching over to the car. "I swear to God you are determined to find my last breaking point."


My mother's last breaking point arrived on the morning of October 3, 1974. All worn out with doctors and tests, she decided Dr. Boni was right: my voice was not a thing gone, but missing. So, on my fourteenth birthday, we set sail to find it. She never said this was the case, exactly, but I could read the truth in the deep weariness casting webs of wrinkles around her eyes.

The morning arrived not to the mountain of brightly beribboned gifts every girl wishes for, but to three mismatched steamer trunks propped beside our front door and my mother's rear end peeping into the room over a small crate. Halfway down the stairs, a small whimper caused me to stop and try to make sense of the scene while my mother wriggled herself free.

"Happy birthday, Iz!" Lifting a handful of wrinkles, she popped the small animal into the crook of my elbow. "He's a shar-pei."

The puppy studied the room with watery bronze eyes, laying one tiny paw flatly against my jaw as if searching for some piece of familiarity, a paper-strewn corner, a brother or sister to nip his tail, the warm teat of his mother. A small shiver moved over the animal's body, causing my fingers to quiver right along with him, and I realized at the same moment he did that he was alone. Some small corner of the fabric of me snagged, threatening to unravel. With another whine, the puppy snuggled into me, tucking his nose under the fold of my robe and licking my wrist.

"He's yours."

Squiggling my pinky between the puppy's ribs and my neck, I rubbed his soft fur as he chewed my finger softly then sucked at it, the shiver subsiding. A moment later, the quiet sniffing deepened and the puppy's head tottered into my curls with a sleepy weight tumbling right into an empty hole inside of me. In one flat half second, I knew I would never let him go, never let him be scared or alone again.

I rubbed the puppy's ear, eyeing the trunks at the front door.

"I thought we'd name him Luke. You know, like in the Bible. I always liked that name. It would have been yours if you'd been a boy. We can bring him with us."

My hand froze halfway down the soft spine, and she must have noticed because she turned abruptly toward the kitchen to answer the ringing phone, which she'd been ignoring for a solid minute. I gazed down at the puppy trying to fish the Gospel of Luke from a million daydreams during Sunday school. All I could recall was the part about Jesus's resurrection, and I realized that my mother wasn't just searching for my voice. She was trying to breathe life back into everything that had withered around us. "It's going to be okay, Iz. You'll see."

She didn't say where we were going. She didn't have to. Since there seemed to be no going forward, we were going back. Back to the spot where my voice had fallen against the night and shattered into silence eight years earlier, to the moment my father disappeared.

# CHAPTER FOUR

The ferry's hull knocked against the landing like a bloated white whale, thudding in time to the argument my mother was having with the ticket agent. *One, two, three, four . . .* , I ticked silently, as though the same laws of nature choreographing thunder and lightning could rule over a knocking ferry.

A large poster on the side of the boat read: PARDON AMERICA! NIX NIXON Making clear the fact that whoever owned the ferry, like most of the country, was still chewing sour grapes over the Watergate scandal.

Tracing the shoreline to the tip of the cove, I studied the jagged granite face of Anawan Cliffs steepling into the sky. I had been there a hundred times with my father, but I wasn't allowed to tell because the drop-off plummeted three hundred feet into a sea dappled with boulders of smoky quartz and there were no railings to keep you on top. The very type of place my mother would not have allowed me to go. The cliffs were just as famous for the number of miles a person could see from their crests as the number of people who had tossed themselves off them. My father and I had climbed the trail up to the rocky crest a dozen times together. The sky was so clear the last time we went you could see the pointy peaks of the Newport Bridge poke straight into the clouds. I remembered thinking it looked like a giant skewer piercing a marshmallow.

"Over there, Be. Can you see it?" My father had lifted me onto his shoulders like he was tossing a scarf around his neck. "Don't be afraid. Nothing is going to happen. Just don't let go." *Don't let go.* Weaving my fingers into his hair, I'd clenched my fists while he crept up to the ledge until his toes were close enough that pebbles had skidded down the edge and into the waves below, sending three tuxedoed gulls into flight. "Look at that."

The gulls stretched their wings until they were paper airplanes sailing gracefully over the rocks. My father watched them wistfully, his voice drifting a million miles away. "Someday we're going to fly straight into the clouds like that."

I can't say where his mind was then, only that it had been elsewhere, because that was when I first came to realize I was afraid of heights. My stomach lurched, spinning my head into a somersault and setting my body teetering as I tilted sideways. The jerking must have snapped him to, because he grabbed my wrist as I slid down his shoulder, stepping sideways so that I swung over the ledge and back onto the cliff with a screech.

"You flew!" My father laughed, kneeling down to brush the bangs from my brow. Then his laughter died and he looked me deep in the eyes. "What did it feel like? Was it amazing?"

How do you answer a question like that? *It felt like a father tossing his child to the rocks to be smashed into a million bits. It felt like tumbling to my death.*

"Was it?"

The memory was so clear I could almost hear his voice on the wind and I found myself nodding.

"Ma'am." The woman at the ticket counter's voice jolted me back to the present. "Like I said, I got room for you and your girl. I can even squeeze in the mutt, but the carport's full." Wild mahogany curls spilled out of a loose pile pinned to the crown of her head with a broken pencil. Folding her arms onto the counter, she leaned in toward my mother. The milky porcelain of her skin was slapped pink at the cheeks from too much sun.

Luke gave a little whine. I bent low, popping the crate open and snuggling him close.

The muscles along my mother's neck visibly tensed, drawing her shoulders into an involuntary shrug as she dug the wallet from her bag. "Here, Iz, hold this." She shoved the purse in my direction. "He isn't a mutt; he's a purebred shar-pei puppy."

Luke licked his nose, stretched, and curled into a mound of toffee-colored folds as a hollow whistle rolled forth from the boat's stern.

"What I see," the woman leveled steely blue eyes at my mother, aimed, "is that some smart Sally went and got you to give your purse for hauling away an old mass of wrinkles and called it a dog." And fired. "And if you would like me to haul *your* wrinkled old mass out to the island tonight, it'll be twenty-two dollars for the lot a' ya, minus the auto, 'cause there's no room."

Bull's-eye.

I bit the stiff collar of my jacket so my mother wouldn't see the grin spreading over my lips, but not before the woman behind the counter saw it and tilted her head inquisitively.

"But, if you'd like to write your name and number on this tag and leave the keys, Telly over there would be happy to deliver it to you sometime next week, or the week after." The woman nodded at a too-thin man who might have passed for twenty-five years old as easily as seventy-five. The remnant of a single tattoo, which could have been either a naked lady or a parrot with a broken wing, had faded to a purple splodge on his left arm. Telly gave my mother a how-do nod, letting flash a golden stud where a front tooth belonged.

The woman dropped me a quick wink, and in that instant I knew two things for sure: my mother's shiny silver BMW was not getting on that boat, and this stranger was somebody I could quickly grow to love.

"Next week! Next week?"

"Or the week after."

"You expect me to just leave it here until whenever? What if I pay more?"

"Miss, I don't expect anything from anybody. But I have a boat full of people waiting to leave, and the Yemaya Festival is coming up. My carport's crammed tighter than a nest of rats until it's over. I don't give two hoots about your money or your dog or your uppity attitude. Unless you're using any of it to build me a bigger carport you're out of luck, because there isn't any more room. So you'd better make up your mind where you fancy sleeping tonight, here in Suttersville or across the sound on Tillings."

I slid my hand into the compartment my mother had unzipped in her bag and slipped three cigarettes free before tucking them into my own bag. It wasn't true that we were wealthy. My mother had bought the car used when my father's Jeep finally refused to be coaxed back to life with money from my father's pension and insurance, which the university had released when it became clear he wasn't coming back. The difference it made was not one of shifting from glass to crystal but from recycled Dixie cups to the variety that could withstand a dishwasher without dissolving.

It was true, though, that in the years since my father went missing my mother had become guarded and cool in a way that gave her an uppity air. My father's disappearance had been an all-you-can-eat buffet for the rumor mills around town and I guess it was just easier to freeze the world out than be burned each time you trusted another person. There was a lot about my mother that confounded me, but that was a thing I understood.

"What's your name?"

"Excuse me?"

"Your name. You do have one, don't you?"

"Remy. Remy O'Malley. Well, technically Mandolin, but I go by O'Malley."

"Remy." The name escaped my mother's lips in the form of a whisper that seemed aimed at nobody and the color seemed to wash from her face. Studying the lines of the woman's face like they might give up some secret about her, she cleared her throat then lowered her eyes down to the counter. "Fine. Ms. Mandolin."

"Remy."

"Remy." My mother's jaw tightened, forcing the name into the air in a way that appeared to hurt. Giving the Anawan Cliffs one last glance, I gazed up at my mother, who seemed suddenly discombobulated, nervous almost, in the company of this woman. "If it's not too much trouble, I'd like to speak to your boss."

"Suit yourself. Telly! This nice lady would like a word." Remy Mandolin tossed her head back with a deep smoky laugh and flipped the sign in the window to CLOSED. I wondered if she would really leave us standing there on the dock with a tattooed gold-toothed pirate or mass murderer—it was hard to tell. My mother glanced between the two of them before coming to her senses, or at least admitting defeat.

"Arrrgh! Fine, here!" The keys to the BMW tinkled onto the counter and my mother scribbled the information onto the tag, giving it a nudge toward the window with her finger. "First thing next week," my mother huffed, grappling with the last trunk and Luke's crate.

"Or the week after," Remy quipped, scooping up the keys and sliding the Plexiglas closed before my mother could reply. On the other side of the window, she hung the keys on a little brass hook, pausing to read the tag. I couldn't help but notice her face twist up a bit as she mouthed the name, or the way she glanced back at my mother with a contemplative expression while my mother kicked the trunk, mumbling something about a royal pain in her ass, and stuffed the tickets in her back pocket.

"At least we're rid of her," she grumbled.

Staring at the sea, I could not stop the butterflies fluttering in my stomach. Here is the thing about an island . . . there is no escape; you are stuck with whatever is there. At least on the mainland running away was an option, if only I could figure out which direction to point my legs.

"Okay, got everything?" My mother sighed, looking down at me.

I patted my jacket pocket seeking the crusty rectangle of a map Grandma Jo had given me three years earlier, and then slid my right hand down to the pocket of my jeans, running it over the hard edges of the Yemaya Stone from Potter's Creek. It was the one thing left on this earth that connected me to my father, and although I was too old to believe he could hear me if I wished into a dead piece of amber, I still tried. Just in case. I wanted him to know I hadn't forgotten him, that I was still looking even if everyone else had given up. I didn't want him to forget me.

I nodded, snuggling Luke back into his crate for the trip.

The *Mirabel*, a reincarnated fishing rig serving its second life as a passenger ferry, teeter-tottered over the waves, dragging my stomach along with it. In my experience, there are three types of boats: boats big enough to barrel gracefully through the waves, boats small enough to zip roller-coaster fashion over them, and every vomitous size in between. The *Mirabel* fell woozily into the final category, climbing each swell lazily before sledding slowly down the opposite bank of the swell until my breakfast washed rhythmically over the back of my throat. Even Luke had resigned himself to the back of his crate amid a banter of whimpering.

"Do you want your mittens, Iz?" My mother dug into her jacket pocket, pulling forth two bright red mittens. "You look cold. Why don't you let go of the bar; the metal's going to turn your fingers raw with frostbite."

I shook my head in small calculated wags, not wishing

to give the *Mirabel* any further cause to rock. My knuckles were not white from the cold but from clutching the handrail in an attempt to steady the boat, or at least my place on it. The cold would need to outwrestle my nausea to make me let go, and I was pretty sure that wasn't going to happen.

My mother tucked the little red mittens away again and pried free a rumpled pack of Merits. I was retching before the match even took.

"Iz?" Flicking the cigarette overboard, she pulled me upright, tucking my hair into my collar in time to save it from being caught in the splash of undigested pancakes left over from my birthday breakfast. "Here, I've got a soda in here somewhere." She rifled through her handbag, digging loose a half-sipped Coca-Cola covered with loose tobacco and lint bits.

By the time she actually managed to unscrew the top, my vomiting spell had set off a chain reaction and Luke was now collapsed in a pool of regurgitated kibble, as well. My mother was handling the mess and the stench with clinical efficiency until a familiar voice sounded over her shoulder.

"Are you trying to see if that child can turn her intestines out onto the deck?" Remy sauntered up. "The only sound reason for feeding cola to a person with sea stomach is if you don't particularly like them."

I have found it generally bad wisdom to share a thing like that before you have determined the nature of a relationship so I clenched my jaw tight, now that the cat was out of the bag, half expecting my mother to shove the whole bottle down my gullet.

"The only thing worse is fried clams, which have the God-given power to knock you to your knees to pray for death. And don't stand her up; lay her flat so she moves with the boat."

"Don't you have something to do?" Twisting three directions trying to steady me, my mother looked like a porcelain doll whose limbs some angry child had bent into broken and unnatural angles. "Eat some fried clams, maybe?" It was meant to be snotty, but my mother was too busy trying to keep us aboard to really pull it off.

The snowy skin pulled tight over her flushed cheeks as Remy Mandolin popped the top off a metal canister with a tinny snap. Her lack of fear, primarily of my mother, filled me with the urge to climb into her lap and stick my tongue out at the world. The only other person I knew who was completely unafraid of my mother was Grandma Jo. Everything about Remy Mandolin was bold, like the wild samba of the djembe drums my mother had taken me to see last year during a Brazilian festival in Mystic, Connecticut. I could almost see her bare feet stomping gypsy circles, a rainbow skirt twirling wildly to and fro at her ankles. Still, as much as I respected her, I wished she had not opened the tin so close to me, for the strong punchy scent of fresh ginger hit me full in the nostril, setting me on another retching spell.

"Here, this is what she needs."

"Don't tell me what my daughter needs," puffed my mother as she made a valiant attempt to keep me from flopping over the handrail. "Look what you did!"

Once I had emptied my stomach of its last crumb, Remy stuck a thread of fresh crystallized ginger into my mouth. "Chew." My eyes must have widened to the size of horse chestnuts, because Remy laughed right out loud. "Chew."

Never having been forced to chew raw roots of any kind before, I was unprepared for the intense burn in my mouth. Tears pooled in my eyes, and the rush of warm sugary heat left a trail clear from my tongue to my tailbone. Within seconds the lurching in my stomach slowed and, with two more straps of ginger, stopped altogether. When it appeared I was no longer at risk of dropping off the edge of the boat, Remy bent low and tossed a strap of ginger inside Luke's crate. He sniffed the string of ginger tentatively before gnawing halfheartedly at one corner while holding the other to the floor of his crate with one paw.

"There now, lay her flat, belly down, so she doesn't drown in her own bile."

My mother did as she was told with surprisingly little rebellion, balling up her jacket and tucking it beneath my ear. Waves lapped up the boat's hull. I watched them carefully, every so often glimpsing a flash of silver darting below them. I wriggled the small hunk of amber from my pocket, tucked my hand below my head, and watched for Yemaya until the bounce of light off the waves made me retch again. For an instant, I fantasized about rolling myself off the edge and into her arms just to free myself of the boat.

"Let her be while you use the hose there to rinse that crate clean," Remy directed. "Otherwise, I'll have to charge you a clean-up fee for hosing down the deck. Besides, I'm dead certain my father will appreciate not having regurgitated dog chunks dropping all over his car. Runs the taxi stand on the wharf." Remy tucked a loose bronze curl back into her pencil knot. "Even if he lets you aboard with that mess, I'm betting whoever you're lodging with on the island will not."

"Thanks, but I can figure out how to take care of my own dog." Looking her over carefully, my mother appeared to have gone the way of Lot's wife, paling to the color of salt.

Had I not still felt too woozy to write, I might have reached for the notepad I always kept in my pocket and reminded her that according to the governing rules of birthday gift giving, Luke was technically all mine and not hers at all. "And we're not lodging with anyone. We're staying at the Booth House." She seemed preoccupied, as though turning a thought over and searching for a spot to set it down.

Now Remy, too, appeared to be reaching, trying to pull forth something that refused to come loose. She followed my mother, letting a steeliness settle in her slate blue eyes.

When she spoke again, her voice hit the air in measured tones. "The Booth House?"

"It was my husband's grandmother's cottage." Her eyes seemed suddenly far away as she gave Luke's cage a shove.

I rolled onto my back, trying to remember the last time my mother had referred to Daddy as her husband. Was he still? I mean, technically speaking. It wasn't as if there had ever been a divorce.

"Well then . . . ," Remy whispered. I squinted up at them, watching the expression on her face change, as though the thought she'd been tugging at had finally broken free. "I suppose you already know my father." A moment of perfect silence passed between them before Remy added, "I guess that explains it. Why don't you bring your girl into the cabin? There's a cot in back she can lie down on."

"Explains what?" My mother dug another cigarette from her bag, lighting it and taking a deep drag before leveling her eyes at Remy. Annoyance hung tight to her words, but Remy Mandolin's back was already turned.

"Like I said, there's a cot. She's welcome to it while you hose off that mutt and its cage." She shook her head halfway across the deck as if in wonderment about something. "I don't want it stinking up my boat." Breasts as round as grapefruits pushed her shirt into soft bouncy curves, the sort of which I dreamed would one day sprout from my own chest. She was dressed in faded jean cutoffs torn high enough for white crescents to peep out from the fringe and a man's button-down shirt knotted at a waist as thin as a chopstick. Fleshy hips rounded into a peach-shaped rear end, which gave a mighty shake in my mother's direction as she slipped into the control cabin. The gesture was as good as any four-lettered word. I could not see my mother's expression but—my right hand to God—her hair tensed, pulling the black tresses up a notch.

"He's not a mutt!" My mother watched the engine room door until the tip of the cigarette burned her finger and she stomped it out on the deck. She took two steps in the direction of the door, stopped, and turned back to help me up. She must have seen the question scribbling itself across my face as I looked back and forth between the cabin and my mother, because as I struggled to free my notepad she stopped me with a sigh. "Her father takes care of Grandma Isabella's house when we're not here. That's all she meant." And with that, she tottered me into the cabin before heading for the hose.

Closing my eyes once I was in the control cabin, I willed the sea to stop churning. Somewhere behind me a radio station was warbling in and out of range. The announcer was saying something about the Watergate trial, but I couldn't zero in on what.

"They ought to throw Nixon's sorry ass in jail," Remy grumbled, more to herself than me. "Anyone too flipping stupid to burn a few audiotapes shouldn't be wandering around free society." She spun the dial, stopping on John Lennon crooning "Sweet Bird of Paradox."

Prying my eyes open to glance at her, I pulled Luke close, letting him curl into a comma beside me. Taped to the metal ribs of the cabin, a tall pretty woman with red hair looked down at me from a yellowing photograph. Cradling an armful of puffy pink flowers, she appeared to be laughing at the lumberjack of a man standing beside her who was planting an exaggerated kiss on her cheek as she tousled his hair with her free hand. Remy glanced at me, then back through the window.

"Pretty, isn't she? That's my mom."

I nodded, staring at the woman, understanding clearly from what fire the blaze in Remy's eyes had been lit.

"There must've been a thousand peonies in my garden that year. Your grandmother and father knew her. They used to come to Tillings every year." There was a slight catch in the statement, like the needle of a record player hopping over a scratch. An untrained ear might have missed it, but I didn't.

*I spent my summers on a sandbar,* my father used to joke about the island. *One good wave and we all would have been swept out to sea.*

"But that was a long time ago." It was barely a wisp of air, as though Remy had wholly forgotten I was in the cabin and was speaking to herself. "Before everything."

I waited for her to go on, but she didn't say another word until the boat's radio squelched to life and she started barking orders into it, leaving me staring at the photo and wondering over her choice of words. *Before ev-*

*erything*. A chill began to move over me, and the more I wondered, the colder that chill became until I was frozen right up solid with a desperate desire to turn the boat around and go home—with or without a voice.

The *Mirabel* wobbled into dock just before five o'clock. The effects of the ginger were wearing thin and the sharp aroma of vomit clinging to my clothes only made matters worse. On shore, bicycles belonging to another century with huge metal rims and woven baskets strapped to the handlebars littered the wharf. Women wearing floppy-brimmed hats tied to their heads with satin scarves waited on the dock waving at visitors as they shuffled off. The only hint that the 1970s had made it across the bay to Tillings Island came in the form of a young couple snuggled close together on the break wall dipping their toes in the surf so that the cuffs of their bell-bottoms boasted dark rings from the water. The collar of the girl's paisley shirt, cut too low for fall and tied in a knot around her waist so that she showed an inch of belly, whipped in the breeze.

At the base of the *Mirabel*'s ramp, a rickety sign weathering in the salt air read: COME ALL YE FAR AND WIDE TO THE FESTIVAL OF YEMAYA OUR LADY OF TILLINGS. And then I saw her standing there, tall and lovely, gazing over the ocean with soft gray eyes the color of a perfect storm. A dolphin swam at her side, where the sea foam and her thighs tangled into one wave. Carved from a slab of mahogany, she looked a thousand years old, with one hand cupped in the air. Beads of water dripped from her fingers into a pile of pearls at her waist like the pearls of water my father had sent skipping over Potter's Creek. Beneath a seaweed shawl, tiny rivulets snaked down her naked breast. A halo of cowry shells pushed the hair from her eyes, which appeared to be studying the horizon thoughtfully.

*If you are very, very lucky you will see her.* My father's words rolled across an ocean and nine years. Closing my eyes, I felt them tinkle into the hollow space he'd left behind. I grasped to hold on to the sound of him, but as always, it slipped away.

The deep mournful bawl of the ferry's horn snapped me back to the present.

"Move along, please!" bellowed a deckhand.

Beside me, my mother wrangled the canvas bag and Luke's crate, rendered all the slipperier from having been hosed down. Before I could gather my ground, a fat woman with tangerine lips tottering on clunky green sandals, dyed to match the ribbon of her sombrero, knocked me forward and I was swept into the rapids of windbreakers, sweaters, and L.L. Bean tennis shoes. When I came to rest at the bottom of the ramp, it was just me, the cobblestones, and Yemaya.

The crowd was just starting to disperse when Remy whisked my arm up in an iron grip, hurrying me toward the statue. As we got closer, I could see three sea stones in Yemaya's outstretched hand. Instinctively, I ran my hand over the lump in my pocket. Behind Yemaya's tiny waist, the hood of a purple Ford Thunderbird poked into the day with TAXI scrawled across it in a bow of red cursive. A fat white gull had settled on its roof and was screeching at the boat.

"Come on. They'll be driving the autos off any moment and the way these blokes drive they'll make a flapjack out of ya. Where's yer mum?" Remy looked at me, prodding. An old familiar wave of guilt sprang up in my chest from my inability to answer her. "I see. Well, I can't say I blame you. If it'd taken me this long to lose her, I wouldn't want someone traipsing behind me undoing all my hard work either."

I tossed her a grin, chewing a tuft of skin hanging tight to the inside of my cheek by one corner.

"Still and all, the law says she's got to feed you and keep you warm. So, I guess we should track her down." Remy glanced up, letting her eyes rest on a huge man with white wavy hair and a round belly leaning easily against the statue. She led me over to his side while he tapped a pipe out on the heel of his shoe before stuffing it with fresh tobacco. Behind him, the purple taxi sat with its passenger door open. He had only begun to suck the flame of the match upside down into the bowl, making the tobacco glow orange, when Remy Mandolin turned me by the shoulders so she could look at me squarely.

"I know just what you're going through. You see this old giant with a shipwreck for lungs?"

I nodded.

"He's my father, and I've been trying to rid myself of him my whole damn life; just keeps coming back to stink up my life like that dog of yours." The grin on my face deepened, touching one off on Mr. O'Malley's face, too. He swatted his daughter on the backside with a rolled-up copy of the *Island Beacon,* shaking his head in the same manner Remy had done onboard. "And that," she pointed at the car, "is the Great Purple Monster of Millbury. Now I'm going to go find your mother and your mutt; I'm sad to say you're stuck with her."

I nodded again.

"It looks like we're going to be neighbors. Way back when the Booth property belonged to an old sea captain, he built two small houses that used to belong to care-takers. Those houses got sold off after he died. I live in one and this old goat lives in the other. I can damn near spit out my window into yours." She laughed, sending the curls along her nape bouncing gently. "I bet your mum is real happy about that."

Curiosity, and a grain of respect, sprouted in my eyes as I tried to make sense of this renegade of a woman that had just come crashing into our lives. She was either awesomely cool or awesomely crazy; it was difficult to tell. Clearly, she threw my mother entirely off kilter for some reason. But there was something else. She had said something on the boat. She knew about my father, and I wanted to know how.

"Okay, then. I'll be back. Since there doesn't seem to be an adult anywhere in the vicinity, I'll leave you in charge. Don't you let him smoke another pipe, you hear? Or his chest is going to collapse right where he stands. Then we will have to roll his big black lungs over to the edge of the dock and dump him, and I just haven't the time nor inclination for that today." Then Remy disappeared, leaving me shifting awkwardly from foot to foot studying the statue Mr. O'Malley was leaning on.

I had never dumped a parent off the side of a dock, but after my father left, I had been plagued by a recurring dream in which I tossed my mother off the edge of the earth.

I could hear my father calling for me from within a dark jungle, could see his hand reaching through the branches, saying, "Don't let go, Be. Don't let go!" Each time I tried to run after him, my mother held my wrist until I was kicking and scratching like a bear in a trap. When my father's hand began to slip away, I used all my strength and shoved her into the mouth of a volcano to free myself of her grip. But I only made it three steps toward the darkness before I saw her pulling herself right back over the edge, yelling, "Jesus, Iz. Don't do it. Just this once, don't follow him." I always woke from the dream pissed as a polecat at my mother for stopping me.

*Why are you so angry with your mother?* Dr. Boni's voice flittered on the breeze.

That I wanted her gone was a lie. Once you have a

parent plunge off the planet, you live the rest of your days haunted by the knowledge that the one you have left could follow at any time and then you will be alone for the rest of your life. Life becomes a wrestling match between holding on tight so they won't leave, and shoving them away so your heart won't dry up like a dandelion and puff into the wind when they do. It isn't pretty and you won't find it in any poem, but it's the truth.

I glanced at Mr. O'Malley, who was now also standing back and tracing the sea witch's soft curves with his eyes. "This is Yemaya, the Great Mother." With his toe, he nudged a stack of white sticks on the ground, sending them scattering apart. "Offerings. Fish bones and such. People come from all over to lay their dreams and secrets at her feet, hoping she can help them find whatever's missing—money, health, love. Those were probably from some sailor going out for a haul." He pointed with the barrel of his pipe to where several alabaster bones had become caught up in the stained blue and white folds of Yemaya's skirt. "The festival starts in a week or so and ends with the Great Feast. The whole island turns out. Somethin' to see."

When he turned quietly back to his paper, I looked up at Yemaya's brown face, studying it so intently I never felt my fingers creep up to touch her hand. Her eyes were haunting as they looked out over the ocean. It was as though she, too, were searching for a thing lost. I could not help wondering what it was.

# CHAPTER FIVE

I was already in the backseat of the taxi sketching the wooden statue on the inside cover of my notepad when I saw Remy locate my mother at the ramp, taking Luke's crate from her hand and setting it on the wooden planks. I cannot say how long they were talking out there, or about what. But it was long enough for my mother's face to grow pale and her mouth to draw into a surprised little O. So I figured Remy had just told her about the three of us being neighbors. Up front, Mr. O'Malley flipped his pipe end over end with his fingers, studying my mother with interest, until they turned for the taxi and he unfolded himself to open the trunk for our bags.

"Mr. O'Malley." All the bark had gone from my mother's voice as she took his hand briefly.

"Thomas," he corrected, taking her gently in his arms, as if he worried he might break her. He gave her a warm hug without letting go of her hand. "It's been a long time."

I let my eyes ping up from my sketch long enough to trace the hint of sadness in his eyes, wondering what he meant by that. "Welcome back."

"It has." My mother nodded, patting his hand. "Too long. How have you been?" A gentleness moved over her tone in a way I hadn't heard in a very long time, and I believed she really wanted to know.

"Disobedient. Ornery. A generalized pain in the ass," Remy interjected, dodging Mr. O'Malley's free hand when it shot out to rumple her hair.

What felt like an awkward hour passed before Mr. O'Malley dropped my mother's hand. Both of them stood motionless for a moment, and I couldn't help but wonder at the familiarity that seemed to pass between them. Remy's back was turned to the cab, but I could make out her hand touching Mr. O'Malley's right shoulder briefly before she dropped down to pick up Luke's crate.

"I'll ride with you," Remy interjected, tossing a bag in the truck. "I've got too much to get done for the festival to sit around waiting for this one to wander back around for me in three hours." She gave Mr. O'Malley a pointed glance. "You can drop me at home after we get these folks unloaded."

"Have it your way." Mr. O'Malley grinned. "But paying passengers sit up front." He tossed my mother a wink, swinging the passenger door open for her to slip in.

"Fine by me." Remy slapped the trunk shut. "The smell of that hell pipe gives me a headache anyway."

We drove through the village of Tillings quietly, Mr. O'Malley's taxi bumping along over the cobblestones. Outside the car, a frenzy of activity seemed to be exploding along the streets and inside the shops, which were preparing for the festival. Two men curled over a walkway popping cobbles from their bracings and hammering new ones in their place. A tall heavyset woman balanced on a ladder as she stitched up the corner of an awning in front of a sweets shop. Four people with rags and small tins polished the brass trappings of a small white church while the pastor plopped clumps of pink mums along the brick walk. The sign read:

THE BLESSING OF YĚMAYA
SUN. 10:00 AM. VISITORS WELCOME.
THE GREAT MOTHER'S CHILDREN'S BLESSING
TO FOLLOW AT 11:00 AM.

"Most summer vacationers leave after Labor Day," Remy said, eyeing the bustling street. "Then we all go a little crazy preparing for the crowd that comes over for the festival. After the Great Feast is over, Tillings will be dead as a beached whale until next Memorial Day."

I didn't know if I would be there to see that. My mother hadn't said how long we were staying, but I had the feeling that my voice wasn't the only reason we were on the island. Over the last few years, my mother had worked primarily from home as a consultant for estate liquidators assessing fine art and pricing it for auction. At least, that was what she did when she wasn't busy scribbling down assignments for me from the room in the back of our house, which she had designated as a home class-room. I was the only kid I knew who had to live with their teacher, and while every kid in the universe got to go out and play for recess, I got to go and make my bed. Over the last three weeks, my mother had packed up her office to work from Tillings and every last pencil from my home-school kit was in my trunk. If she knew how long she intended us to be gone, she didn't say. It wasn't like there was really anything to leave behind, or anyone who would miss us.

Other than Grandma Jo, my mother had frozen the world out so thoroughly there were times she didn't even open the door for the UPS man. A month earlier, I had found her sitting on the living room floor with a bottle of Kendall Jackson, crying in a sea of loose photographs like some sort of rogue planet trying to hold its universe in orbit. Or maybe it was a black hole and she was will-ing it to swallow her up—I can't be sure. But this is what I do know . . . sometimes the only place left to hide is in the shadows of your own mind. Mr. O'Malley wove up and down a labyrinth of streets dotted with people repair-ing pickets and toting rakes. Behind them, small children dragged yard bags and jumped in leaf piles before stuff-ing them full. Finally, the taxi headed out of town on a road skirting the ocean until only a few homes speckled the fields. We drove past the jetties, where a small boy in rolled-up jeans hopped up and down splashing the water from a tidal pool with bare feet. A starfish dangled between his fingers, its tentacles so orange in the sunlight that it appeared rusted. The girl behind him scrunched her face up, trying to force a small shovel into the sand beside a clam hole, working it with such force she kicked the tin pail at her toes, toppling it onto its side. Their parents sat on the rocks along the dunes, laughing.

We drove for another five minutes before Mr. O'Malley flicked on his blinker and a small green arrow winked to the left. I had just remembered to add the drips of water cascading into pearls off Yemaya's arm when the taxi passed a sign marked KNOCKBERRY LANE, which turned out to be about a mile of crushed oyster shells sparkling like pink snow in the dying sun.

The tires of Mr. O'Malley's Thunderbird crunched past a tidy stone carriage house through whose doors I fully expected seven midget men to whistle their way into view. It was cinnamon-sugar warm; the sort of place where a chimney fills the yard with applewood smoke in the fall, and whose shallow knolls seemed to tremble with children giggling their way through a toboggan race. Autumn roses climbed the chimney bricks and spilled over the roof in huge cotton-candy tufts; wisteria tangled so thickly around the garden its vines had long ago wrestled the chicken wire to the ground. The whole scene shooed away formality in a way Grandma Jo would have adored.

"Sit back and relax." Remy laughed. "That old hovel belongs to me. The Booth House is at the very end of Knockberry Lane." Remy must have noticed the corners of my mouth change direction, because she gave my knee a quick squeeze, adding, "But I have high hopes that you'll visit. Lord knows I could make good use of two more hands bringing in the cabbages and carrots. If I don't get 'em harvested just as soon as they're ready the wildlife around here will have them for supper. That crazy old Goliath in the front seat has a history of putting out salt licks. Now every form of cotton-tailed rodent on the island lives in my back orchard. There used to be gardens all through here. My mother would save her potato shavings all winter long and at the first thaw, she'd be out seasoning the soil. Priming the pot, she used to call it." Remy laughed again.

My mother jerked around in her seat, locking eyes with Remy, and for a long second not a peep came from anyone. I looked back and forth between them curiously.

"Anyway . . . ," Remy finally said. "Well, they aren't so grand anymore, but the damn deer seem to like them just the same."

There came a chortle from the driver's seat, followed by the muffled *chhh* of a match striking against Thomas O'Malley's jeans. He dragged the flame to the pipe bowl in slow motion and touched it to the ball of tobacco, setting Remy to shaking her head again, the thin red ringlets at her neck bobbing like miniature Slinkys.

"Go ahead, grill your damn lungs. But don't think I'm feeding those rabid mongrels you're so damn fond of when you drop over gasping for air," she grumbled.

"My lungs are just fine. It's my ears that are aching." He chuckled, smiling at her in the rearview mirror. The statement said "Go on and zip your lips," but the way Mr. O'Malley wrapped it all up sounded a lot more like "I love you, too."

I glanced down at the journal in my lap. That was the problem with getting a phrase to sing the way you wanted it to. You could get the words all straight and neat between the lines, but the meaning was in the way they zigzagged toward a person when you gave them life. Mr. O'Malley and Remy tossed words into the space between them like a father tossing a child in the air and spinning around until both were laughing great big belly laughs. They could say, "You're a big old pain in my ass," and know it really meant "You are the sparkle in my stars and the wind in my wings," because each knew no matter how dizzy the universe got, the other would never let them hit the ground when it went off kilter.

The small stone inside my front pocket grew heavy, and my throat tightened. During the last eight years, I had rubbed its edges soft. In my back pocket, the corners of Grandma Jo's map poked into my hip and I wondered, not for the first time that day, where my father was, if his fingers missed the feel of my hair running through them.

For months after my father left, I slept in my parents'

bed with my mother on one side of me and Grandma Jo on the other, my face buried in my father's pillow. The fact of the matter is, I knew in the darkest crevices of my heart that he was gone, even if I didn't say so. In the middle of the night, I would wake with the cold fingers of that knowledge strangling me until every last memory of him was squeezed out of me, and the only way I could get them back was to bury my nose in the pillow, searching for the smell of him.

Inking in the final pearl, I held the sketch of Yemaya out in front of me, looking at it. Sea witches were supposed to be old hags, ugly creatures with snakes for hair who had been banished to darkness. But Yemaya was not. The sketch was clumsy, but even in its awkward state you could see the love in her eyes, the way she longed to let the arms of the ocean wrap her up in them. I knew precisely how she felt.

"What've you got there?" Remy's eyes rested on the picture in my hand. "Hey, that's not half bad. Can you make me one like that?"

Tearing the page from my notebook, I handed it to her.

"You know how she came to be our matron witch?" Remy tilted the sketch, studying it while she spoke.

I shook my head, closing the pad.

"The British were the first to arrive on Tillings. But settling an island is a whole lot of work, and let's be honest, have you ever known a Brit who liked getting dirt under their fingernails? So they brought slaves from Africa to do it for them, and those slaves brought Yemaya. Turns out, she liked it here, and to this very day she protects the island and everyone on it. Anyone who doubted the fact came to believe it was so in 1920, when Hurricane Gilbert leveled every one of these barrier islands then set its sights on Tillings. It was barreling right for it, and then stopped—just stopped—four miles out, did a forty-five-degree turn and went right back out to sea without knocking a single branch off one tree. Old-timers, like the one up there," she waved toward Mr. O'Malley, "say Gilbert came close enough to get a good look at Yemaya's eyes and thought better of it.

"Then there was Captain Booth, who built this property. He swore until his dying day he'd been rescued from the sea by her in the spring of 1936, when his ship went down on the ledge rock out there." She pointed vaguely toward the ocean beyond the cliffs. "Legend says when he cast his line, Captain Booth pulled in the biggest marlin anyone here had ever seen. He drew the harpoon back with two hands, ready to put it out of its misery. But when he looked in that fish's eye he couldn't kill it, claimed God's hand reached down and stopped him in his tracks a split second before he ripped through the fish's heart. I know it sounds crazy. . . ."

*Not to me*, I thought. The memory of the dead salmon bobbing pathetically onto its side in Potter's Creek drifted back to me.

"Anyway, he cut the line just before his skiff ran against

the reef, ripping it in two. Every single man on deck drowned. But not Captain Booth; they found him two days later half-conscious on the beach mumbling about a marlin who'd taken the shape of a beautiful woman and carried him home. The islanders say she fell in love with him when he spared her and couldn't bear to see him drown. They say she watched over him for the rest of his life, that you can still see her pacing the cliffs up here on stormy nights watching for him to come home." I squinted out the window toward the cliffs of Knockberry Ridge with a sting in my chest.

For an instant, the purple nose of the taxi headed straight for the ocean, looking as though it might plummet right off the edge of the cliff. Then twenty yards before reaching it, the car rounded a bend where a driveway veered to the right.

"You see there?" Remy was poking her finger toward the cliff where a proud pointy-roofed Cape sprouted right up from the hill. Small white bricks littered the lawn on all sides. "That house's where Mr. Audubon up front resides. Do you see those white blobs scattered all over his lawn? Salt licks! Brunch for all the deer and fox and rabbits on the island; and I am here to tell you every last creature on this island has moved into our backyard. When they come cart me away to the hospital on a stretcher paralyzed with Lyme disease, you be sure and tell them to send the bill to Mr. Thomas O'Malley, the old fool on Knockberry Ridge!"

She was joking, I'm pretty sure. However, something in the underbelly of her words was not, and I knew if any sane woman on the planet could be driven to loathe a hunk of salt I was sitting beside her. A mighty puff of sweet smoke billowed into the air from the front, followed by a deep chuckle.

"And behind that house is a corner of the property you'd do very well to steer clear from. There's a hundred-and-twenty-foot drop lined up with the corner of a reef, which has made a widow out of many a sailor's wife. If you walk the basin from below, you'll see the sand is the color of chestnut husks due to the smashed-up hulls of whaling ships. They get caught in the currents and dashed into the rocks." Her story seemed to be gaining steam, when she caught my eye and suddenly deflated, adding quietly, "There's nothing up top to keep you from the dive. So explore all the other edges of the property you like, but leave that one alone, okay?"

A certain gravity took hold of Remy's words, slowing them to a snail's pace, and I noticed my mother eyeing the ridge with a faraway look in her eyes. The normally faint crow's feet around her lips had pulled into tight creases. Beside her in the front seat, Thomas O'Malley's wavy white head nodded in silent agreement all the way past an overgrown field spattered with fruit trees and a thick hedge of evergreens.

A moment later, the Thunderbird's purple hood pointed in the direction of a huge white house with large black-shuttered windows and a rickety widow's walk peeping out over the Atlantic. The cottage looked to have been empty since the beginning of time, except I knew that wasn't true. I had been here before. The clapboards, the windows, the stairways, were all stuffed with the secret of what had really happened to my father. My stomach churned violently at the thought of going inside.

Three stories high, a stone chimney climbed out of the cottage at one end. A tall proud turret poked into the sky at the other with leaded windows sparkling on all eight sides. Four gables pointed upward from the straight lines of the second floor like fat arrows pointing to heaven. At the foot of the second story, the roof slanted sharply away from the home like a hoop skirt covering a full-pillared porch wrapping around the entire base of the house.

"Is there anything you'll be needing to settle in tonight?" Mr. O'Malley asked, eyeing my mother gently.

"We'll have to make a run to the market tomorrow, but I think we have everything we need." She looked at him thoughtfully with a nod before glancing at Remy and adding, "Except a vehicle."

Remy ignored the comment and studied my face, as if she knew inherently that was not true, as if she understood that the very reason we had come to this place was because we had nothing that we needed to keep us going. What we needed was love baked into our walls and the sound of laughter, and there was not a market in the world that could fix it.

Mr. O'Malley unlatched Luke's crate and scruffed the fur behind his ears. Luke gave a thank-you wag, poking his snout into the air for a sniff.

"Out with ya, then." Thomas O'Malley's voice was soft and gravelly, an utter contradiction to the enormity of him—like one of those Saturday-morning cartoons where Tweety Bird pipes up from the depths of Sylvester's stomach. I liked the sound of him, and so did Luke, who lapped at his open hand before bounding into the yard, tumbling over his own legs. I clamored out of the backseat while Remy flipped open the trunk, placed the suitcases at my mother's feet, and turned back to the larger steamer trunk. She took hold of the handle with the authority of a woman fully prepared to level a great sequoia armed with nothing more than an emery board.

"This one yours?"

I shook my head.

Remy looked my mother in the eye and plopped the trunk on its side no less than an inch from my mother's toe, thereby clarifying what was to become the terms of their acquaintanceship. Taking up the smaller trunk and my art case, she headed down the walk toward the arched French doors. To picture Remy Mandolin as anybody's servant was a difficult image to conjure, and yet there was something about her determination that whispered she'd been down that road once before—and blown it to smithereens behind her.

My mother planted both hands on the shelves of her

hips, watching Remy stroll to the door with my trunk in hand. There was not one thing bony about Remy. She had a Betty Boop body and walked with the swagger of a woman carrying a basket of fruit atop her head.

Two weeks ago, the black-eyed Susans at home had crumpled up into brown papery sacks, sad as spit wads upon their stalks, but here the lawn beyond the porch was speckled with them. Luke barked and I followed him around the corner of the house, sending him racing in lopsided circles around the yard. Overhead a gull screeched, sailing below the cliff and unexpectedly taking my stomach with it. My legs froze right up solid, refusing to go even one inch closer. The gull soared back into sight, tipped its wings, and dove again. In the distance, the cliff swam in and out of focus and the world tipped dizzily off its axis. It was still daylight, but over the waves the evening star winked above the clouds. It wasn't really a star. I had learned that when my mother forced me to make a model of the universe out of grapes and oranges tacked together with toothpicks. It was the planet Venus, named after the Greek goddess of love. The honest truth is, I didn't remember a lot about it. But I remembered this: it didn't have a moon to dance with or throw the tides off balance—just a field of stars to spin inside.

"Someday I'm going to catch you a star." My father and I had been lying in the field behind our house watching the Perseids. Resting my head in the pit of his arm, I blinked sleepily as meteors zipped overhead, pulling trails of white across heaven. The bonfire behind us sizzled at the remnants of a marshmallow, which had wriggled free of my stick and been broiled to a bubbling blob, sending a sugary sweetness into the night air.

I don't recall dozing off, but I awoke to my father dancing and darting through the field in nothing but his tighty-whiteys, chasing lightning bugs.

"Be look, stars." He laughed wildly. "I got you one. I caught you a falling star." He shook a mayonnaise jar in the air, setting a tiny green light flickering inside.

The commotion must have woken my mother, too, because she'd come jogging out in her robe and sent me to bed.

The next morning I found him in my bedroom jiggling the jar sadly as the small dead bug slid around the base. "It went out." I remember his voice as that of a child. "The light went out."

I was brought back by the chatter of Mr. O'Malley and Remy around the corner of the house. Occasionally, my mother's voice cut in to ask about the oil tank or fire-wood or, for the millionth time, when Remy intended to deliver her car. Inching away from the cliffs and toward the clapboards of the house, I put on my best eavesdropping ears.

"So it should be here by Thursday," my mother stated more than asked.

Remy ignored the question outright. "Does she remember?"

"No." My mother had lowered her voice.

"Did you ask her?" Remy and my mother were talking like they'd known each other all along now.

"Her doctor thinks she needs to come back to it on her own. So I don't try to talk about it anymore and I don't want anyone else to, either."

"I do not meddle in other people's business," I heard Remy say.

Mr. O'Malley let out a chuckle of amusement that said he didn't believe her.

"But if you ask me—"

"I didn't." My mother cut her off short.

"Right. But if you did, I might say that sometimes a situation calls for a good old-fashioned honest heart-to-heart."

"She'll come to it on her own."

"In this lifetime?" Remy lobbed back. "Because forgive me for saying so, but your method seems to really suck. I mean, eight years—you can become a damn doctor in eight years and cure yourself."

"Let me know when you've done that, and then we'll talk. I'm not sure why the hell you care, anyway. Don't you have someplace you need to go?"

"Not really. And maybe I know something about all this," Remy's voice challenged.

"You're not her."

I patted my hand to my knee, calling Luke back, and came around the corner in time to see my mother disappear inside with Remy hot on her heels.

Thomas O'Malley propped his huge frame against the purple Thunderbird, causing the red cursive letters to read T _ _ I, the word's middle lost under the expansive girth of his waist, and shook his head, letting the corners of his mouth tilt up.

"Izabella, come see your room." Remy was leaning out the front door, craning her neck around a porch pillar, apparently having won yet another round with my mother, who was climbing back down the steps to haul in the last of the luggage.

Luke bounced through the door with me behind him. The living room of the Booth House was scattered with Oriental rugs, big splashes of red and blue against the white room. There were two staircases, one that climbed to the second floor from the living room, and a second, narrow utility staircase from the back of the kitchen. A beach-stone fireplace took up one entire wall. From the corner of my eye, I could see my mother pretending to unload a bag of food as she watched me.

"Upstairs," Remy hollered from the top floor.

Luke bounded clumsily up one flight of steps, disappearing around a corner. Two seconds later, I heard the pitter-patter of puppy paws up another flight. When I caught up with him, he was parked inside the doorway, tail drumming back and forth against the jamb.

"Boy, I haven't been in this room in a long time." Remy pushed open a window.

The room was tucked right inside of the turret and shaped like a huge stop sign, only instead of arrest-me-red it was Pepto-Bismol pink: pink wallpaper, pink quilt, pink rugs, and heavy white velvet curtains to hold it all in. There was no lightning bolt of memory, just a soft tickling déjà vu, as though the walls were trying to whisper something to me in a voice too low for me to hear. Luke sat upright and cocked an ear politely in her direction. I came up close behind Remy to peek out the three-story-high window, keeping the pillowy crescent of her hips between it and me.

"Look at that. Ocean view on six walls!"

She was right about that. From the middle of the room, every window seemed filled up with water like a huge tank.

When my fifth birthday rolled around, my father's apology about the trip to Potter's Creek had materialized in the way of a tank of fish to call my own. While they were not dancing salmon, it's true, my father had filled the tank with as many fish as it would hold and covered the whole thing with a sheet and bow. The morning of my birthday, I'd run to unwrap it with thoughts of angelfish dancing in my head. Instead, I was greeted by ten golden bellies bobbing grotesquely across the surface and not one living fish. My father, having failed to take into consideration the radiator behind the tank, had cooked the whole lot of them into the here beyond. With the last flush of the toilet, my father had turned and plodded downstairs.

"Perfect." My mother had sighed once he'd gone. The letters added up to *p-e-r-f-e-c-t,* but her tone added up to *s-h-i-t-h-e-a-d.*

"Izabella?" I turned toward the sound of Remy's voice. "Do you want me to open the rest of the windows?"

I shook my head, sweeping the memory back into the corner of my mind. It was hard to sort out exactly when my parents' marriage started to unknit. When I tried, the memories got all knotted up together: one moment I recalled my parents tangled up on a blanket in the backyard whispering to each other and laughing, and the next they were standing a world apart screaming at each other and crying. Not for the first time, I wondered if my mother missed him, if she ever longed, like me, for him to come home.

As I stepped closer to the window, the sharp crags of Knockberry Ridge pulled into view. The sight of them snagged at my gut and I had the distinct feeling one good yank might just go ahead and unravel the entire fabric of me.

"Hey, come have a look at this." Remy crossed the room, pointing out the northern window. "You see the really

tall boulder out there? That one, down the path there."
I squinted out the window where a huge rock seemed to
pitch over the side of the cliff in the shape of a curled
wave. Behind it was a ramshackle shed with a broken
weathervane on its roof. "That's Witch's Peak. It's where
Yemaya watches for the sailors to come home."

I nodded, leaning over to scoop Luke up before turning
back to study the room where two stained-glass side windows threw braided rainbows wavering along the pink
walls in the shape of ships. It reminded me of Jesus flying
up to the rafters of the Talabahoo First Congregational
Church.

When we returned downstairs, Mr. O'Malley was fighting with a damp match to light a fire in the hearth. Remy
went over to help him.

"These matches are no good," she muttered, tossing the
entire book into the fireplace. "They can start their own
damn fire."

"I said I'd have the place ready, and I intend to do so.
I'll get mine from the car," Mr. O'Malley said, stepping for
the door, and I recalled what my mother had said on the
boat about him looking after the house in our absence.

"No, you will not!" Remy bounced to her feet. "You'll
just light that damned pipe of Satan again. I'll get them."
She vanished through the door, trotting back two seconds
later wielding a Zippo in her right hand. Bending low, she
fiddled with the stack of kindling then touched the lighter

to the paper's edge, tending it as if it could not be trusted to burn on its own.

From the kitchen, the phone rang and my mother knocked something to the floor with a thump trying to answer it. It was not until her voice picked up volume in the way of panic that I could make out what she was saying.

"Really, Mother, now probably isn't the best time. . . ."

Across the room, Remy drew her head out from the ashes to raise an eyebrow at me. I shrugged.

"I'm fine, Mother. Iz is fine. We are all fine. Really, you needn't come right away."

Pause.

"Well, I don't care if you believe me. It's true."

Pause.

"Yes, I'm eating."

That was an outright lie. Several times a day plates appeared in the kitchen sink full of food she hadn't bothered to touch. She prepared meals for me . . . well, at least in the way of pouring some milk over cereal or boiling noodles, but she never ate them. It was a small wonder she needed to wrap herself up like a mummy to stay warm.

"Maybe later . . . another week or two . . . "

A weighty sigh and, "Fine."

Remy shoved another log in the grate as the phone clinked into its cradle. A second later, my mother made her way into the doorway, leaning heavily against the frame. "Who the hell hooked up the phone service?"

"Sorry about that." Sincerity was lacking in Remy's words, which were muffled by the stone hearth. "I just assumed—"

"Incorrectly."

"—incorrectly, that you might like to be able to ring the operator in the event your house catches fire or you break a leg or something. I radioed ahead from the boat."

"Raving lunatic," my mother grumbled under her breath.

"And damn proud of it," Remy chirped, but whether my mother was referring to Remy or Grandma Jo wasn't plain. I figured it was a fifty-fifty gamble.

I bit my cheek trying to force back a smile. It was too late.

"Your grandmother's coming," my mother huffed before letting the door swing closed behind her. "Tomorrow."

# CHAPTER SIX

It was our second day on the island and I had spent a good portion of the afternoon just wandering from room to room, peeking through closets and under carpet edges. There was no shortage of small hidden doors fit for a leprechaun, which Luke took to wiggling in and out of, and cabinets leading to nowhere. I'd decided Captain Booth must have built his whole house around the notion that he'd someday have a lot of treasure to stash. If he ever did, all he'd left behind was a small brass monocle I slipped into my back pocket.

I found my mother sitting cross-legged on the floor of her room, staring at the closet door among piles of half-hung shirts. The dresser drawers were pulled wide open, but not one pair of socks had yet been put away. From all evidence, there had been a struggle and the shirts had clearly prevailed. The closet door hung lopsided from one hinge with a big chip in the frame and my mother was staring hard at it with bloodshot eyes while holding a screwdriver in one hand. In the back of the room, a stack of my father's old stories tilted against the wall covered in splinters and dust. He'd brought them over with us on our last visit, but in his rush out of our lives, he'd left them behind. Whisking the corner of her hand across her eyes, she gazed up at me and cleared her throat.

"All this dust is setting my allergies off," she croaked, as though I were expected to believe a huge dust bunny had wrestled her to the ground, leaving her crumpled there on the floor sniffling. However, something clearly had. Luke whined, stumbling over to her, and lapped at her wrist.

Giving Luke a gentle shove, she got to her knees, trying to wriggle the bottom hinge back into place. It slipped away from her, catching the joint of her thumb in the process. She kicked the door then threw the screwdriver at it as if to finish it off.

"Son of a bitch!"

The words drifted in like fog, leaving me disoriented and reeling through the years to this very spot on my sixth birthday. And then it was not her but me on the floor just like that, blood trickling down my shin from landing on the closet door. I had followed him that night, had tried to take the wish back and make him stay. The memory knocked the wind out of me.

My father had stormed upstairs after my tantrum in the kitchen. Standing in khaki shorts and a sweater, he'd already made one attempt at sliding back the closet door before kicking it squarely off its track when I ran up behind him. His shoulders were cocked back with a cowboy's readiness to take the quarrel outside and end it once and for all, which, in a way, is exactly what happened. I could feel it then, the secret of what I had done taking its first breath, burning its way through me the very way I had imagined the air burning through the gills of that salmon in Potter's Creek.

There are times when a person is so mad that a bubble of rage circles right around him so tightly nobody else can get in, and that is how my father was that night. He grabbed my mother's suitcase, the one printed in Wedgwood blue roses, and flipped it open. Him being fond neither of the color blue or flowers of any sort, I knew then he was bent on leaving at any cost, that he was going with my mother's suitcase tucked under his arm and my "I hate you" tucked in his ears.

"I didn't mean it!" It had started as a whimper climbing up my throat but came into the world as a full-blown wail. "Don't go!"

In hindsight, the words should have been more poetic, or profound, or tragic. But I was six and in a hurry to get them out. Throwing myself at him, I latched on to the arm of his purple striped sweater, the very one I had picked out on my own for a Father's Day gift that year. It had taken me three months, and a thousand extra chores, to raise enough money for that sweater; but I did not care one stitch if I tore it in two stopping him.

The weight of me hadn't slowed him down; he continued to toss clothes among the blue roses while I swung like a monkey from his arm. The reason he was leaving was my stupid, horrible fault, and I was trying desperately to undo the words I had spoken.

"Please, please, don't go. I didn't mean it. Honest, I didn't. Daddy, don't go!"

"Don't, Be." The command came at me just like that, *don't be*, as if he wanted me to drop from existence right there. For the first time ever, my father, who had always acted as if the whole world spun just for me, stared straight through me, plucking me from his arm and letting me tumble to the ground like an old winter-scorched burdock. I'd hopped to and latched on again, pleading with all my might.

"Noooo, Daddy, pleeeease, no!"

"Goddamn it!" He roared, pushing my foot so it hit a stack of papers and sent them flying to the ground. "Knock it off! *Knock it off, I said!! Let go!*" Let go, let go, *letgoletgoletgoletgo.* "Don't, Be!" The words hit me with the smart of a firm slap on the cheek as a request to God to take my last breath. *Don't be.* They tinkled down around me in broken bits. When I looked up, my father's gray eyes had narrowed to razor shards of shattered glass.

This is the first and only memory I have of my father

hating me; still, one moment of hating does not seem like enough to make someone go away forever.

With a final whisk, my father shook himself free, sending me flying into the broken closet door with a thump, leaving me crumpled up beside his shoes with air hissing out of me like a popped tire, but he never looked down. Tears bit the corners of my eyes as I untangled my legs, wiping a streak of blood from my shin where the splintered corner had grated the skin. The severity of the situation became water clear: my father was leaving. It was my fault and I could not stop him.

"Son of a bitch!" My mother had rushed into the room behind us, planting herself firmly between my father and me. She was half my father's size, but twice mine, and her legs blocked me with two pillars of tan corduroy. "Are you totally fucking crazy?" My father's eyes dropped to where I'd landed. "Get the hell away from her." She reached down to put a hand on my head. The look in her eye said she did not give a rat's ass how big my father was; one more move and she would cut him down to size two inches at a time.

When the shock of what had just happened cleared, I bolted between the rigid V of my mother's legs so driven that the confused fear in her eyes passed by almost unnoticed. When she swept me up from behind, I felt the wobble of her legs shifting slightly from their fighting stance to stop me. And then I did a thing I had never done before. I hit her. I balled all my six-year-old fingers up into a neat knot and swung at her with everything I had. I was so angry at that moment, at both of them, that I might have killed her flat out if I'd been seven. I wasn't. But the blow hit with enough force to shock her into letting go long enough for me to roll back to the floor and bolt for my backpack. To this very day, I can't help wondering why she didn't grab him instead.

"I give up," my mother now said, sucking the blood from her thumb.

Climbing to her feet, she tossed the screwdriver to the ground. "I'm going to start a fire and make some tea."

I followed her downstairs, snatching my notebook off the dining room table as we walked by. While she started the stove I hopped onto the counter.

*How do you know them? Mr. O'Malley and Remy.* I tossed the pad on the counter beside my mother's mug and studied a scratch on my right knuckle.

"I don't know what you mean. I told you, Mr. O'Malley looks after Grandma Izabella's cottage when we aren't here. You know, mowing the grass, checking the boiler, putting in the screens. You've met him before, when you were little." She glanced my way, but I noticed she didn't look me in the eye. "They live down the lane. They always have—well, Mr. O'Malley, at least. I think his daughter lived in Boston or something. I haven't seen her in years; I didn't even recognize her."

I leaned over the paper and scribbled, *She knew Dad.*

My mother paused over the statement before clearing her throat. "Yes, she did. It's a small island, Iz. Everyone knows everybody else here."

I went to reach for the paper again, but my mother put her hand over it.

"Go get the matches, please. Mr. O'Malley left a pack on the bookshelf." She turned and walked into the living room. "I want to set the fire before Grandma Jo gets here."

**The kettle had** just begun to shrill and my mother was head down in the mammoth stonework of the living room fireplace trying to convince the wood to burn when Grandma Jo came through the door two hours early dangling a pair of leather flip-flops from her thumb. Holding tight to the 1960s, and liking nothing to come between herself and the natural world, she seldom wore shoes and often wandered around the house stark naked, a habit which drove my mother to distraction. "Jojo the naked Hobo," my father used to tease her.

She paused to examine my mother with a perplexed expression. "No, dear." She laughed. "You've got it all wrong. It's the gas stove you want to stick your head in when you would rather asphyxiate yourself than greet your mother. Don't you keep up with the poets? It's all the rage in San Francisco. Wood won't do at all, at least not unless you can actually light it. Then I suppose it might have a certain poetic cadence to it."

"Mother!" My mother withdrew her head, smudged with soot at the cheeks and chin. "I thought you were taking the two o'clock ferry."

Grandma Jo crossed the room and hugged her tight, kissing her squarely on her smudged cheek. When she finally let go, she turned to me, taking two steps back to look me over. "It is an impossibility that you are fourteen years old. My God! Have you seen yourself in the mirror? You're lovely."

I ran up to kiss her, letting her wrap me up in one of her famous tourniquet hugs.

"You look fabulous, Mom," my mother said, swiping the dust from her hand onto her jeans.

"You look perplexed," Grandma Jo answered. "I'll trade you, a fire for a cup of Earl Grey."

"Deal." My mother's face relaxed.

"And you, my gorgeous, please get the bags on the steps and tear them open before one more moment ticks past your birthday while I go call the Girl Scouts and demand a refund for your mother's woods-woman training." Grandma Jo rolled up her sleeves, heading toward the fireplace.

"You know the reason you can't start a fire, Zorrie?" she called after my mother. "It's that job of yours. Antique chairs, collectible frames, dusty old whoosits, thingamabobs, and whatsits. Those people you work for are so flipping concerned about how much money they can get from old wood you forget that sometimes," Grandma Jo tossed a match into the pile with ease, "it is in a thing's nature to burst into flames just for the fun of it."

My mother managed a genuine laugh from the kitchen, surprising me down to my toes. "Well, I may agree with you, but I won't get many appraisal contracts with that on my business card."

"How many old relics does a person need from a bunch of dead artists before they rejoin the living?"

"A lot," my mother called through the clinking of tea-cups.

"That's the problem with people. Holding on to every inch of the past, while the present speeds on past them."

My friend, Libby, called my grandmother a granola head, and I counted myself lucky for it. While her grand-mother spent hours knitting toilet paper cozies, mine had dragged me to lectures at Brown by the Dalai Lama and traveled all over the world volunteering.

She leaned over the wood shifting the kindling around and in less than a minute the hearth was ablaze. The glow of the fire rendered her cotton tunic transparent. Beneath it, her breasts hung braless in soft mounds. Even at sixty, I thought she was the second most beautiful woman I had ever seen, next to my mother, who looked just like her. Together they could silence a room simply by floating into it together.

Setting down the bags Grandma Jo had brought and

digging through them, I lifted forth a volume of essays by Ralph Waldo Emerson, flipping it over in my hand.

"Oh, and look at these; I got them at the Ben Gurion airport in Israel at one of the kiosks." She pulled a small square envelope from her bag and peeled a sticker of a Tootsie Roll donning a man's dress loafer free. Giggling at the label, which read FOOTSIEROLL, she stuck it to the tip of my nose. "They call them Wacky Packs"

Plucking it free from my skin, I dug back into the bag and pulled forth a compact filled with blushes and tints made from African wildflowers, and a fitted silk shirt with a low-cut sweater to go along with it—styles my mother would clearly not approve of, making them all the sweeter. At the bottom of the bag was a brand-new leather-bound journal and a carved wooden fountain pen that must have cost a fortune. I bolted from the room, shirt and makeup in hand, brushing her cheek with a kiss as I passed.

When I returned my mother gasped.

"Look at you!" Grandma Jo gushed, standing up to blend the blush on my cheeks. "You could join the plastic ranks of supermodel."

"Mother! She looks . . . "

"Stunning." Grandma Jo leveled two hazel eyes in my mother's direction.

"That shirt is cut to her navel. Why didn't you just buy her a roll of cellophane to wrap up in?"

"Because the store was clean out, if you must know. Zorrie, she's a young woman now. Don't you remember being fourteen? I used to have to stand by the door and button you up three notches every time you left, and don't think I don't know you used to undo them once you were gone."

"No, Mother, I didn't. That was me, buttoning you up. You were the nudist of the neighborhood."

"Well, that's neither here nor there. She's growing up and dressing her like a football player will not stop her from going right ahead and doing it anyway. Look, she's even developing beautiful breasts."

"Mom!" Color washed over my mother's cheeks in a rush of crimson. I looked down at the tiniest mounds of flesh barely holding the silk from my ribs.

Grandma Jo laughed at both of us. "Oh, Zorrie! You need to lighten up before those frown-lines settle in for good. With Ansel gone you have forgotten how to laugh." She didn't mean it, but the statement landed on my mother's face like a physical slap.

"And as for you . . . " She tugged the shirttails in line with the waistband of my Levi's. She was studying me closely, as though reading the small print of my body, and I wondered if she could tell I'd gotten my period. "Don't move."

Grandma Jo disappeared for a second, reappearing with a pair of scissors. With a single snip, she poked a hole in my jeans and gave it a hearty tug, ripping the knee casually. "There. That's how the girls are wearing them now." I can only imagine the sparkle in my eyes, but I saw clearly

the shock in my mother's and the way it melted into resigned silence as my grandmother snuggled back into the
sofa, lifting Luke into her lap. "So, this is the newest addi-
tion to the family?" Taking a sip of her tea, she scrubbed
his belly, sending him tottering happily onto his side.

I nodded as Luke's eyes blinked lazily then closed,
content in her care. There was no doubt about it; the air
around us had shifted. Grandma Jo had arrived.

"Any new boys in your life?"

I rolled my eyes.

"Well, you'll have some choosing to do in that outfit!
You just wait and see. What about you, Zorrie?"

"No, Mom. I don't have time for anyone else in my life.
I'm too busy. That's what I was trying to tell you on the
phone. It isn't that we don't love having you, but truly, I
am so swamped with work right now—"

"My love, sometimes the swamp finds a person, and
sometimes a person finds the swamp."

Grandma Jo did not believe in holding on to the past.
When my grandfather passed away, she'd worn fuchsia to
his memorial service and asked a friend to play "Home-
ward Bound" by Simon & Garfunkel on the guitar. Afterward, everyone let a fistful of white daisy petals tumble
into the breeze. And when they had flown away from the
sorrow below, so had she. Since then, my grandmother
had spent most of her time traveling. It was the reason
she'd given me a map of my own, so I could always see
exactly where she was. In the three months since I'd last

seen her, Grandma Jo had lived for two months in Africa teaching at a small school and spent one month farming on a kibbutz in Israel.

"Okay, who wants to see pictures?" Grandma Jo reached into her bag, drawing forth a stack of photographs and waving them in the air.

"Sorry, but I need to finish up my estimates for an auction I'm working on. Iz will show you to your room if you'd like to freshen up." With that, my mother made her way stiffly into the study and shut the door heavily behind her.

"Funny, I don't feel like I need freshening." Grandma Jo looked at me perplexed. "Do I look like I need freshening?"

I shook my head. Watching the two of them together was better than front row seats at a Barnum & Bailey Circus sideshow.

"Well, I guess that just leaves the two youngsters of the family," Grandma Jo winked. "I may not need freshening, but I could air out. How about we go for a walk and you can reacquaint me with this island of yours?"

I hopped off the couch, heading for my shoes, then decided to go barefoot like Grandma Jo.

"I'll bring my pictures, you bring your journal," she called as she opened the door and let Luke scurry between her ankles into the day.

**The noon sun** slipped behind a white puff of cloud in the shape of a powdered doughnut as we followed a thin trail through the meadow. A hundred yards away, the cliffs of Knockberry Ridge curved around us, jutting out over the water. Grandma Jo turned inland, heading toward a hedge of sugar maples that had been tapped and hung with weathered tin buckets. When we reached the first she stuck her finger into the sap, lifting it back into the air dripping, and let the liquid fall from her fingertip in oozy drips. When no more would fall away, she stuck the finger in her mouth and puckered, sending a smile spreading over both our faces.

"Do you think they'd miss one?" She peered back at me, wrestling the bucket off its hook. "I'll hang it back up tomorrow."

I raised a brow at her.

"I made sugarcane syrup and molasses in Africa. How different could it be?"

I shrugged.

"Pancakes tomorrow!"

Lugging the pail along with her, she followed the path to a mound of boulders and sat down, which sent a garter snake slithering out between her feet and me nearly twisting an ankle to let it through. Luke bounced to his feet, nipping the air behind the snake until it dodged under a rock.

"Come. Sit. Tell me everything."

When I was certain no more snakes were going to make their way over my toes, I settled in beside her on the rocks, holding the new pen and journal, intent on hearing all about her travels.

*Tell me all about Africa*, I wrote.

"I spent a month in Porto-Novo helping to build a small school for the village, and another in Monrovia teaching, although I think I did a whole lot more learning than teaching. The children were so smart and friendly. Most of them only had two or three outfits, but they were the happiest little pips I believe I've ever met. Look!" Grandma Jo bent her wrist, showing off a woven bracelet decorated with carved beads. "Isn't it lovely? They made it for me! And the oldest was twelve years old. Each bead has a different meaning. This one means hope, and this one means health and unity. You would love it there, absolutely love it. Next year you'll come with me." She patted my hand.

*Really?*

"Really. Look. This picture was taken at the Ivory Coast. And this is the first village I stayed at, in Lagos. That man is the village elder, and this one is the *Oloogun*."

*Oloogun?*

"Medicine man, but he doesn't just heal people, he watches over the crops and weather and infestations. Stuff like that. Oh! Look." Grandma Jo opened her bag, pulling out a white stick wrapped halfway with leaves and tied with a string. "It's a talisman! He gave it to me for protection. This is the bone of a wild boar, and it's wrapped in rooibos leaves. He blessed it with goat blood." She held it out to me, laughing when I curled my nose up at it. "Oh, and this is Kitzi, the daughter of the host family whose hut I stayed in." Grandma Jo flipped to another picture, but I was barely listening.

*Did they talk about a witch named Yemaya? She's the matron of Tillings*, I scribbled.

"I had forgotten that." Grandma Jo nodded. "Yemaya isn't really a witch. She's an *orisha* of the ocean from Yorubaland. And Yemaya isn't really a name, it's sort of a contraction—*Yeye omo eja* means 'Mother whose children are the fish,' hence Yemaya. She's revered more on the western coast in villages along the River Ogun than where I was. That's really all I know about her. Why?"

*No reason*, I wrote, which wasn't entirely true. *Remy and Mr. O'Malley know all about her.*

"Remy?"

*Remy Mandolin, Mr. O'Malley's daughter.*

"Tom O'Malley?"

*How did you know his name?*

"I met him many years ago. You were still a baby."

*What about Remy and Mrs. O'Malley?* I'd forgotten that Grandma Jo came with us to Tillings several times when I was young, and it never occurred to me that she might know anyone here. I set the journal on the ground beside the bucket of sap, which now had three honeybees crawling laps around its rim.

There was a long pause. "I might have met Mrs. O'Malley and Remy. It was a long time ago." Grandma Jo lazed back on the boulder to watch the honeybees. "I just remember Mr. O'Malley coming to fix things around the property anytime something didn't work." Her toes curled and uncurled over the rock's edge. "So tell me: how are you really?"

By the time I was done writing, I had told her about everything: the crimson stain on my underpants, the weird déjà vu feeling of the house, which made me worry somewhere in the basement of my brain that I might be going insane, and what I had remembered about my mother crumpled up beside the closet. It all spilled onto the page like water from a spring and when she had read the pages, rubbing Luke's stomach the whole while, she sat back and looked at me thoughtfully.

"So it feels like the world is trying to tell you something. Is that so insane, Izabella?" I liked when she talked to me this way—one woman to another, not grandmother to child. She didn't ever shorten my name or try to dig my voice free. "Do you know a lioness can communicate with her mate three miles away? There's just so much we don't really understand. Why don't you stop worrying about being crazy and just try listening to what the world has to say? And as far as déjà vu, have you considered the fact that maybe there is something familiar here, something trying to get in that you may be keeping out?" She set the journal on my knee, looking at her watch. "Oh my, it's getting late. We'd better head back. But first . . . " Words don't glitter, but if they did my grandmother's would have. "Do you still smear honey on your toast?"

I nodded, giving her a "what are you up to" look.

"Me, too. And I think I know just where to find some—watch."

And with that Grandma Jo gently brushed the bees from the lid of the bucket, gazing after them as they flitted through a hole in the side of a poplar tree. Tiptoeing behind them, her whole body seemed to shift into slow motion. By the time she reached the hole, her arms and face were dotted with fuzzy little bodies strutting up and down, as confused by my grandmother as the rest of the world was.

I pulled Luke into my lap, tucking him close to my chest, and held my breath waiting to see Grandma Jo keel over from a thousand stings. Luke must have sensed my heart racing, because every few seconds he would peel his eyes from Grandma Jo and lick my ear gently until the muscles along my neck relaxed.

Slowly, she reached into the hole, made a tiny jerking motion with her hand, and turned back to me with a fistful of dripping honeycomb. The bees lit into the air, buzzing calmly around the mouth of the hive as though bidding farewell to an old friend. By the time she'd reached the boulder again, they'd all disappeared without stabbing one single stinger into her skin. Looking at the astounded expression on my face, Grandma Jo laughed, scraping the honey onto the edge of the bucket.

"It's really no mystical gift. They don't mind sharing, showing off their art a bit. Just as long as you only take your fair share and don't squish any of them in the process. If they sense aggression, they sting. If they sense calm, they just sort of visit with you while you're there. Ready?"

I nodded, hopping off the rock, still amazed that my grandmother's blood coursed somewhere in my veins.

Once the tin pail, with its watery sap and small clump of honeycomb clinging to the side, had been deposited in the kitchen sink, Grandma Jo turned to me with two sticky hands planted on her hips. For a second, I noticed that both she and my mother did that. Then the thought righted itself in my head because it wasn't the same thing at all. When my mother dug her hands into her hips it was as if she was gluing her fingers to something to stop herself from smacking the world silly. The way that my grandmother did it said, "Bring it on—I haven't got all day," like she couldn't wait for life to turn the page.

"*Now* I need freshening up. If you would be kind enough to show me where my room is, I'll shower then make dinner while your mom works. I feel like I'm back at the kibbutz. Nothing feels better than a little dirt under the nails. Someday I'll bring you with me, or maybe we'll go somewhere new, like Holland. I have always wanted to go to Holland. What do you think? We can tumble through a field of tulips and chase windmills like Don Quixote." Grandma Jo winked at me.

I nodded, trying to picture that in my head. The closest I had ever come to leaving the country was when my father brought me to Noatak National Preserve in Alaska, which is kissing distance across the Bering Strait to the Chukotsky District in Russia.

My mother was away working on an art estate sale in Alabama, and I had no idea that she didn't know we were going. Caught up by a burning desire to become one with nature, my father had rented a cabin, packed our parkas, and booked a flight for the West Coast. When we landed, he rented a red pickup eaten through with rust and bought a crossbow with which to hunt our own food.

"Ready to go wild?" he'd joked. "We're going to have so much fun."

And it was fun, until I woke up the following morning in the tiny cabin shivering because the woodstove had fizzled out and my father and his crossbow were nowhere to be found. I might have frozen to death if the owner of the cabin had not come to stack wood and check on us.

"Have you ever ridden on a snowmobile?" The man had tucked me between his legs and hit the throttle.

Shaking my head, I had buried my face in the arm of his parka and let the tears come as he whizzed me away. I didn't know where my father had gone, but I was sure he would come back for me. My mother would be upset that I had gone so easily with a perfect stranger, but my father would be worried. He would go searching.

Five hours after we arrived at the cabin owner's house, and with no trace of my father, the park rangers and my mother were notified.

They found my dad downriver an hour later. He had

painted his face and neck with clay from the riverbank like some ancient native hunter and was using the cross-bow to try to shoot fish in the river. He hadn't come back. He wasn't looking. He'd left me behind.

After that, any time my mother was not home, Grandma Jo came to stay with us. I wondered how far Holland was from Alaska.

# CHAPTER SEVEN

By the time I got downstairs the next morning, every hall in the house was filled with the sweet smell of maple syrup, which Grandma Jo had simmered to a warm golden froth on the stove. Remy Mandolin was teetering precariously on a Windsor chair while edging the last of the storm windows into its frame in the living room, and Grandma Jo had come up behind her with a bottle of Windex and a rag.

"That's what they're saying," she was telling my grandmother. "They have three propaganda videos from the Symbionese Liberation Army and it's Patty Hearst speaking on all of them. It may be that she wasn't kidnapped, after all. She may have gone of her own free will."

Luke wiggled free of my arm and scampered up beside them with a whine.

"Good morning, Sunshine," Grandma Jo twittered, lifting the rag into the air as Luke tried to snatch it.

"More like Rip Van Winkle. The day's half gone," Remy mumbled, snapping the window secure. "Your mother's sending you off to Herman's with me on a grocery run. So, if you're having breakfast, you'd better have at it."

"I'd go myself," my mother said, coming into the room and sniffing the remnants of the gallon of milk she'd brought from home and wrinkling her nose up at it. "But, I've got—"

"A ton of work to finish up before the weekend," Grandma Jo and Remy finished in unison. "We know."

"Actually, I was going to say *no car.*" She gazed at Remy, who ignored her. "I'm the only person on Tillings running a tab with a taxi—and a perfectly good car of my own across the bay."

I suspected the real reason my mother refused to go herself was that she did not want to admit defeat by depending on a ride from Remy while her car sat doubling as a beach chair for Telly.

"First, you are not the only one," Remy corrected. "Second, I told you I'll bring it as soon as I can. That ferry's packed tighter than a wad of chewing tobacco until the festival is over. And third, I'm already tired of listening to you whine on about it. Give it a rest. It isn't like I haven't got better things to do than plop storm windows into your frames and cart you around hell's half acre."

"At least you're getting paid for your misery," my mother grumbled under her breath. She turned to look at me.

"Maybe Grandma Jo would like to go with you." There was a hopeful tone in her voice.

"It's an island, darling. She's not going to get lost. You let that puppy out more than her. Give the child a break from all of us. She's a teenager; they need open space to air out."

"Hear, hear," Remy quipped.

"Maybe she'll meet some kids her own age instead of being cooped up in this house with a bunch of antiques."

"I brought pictures, Mom, not the actual antiques."

"I wasn't talking about your musty old furniture." Grandma Jo laughed. "I was referring to us, or more frankly, you. Besides, I'm going to take a stroll down to the beach. Remy says there's a great place to do yoga not far from here."

"Oh, that sounds nice." My mother's voice perked up. "Iz, grab a pen and make a list for me, will you?"

Still sleepy, I stumbled over to the journal Grandma Jo had brought, tore a page free, and flopped into a chair at the table.

Buried under six layers of clothes like a summer onion, my mother made her way back into the kitchen and began scuttling from cabinet to cabinet calling off items for a grocery list.

"Pasta," she called. Then, "linguini," as though one were not the other. I shook my head at the soft risen dough of Remy's rear end waggling in the woodbin as she tossed a load of kindling in. Although it was not a kinship she admitted to, I felt sure somewhere in my mother's lineage there was a shot of Italian blood. Dinner—when it was not cereal—meant pasta, the only difference being the sauce she poured over it and the chunks of meat tossed in for texture.

"Chicken and honey." With her face shoved in the icebox, my mother sounded as if she were chewing sand. There was a tinkle of ice cubes followed by the light thud of the icebox door swinging shut.

"Izabella and I got honey yesterday." Grandma Jo went to the kitchen, returning with a crock containing the slab of honeycomb.

From her chair, Remy studied the waxy blob with a sour face.

"What?" Grandma Jo looked at the crock. "It's organic."

"So is horse shit, but I don't eat it on crackers," Remy quipped, turning back to the window. "Real honey comes in little jars shaped like bears with the bee poop cooked out of it."

Grandma Jo laughed as she stuck her pinky into the crock and poked it in the air at Remy. "Just try it!"

"Not on your life," Remy answered without turning around.

Grandma Jo marched over to me and stuck her finger in my mouth. I rolled my eyes and licked the remnants from my top lip. It was the sweetest honey I'd ever tasted.

"Well, I'm going to need more than that for honey chicken anyway, so grab another," my mother intervened.

"Tofu," Grandma Jo called over her shoulder.

"What the hell is toe food?" Remy scooped up the stack of screens she had freed from the windows and stuck them outside the front door.

"*Tofu*. You know, bean curd."

"I don't know that Herman's carries bean turd." Remy glanced at my grandmother as if she might be insane.

"Bean *curd*." Grandma Jo laughed. "Oh, and whole wheat pasta. I'm going to make Izabella my famous home-made macaroni and cheese."

"I'll buy it." My mother came back through the kitchen doorway. "So long as I don't have to eat it."

"You will eat it, and you will love it," Grandma Jo said.

"Can Iz pay with a check?"

"Cash," Remy called from the front step. "Maynard Herman only takes local checks."

We had passed Herman's Market, a small storefront with a red and white awning and a broom leaned up against the wall, coming in two days earlier. I vaguely re-membered seeing the crooked old man standing on the stoop with a shock of white hair slicked back as smooth as bleached vinyl to his scalp. He'd waved politely as we passed, but deep lines etched his expression into a per-manent scowl.

My mother dug three twenties free from her wallet, tossing them beside the list.

"Get a sweater before you leave." I rolled my eyes, look-ing down at the shirt Grandma Jo had brought me. I knew she just wanted it covered up. "Iz, I'm not in the mood. Just do it."

Untangling my ankles from Luke's paws, I ran upstairs, pulling on the accompanying sweater, knowing my mother wouldn't dare say anything in front of Grandma Jo, even if she disapproved.

Walking over to the mirror, I tugged the shirttails of my blouse the way Grandma Jo had done the night before, letting them poke out from under the bottom of the sweater. Looking back at me was a snaky tendrilled Medusa with skin the color of curdled cream. Instead of brushing through the knotted uncombed spirals hanging to my waist, I grabbed an elastic band, pulling them into a messy mop at the back of my neck and looked at myself in the mirror, trying to make the word "hideous" come alive in my throat. Even that was just an ugly small hiss of air. Against my pale complexion, the spatter of freckles passed down by my father looked more like a splash of mud that refused to wash away.

Sometimes, I pretended the girl in the mirror was someone else. I brushed through the loose curls until they softened and the light played off them in shocks of auburn. When she smiled back at me, shallow dimples appeared at the corners of her mouth in a way that was one part playful, two parts flirty. Her eyes said she knew something the rest of the world did not. But, all it took was a single shift of light and she always morphed back into me—silent as the moon strung over the world like a fat pearl and not nearly as pretty. Today, she was all me—awkward beyond the help of cheeks pinched pink and lip gloss, one part gawky and two parts weird.

"Gotta go!" Remy called from downstairs.

Sighing, I pulled on a pair of Nikes and trotted out to the driveway, slipping into the passenger seat.

"Okay, kiddo. I'll drop you at Herman's then run to the landing to help Mr. O'Malley unload passengers and come back around for you in about an hour. You okay for that long?"

I nodded.

"If you finish early, there's a soda fountain at the White Whale. Go around to the side and Mrs. Barrett's got a small ice cream shop, any kind of soda you want. But don't go anywhere off Main Street, okay? Your mom'll have apoplexy if I lose you." Remy gave me a sidelong glance. "You remember this place at all? I mean, you were pretty little last time you were here, so . . . "

I gazed out the window at the fields and cottages spinning past as we drove along in the taxi and shook my head. It wasn't entirely true that I didn't remember; there was something hauntingly familiar about it all, but it wasn't anything tangible, just a soft echo bouncing around inside me of something long gone.

"Mr. O'Malley said last time you were here my mother brought you a rag doll for your birthday." She looked at me as if waiting for a response. When she didn't get one, she shrugged. "Well, that's what he said. Who knows, sometimes his memory is like Swiss cheese. Old moldy Swiss cheese." She laughed. "And she used to make rag dolls for a lot of kids on the island." Outside the window, a horse nibbled at the tall tips of alfalfa blowing back and forth in the breeze.

My mind skated back to my room in Tuckertown, where a rag doll with charcoal yarn for hair and a button nose sat covered in dust on my bookshelf. Somehow, I always thought it was from Grandma Jo, one of the kazillion dolls she'd brought back to me from her travels. But there was only one rag doll; I'd named her Mitsey. There was an inky smudge on her dress, the fabric on her left arm was worn, and the stitching had been pulled loose from my dragging her behind me through a good slice of my childhood.

I can't say why the fact that I might have met Mr. and Mrs. O'Malley, not to mention Remy, on one of our trips to the cottage had never occurred to me. Of course, it made perfect sense. I'd been to the island several times when I was little, and they lived right next door. But Remy seemed a person one couldn't forget—ever.

"Of course, I wasn't around," she said, as if she'd read my mind. "Too busy raising hell on the mainland and all." There was a snag in her voice like a scratched record. "Anyway, even if she had, it was a long time ago; it's probably long gone by now."

*No*, I wanted to tell her. I loved that doll, had slept with it every night after my father left, imagining she could read the thousand thoughts racing through my mind even if I had no words to bring them to life. But I didn't tell her that. Instead, I studied the sunlight dancing off the purple nose of the Thunderbird, trying to yank the memory of Mrs. O'Malley free from the rock it was stuck under.

"Alrighty, here we are." Remy guided the Purple Monster up to the curb. "You remember how to get to the soda fountain?"

I nodded, slipping out the passenger door and making a mental note to hold back a few dollars for it. Anxious to have an hour to explore the village, I intended to rush through the shopping so I'd have time to do so. Up and down Main Street, men with white coveralls armed with paintbrushes were slathering the sides of buildings with a fresh coat of color. A small movie theater was changing its marquee from *The Sting* to *The Godfather Part II*. Marlon Brando had been amazing in the first *Godfather*, but my heart belonged to Al Pacino. I decided maybe I'd ask Grandma Jo to bring me. On the corner, two teenagers wrestled with a brass letter *R*, trying to affix it to a sign that read, USTY NAIL TAVERN. Tourists were already beginning to land on the island and it was clear every resident was busy with last-minute preparations for the festival.

"You know," Remy leaned across the front seat, her skin sticking to the vinyl, "I've got a bike in the garage. Got it a year and a half ago with the idea I might take up cycling and fit back into those size eights I refuse to throw away.

Both the bike and the jeans still have the tags hanging from their seats." She laughed her smoky deep chuckle. "You're welcome to cut 'em off if you want. I'd like to think it will get ridden by someone at least once."

I gave her a nod that said I was just the girl to do it and waved goodbye.

Ten minutes later, I found myself fighting with a sticky wheel on an ancient grocery cart that seemed intent on knocking over Mr. Herman's displays while he eyed me suspiciously over a box of Granny Smiths from the produce aisle. I finished the list in less than half an hour, making my way to the woman at the register amid a mountain of boxed dry pasta, the contents of which shook and *shish*ed like a baby's rattle every time the wheel caught, skidding stubbornly over Mr. Herman's polished floors.

"What ya running?" The checkout girl, a gangly thing with stringy auburn hair and eyes the color of creamed coffee, snapped her gum, examining the items on the belt. "A day-care center? Let me guess: tomorrow's macaroni-art day." Leaning over to turn up the volume on the small eight-track player beside her register, she tapped her finger to the counter, keeping time with Terry Jacks as he sang "Seasons in the Sun." When I didn't answer, she flashed a mouthful of braces that nearly blinded me on the spot in the fluorescent light.

Handing her the three twenties and taking three dollars back, I plucked the two paper bags off the belt before heading toward the front door.

"Honey!"

Taken aback at her friendliness, I turned to find her rushing after me, waving in the air the plastic bear full of honey I'd left behind.

Outside, Mr. Herman's broom leaned into the corner of the stoop beside an advertisement soaped onto the front window, reading: PORK LOINS ¢.90 LB ONE DAY ONLY. I stepped off the concrete stoop eager to taste one of Mrs. Barrett's root beer floats. The White Whale was difficult to miss, but the reason that I almost did was because the sign with a picture of a harpooned white whale was hanging from two cast iron hooks directly over my head. I only happened to look up as I passed when the breeze caught it, sending out an obnoxious squeak.

Tillings Island was a crisscross of small crushed-shell pathways zigzagging off to the shoreline, and the White Whale lay just across one from Herman's. Beside the White Whale, two men pushed through the door of Merchant's Hardware with a sack of nails. A trio of kids a few years older than me lazed against the wall of Merchant's while two girls laughed hysterically and pitched stones into a corner. One of the girls was too fat for the polyester shirt she wore, making the buttons strain over the roll above her belt. She was a stark contrast to the pretty girl posed beside her, whose long golden hair had been swept to one side and fixed with a barrette in precisely the same fashion as a Barbie doll.

"Shit! I nicked the enamel. Now it looks like a fucking arrow instead of a star. Look." She shoved her polished fingernail under the fat girl's nose.

"Jesus Christ, Lindsey"—she gave the polyester shirt-tail a tug, pulling the hemline over the bulge around her waistband—"It's a goddamn nail. Come on. See if you can finish him off."

"Fuck you. It took me a whole hour coming up with that design."

Taking a deep breath, I willed myself invisible and moved forward. I had not spent much time praying— okay, *any* time praying—during the last few years, but I sent up a small prayer now hoping they would be too busy focusing on Barbie's chipped nail to notice me walking by.

"Tell you what. That sucker drops with the next stone and I'll paint your stupid nail back on myself. Tell her to pitch the damn stone, will ya, Riley? Everyone knows she'll do whatever you say."

"Shut the fuck up," Lindsey growled, pitching the small stone in her hand at the fat girl instead, bouncing it off the deep panty bulge of her hip.

"Ouch!"

Lindsey smirked, glancing at a tall boy with mussed hair the precise brown of nutmeg. Dressed in raggedy painter's pants with oil stains spreading over his knees as big as Dr. Boni's inkblots, he gave her a weak smile before turning eyes as pale and green as sea foam in my direction. Balancing the two grocery bags clumsily on my hips, I studied the crushed-shell path as I crossed.

This was the reason I missed the glance, the one that must have passed from Lindsey to the boy to me before she chirped, "Hey! You're new around here, aren't ya?"

I looked up in time to see the fat girl behind her laugh, nudging her softly on the shoulder. Lindsey stood with one hip jutted out at an exaggerated angle as she ran the pad of her thumb over the chip in her nail polish. Apparently, her mother did not share my mother's misgivings about makeup, because her hazel eyes peeped through dramatically lined charcoal lids and an unnatural tan lit her face.

Behind her, a watery squawk and a ghost-like shift of white drew my attention into the shadows. A seagull huddled in the corner: one wing bent unnaturally upward, a slew of pebbles circling its talons. For an instant, it looked at me before casting its yellow eyes downward. The girl in the too-tight polyester shirt bent over, plucked a stone from the alleyway, and pitched it at the bird.

"Damn bird's too stupid to fly away." She shook her head in disgust. But I knew that was not the case. When a thing is that scared and hurt there is only one place to go that's safe: deep into a small crevasse inside yourself where nobody can follow. And if you died in the process—well, so be it.

"What ya got there?" Lindsey turned her attention fully back to me. "Mommy's groceries? Isn't that precious, guys?

She's got her mommy's groceries." The group laughed, except for the boy with nutmeg hair, who was still staring at me intently. "Come on over here. Don't be scared. I'm Lindsey. This here's Carly, and that guy standing there droolin' is Riley. Come on."

As it turned out, I didn't need to come anywhere, the two girls were already making their way toward me. I glanced at the seagull again, letting my eyes linger too long. Lindsey followed my gaze, laughed, and picked up a large stone.

"What's the matter? You shy or something? It's okay. You wanna play? Sure. Here. The one who finishes him off gets a free soda at Mrs. Barrett's courtesy of the rest of us." She took the bag from my right arm and shoved the rock into my palm. It was heavy and surprisingly warm. The bird followed it from her hand to mine, hobbling back against the sideboards of Merchant's Hardware. "Go ahead, get it in the head. You can show them how it's done, can't ya?" she crooned, beginning to pick through the bag of groceries.

"She won't do it." Carly smirked at Riley.

"Don't count on it. She's a Haywood," the boy growled under his breath. "Killing's what they do best."

Turning away from the alley, I stared at Riley, feeling small bubbles of rage pop against the sharp edges of what he'd just said. I had never killed anything in my life, unless you counted my mother, who swore I was killing her another inch each day that I refused to speak. He didn't know me, even if he somehow knew my family's name. Still, he seemed to be wresting back an urge to spit in my face.

"What's the matter with her? She a retard or something?" Carly whispered. Riley ignored her, as though watching to see what I would do.

I wanted to speak. I wanted to tell her to shut the fuck up. The words were there, I could feel them splashing around like water in a well. But every time I tried to scoop them up and reel them into the day, they sloshed back over the bucket's edge and washed into the shadows.

"What will happen if you speak, Izabella?" It was my second session with Dr. Boni, and once again, it began with an impossibly simple question.

I knew exactly what would happen. Words would tumble into the wind like butterflies and I would not be able to catch them before they fluttered out of my grasp forever. Secrets would escape. The stars would stop falling. The moon would stop dancing. The magic would die.

*Nothing*, I'd scrolled on the paper before sliding it over to Dr. Boni.

*Retard.* I glanced at the bird, letting the word roll around inside me until it crackled and burst to life and I was six years old again with Robert Goober Head calling me a retard and leaving my ant squashed into the playground mud with its legs pedaling in the wind. In two seconds flat, the same anger and embarrassment of that day lifted itself upright inside of me.

Lindsey pulled free the small plastic bear filled with honey, holding it up with a tinny high-pitched laugh. Biting the inside of my cheek, I slid the other bag onto the crushed shells with a *crinkle* and drew my hand back softball style.

The bird shuffled again and I knew exactly how it felt. The idea crossed my mind to overthrow the rock, intentionally missing the bird, and be on my way, never looking back. I could do it; I had a damn good pitch and I was downright masterful at never looking back—not ever. The bird cowered back another inch, as though the shadow could harden in form and create a shield capable of saving its life.

Lindsey unscrewed the bear's red plastic head, peeled back the foil, and stuck her pinky into the honey before licking her finger with a grin. "Go, girl, you can do it! Put it out of its misery."

I let the rock reel me into a half circle, pitching it into the wind with conviction. Lindsey squealed. There was an ugly *crack,* followed by a watery feeling in my stomach as Mr. Herman hollered from the other side of the hole the rock had left in his front window. His soap-scrawled ad now read: P- - - - -INS ¢.90 LB ONE DAY ONLY.

"Ha! I knew she didn't have the guts to do it!" Lindsey

twittered, giving the plastic bear a squeeze over my head so honey oozed through my hair and dripped in gooey little globs onto my eyebrow. Small blobs plopped to the collar of my new sweater while Lindsey and Carly darted down the path from sight. Still leaning into the corner, Riley studied me with interested eyes.

"You, there!" Mr. Herman barked at me. "I have Betsey calling the sheriff right now."

Turning around, I pushed a gob of honey from my eyelid.

"Look what you did to my window! And if you think you're not paying for the damages, well, we will just see what the po-lice have to say a-bout that." Mr. Herman looked up and down the pathway, red-faced and huffing like a steam engine. A thin film of sweat shone on his brow and he was brandishing his broom like a knotty old sword.

"*In!*" He thundered. "*Now!*" Mr. Herman took me by the sleeve and began tugging me back toward the store.

I tripped alongside him, stupid in my silence, wishing Riley would just go away.

"You're that girl staying up at the Booth House, aren't you?" Mr. Herman said.

I nodded weakly.

"Well, I don't know how they do things wherever you're from, but here we don't let hooligans tromp around town damaging people's property. Do you hear me?"

I nodded.

"I said, do you hear me!"

"I—I . . . " The sound was little more than a belch of air. Mr. Herman's face contorted into angry red pools of wrinkles.

"And we do *not* ignore adults when they're speaking."

Two police cruisers pulled into sight before we reached the door. I did not have to look back; I could feel Riley watching me from the corner. I did not want him to see me blushing, did not want him to know I was too dumb to speak up and defend myself. A youngish police officer with sun-streaked hair stepped out of the car. Dressed in jeans and clutching a flip pad and gold pen, he looked anything but rushed.

"Sheriff," Mr. Herman greeted him with a scowl.

A second, older officer in uniform stepped out of his car, coming up behind the sheriff with a friendly slap on the back.

"What're you doing here, Dillon?" the sheriff said. "I thought we were meeting for lunch at the Anchor."

"A-yup." The uniformed officer was a head taller than the sheriff, with salt-and-pepper hair; his blue eyes lit up like lanterns even though his mouth did not follow suit. "But when I heard the call come over the radio, I knew you'd be late for lunch and I'm already hungry." He gave a shallow nod in Mr. Herman's direction, sending the corners of both policemen's lips tilting skyward. "Thought maybe if I shot down to lend a hand we might make it in time for dinner."

"Deputy," Mr. Herman growled, still holding tight to my elbow. Biting my cheek, I fought back the tears pooling in the corners of my eyes.

"Okay, Maynard, I suppose you can let that child loose now. I don't guess that she's going to jump into the Atlantic and swim away anytime soon." The sheriff leaned against his cruiser, studying the hole in the window. Across the street, Riley stuffed his hands in his front pockets and slipped quietly down a small lane.

Grudgingly, Mr. Herman released my sleeve. "Do you see what she's done?"

"I see," he said.

"Hell of a deal you've got going on, Maynard. Man, people will buy anything these days as long as it's on sale. What exactly is the *pee* in, a sauce or something? I guess you'll need to tell Sarah about that, Jim." The deputy chuckled.

"There is nothing funny about the damage this hooligan caused to my shop, Dillon!" Mr. Herman glowered, turning to the sheriff. "Jim, do you know how expensive this window was? It is going to cost a small sack of gold to fix. And it's not coming outta my till; I'll tell you that plain as day right this minute!"

"Okay, okay. Settle down before you set off your arrhythmia. Let's go inside and figure this all out, shall we?"

"What's your name, darlin'?"

"Good luck getting an answer," Mr. Herman grumbled, knitting his arms over his chest.

I felt my face flush, that same old embarrassment taking hold of my stomach. Digging my pad free I wrote, *Izabella Rae Haywood*. It was barely legible because of the way my hand was trembling and I was relieved that he didn't ask me to write it again.

The sheriff watched me, perplexed, reaching for the pad when I handed it to him.

Gazing over the sheriff's shoulder, the second officer read what I'd written with a bewildered expression. They exchanged a look I couldn't quite decipher. "Haywood?"

The sheriff blew air through a small opening in his lips. "Are you staying up at the old Booth place?"

I nodded, taking back the pad.

"I think you'd better write down what happened and your mother's number for us."

The fact that he didn't ask me about my voice, or yell at me for not speaking the way Mr. Herman had, surprised me. It was a thing I had never grown used to, but it happened all the time. Usually, it took a person a few tries before he figured out something was wrong with me. And then he almost always decided I was either born deaf or mute. One of first words I learned to spell after my father left was *laryngitis*. I had scribbled it so many times I didn't have to look at the paper anymore to do it. That was for the times a person did not come to his own conclusion first. But, for some reason, the sheriff hadn't even asked.

I was just writing down my mother's name, wondering why he'd chosen not to ask for my parents' number, or even my father's, when Remy pulled up in front of the shattered window, tilting her head to study the jagged edges. After giving it a good look, she stepped from the Purple Monster, kicking the door closed with her boot, and sidled up to where we were standing.

"What in God's green earth happened here?" She hugged the sheriff warmly before laying a hand on my shoulder. "Jesus Christ, you're shaking like a naked cat on a glacier."

I looked at her, pleading for help.

"It seems your young friend here has a hell of a pitch." He drew his fingers across his mouth as though trying to stop a chuckle from forming.

"And piss-poor aim." Remy gazed at the hole.

"Can't have everything, I suppose."

"I'm glad you all find this so blasted amusing," Mr. Herman growled. "I guess if I come down to the police station and knock a hole through your window you'll really have a good laugh."

"At least no one was hurt. Why, that rock could've hit Betsey, but it didn't. That's something to be grateful for." The sheriff patted Mr. Herman's back.

The thought hit my gut with so much force I actually felt it. Glancing at the girl inside the store, I swatted a tear from my lashes.

"Betsey's cheek I can stick a Band-Aid on. What am I supposed to do, stick a Band-Aid over my window? We got a thousand people coming for the festival, and I've got no front window. I make more than a quarter of my annual profits during festival week. People aren't going to come into a boarded-up shop unless they're looting it. And there's no way I can get someone over here from the mainland to measure and set it before that. Someone could march right through that hole and rob me blind."

"Well, I don't know. It'd have to be a four-and-a-half-inch-tall thief to get through that. How much do you guess a four-and-a-half-inch bandit can make off with, Remy?" Officer Dillon quipped.

"All right now, you two. He's got a right to worry. That's a good chunk of change." The sheriff's tone took on a hint of concern.

"It's enough to close me down for part of the winter. You got tonight to figure this out, Jim. Then I have to press charges. My insurance isn't going to cover losses that I didn't file a formal complaint on. I'm not playing here." Mr. Herman snatched up the broom, which was still standing on the stoop, and began to beat the sidewalk with it as though hitting it hard enough would make it cough up the slivers of glass stuck in its crevices.

"Don't get yourself all worked up." The sheriff gazed at me. "I'll figure it out. Maybe Merchant's has enough glass in stock to cut you a pane."

"I've still got to get someone to board this up tonight and then get the broken one out and scrape the edges before it can be set and glazed."

"I'll send my boy by to help hammer this up for the night."

"And Izabella will come down and help knock out the window and scrape," Remy added, leaving me wide-eyed and trying to catch her attention, which she skillfully averted.

"That be okay, Maynard? And whatever Merchant's charges, it comes out of her pocket."

"You'd better believe that's true," Mr. Herman huffed.

"I'll see to it," the sheriff assured him. "I'll go over right now and find out how much that will cost and call this young lady's mother to let her know."

Remy kissed the sheriff on the cheek like an old friend and watched him get into his car while Officer Dillon shuttled me and the grocery bags into the passenger door of the Purple Monster. I just gleaned the question scuttling over his expression as he caught Remy's eye, nodding in my direction.

"Hasn't said a word since the stuff with her dad," I heard her say before the door slammed shut. I couldn't make out the rest of what they were saying on the other side of the window, but it was impossible not to notice the strange look coming over his face while Remy spoke.

Officer Dillon opened the door for Remy. "I guess it goes without saying you should make sure she's back here tomorrow to help clean this up. You, yourself, might want to do your shopping at Salva's for a few days. Better yet, you could break down and let me take you out to dinner and then you wouldn't need groceries at all. I'll even make you breakfast the next morning." He winked.

"Well, thanks for the offer," Remy said, folding herself behind the wheel. "But I imagine Maynard will touch back down, soon as he needs a ride to shore to cash his checks."

"I'd imagine." He shut the door, leaning into the window as if I wasn't sitting right there listening to their conversation. "Remy, let me ask you a question."

"What would that be, Officer Dillon?" I wondered if she realized that despite her gruffness, an affectionate light danced into her eyes when she spoke to him.

"How many more years are you gonna keep turning me down? It's a meal—food, wine, maybe a dance. I'm not askin' you to accompany me to a human sacrifice."

"Well, there's not much difference, now is there?"

"Is the idea of sitting across a table from me really all that bad?"

"Yes." She smirked.

"Well, you can't blame me for trying."

"I don't blame you one little bit, Dillon. I can't hold you responsible for being part of the male gender any more than I hold a skunk responsible for stinking. But that doesn't mean I'd hold hands with one." Winking at the officer, Remy turned the key, igniting a deep roar under the hood of the Purple Monster, and pulled away from the curb, leaving Officer Dillon standing there alone watching her go.

It was five minutes later and we were just turning onto Knockberry Lane when she finally spoke to me.

"You want to grab that pad of yours and tell me what the hell's eating you?"

Yes, I thought, shaking my head no.

"Okay then, you want to tell me what bird of fancy flew into those curls of yours and made you think it might be a grand old idea to skip a rock through Herman's windowpane?" Remy pulled the car to the side of the road, throwing the stick shift into park.

I shook my head weakly.

"They overcharge you?"

I shook my head.

"Kick your cart? Give you the wrong damn pasta? Call you a green-faced alien?" She grabbed a crumpled envelope from the console, dropping it in my lap, and poked a pencil at me.

*Some girls were trying to kill a bird with the rock. That's all*, I scrawled, before tossing the pencil back at her and fixing my eyes on the crest of Knockberry Ridge, where the sun was slipping over the cliffs in a ribbon of orange.

"Ah." Remy's voice sidled down a notch, edging on a whisper. "Well, are you done throwing things? Because I don't know what those girls said to set your belly ablaze, but I have a bad notion it may not be the last harsh word you hear today." I followed her gaze down the lane to the Booth House, where the thin form of my mother was pacing back and forth in the front yard.

I rolled my eyes.

"I guess it's not easy having a mother sitting on your shoulder, watching everything you do." She pulled the car back onto the lane. "But, I can tell you this, it's easier than not having one around to do it."

As soon as I opened the car door, my mother turned sharply on one heel and pointed to the house. Remy followed us, balancing a bag of groceries in each arm.

Once the front door closed, my mother spun around, planting her right hand on her hip. I could not remember the last time I saw her naked—unlike Grandma Jo, who romped around on a daily basis without clothes—but under there somewhere I was positive her hips donned five permanent dimples from always pushing her fingers into them.

"Two days!" Her voice cracked. "We have been on this island for two days, and I get a call from the police saying the owner of the local grocery is threatening to sue me for damages for a broken window from a fight. Seriously, are you enjoying driving me stark raving mad? Is that it? Really, I want to know. Do you just walk out of the room and have a good laugh?"

"Well," Remy quipped, "maybe not an outright belly laugh. Perhaps a chuckle—"

"I'm not asking *you*!" My mother reeled. "And I don't appreciate you making a big old joke out of it!"

"There seems to be some agreement on that point." Remy sighed, winking at me. "But in all honesty, it wasn't a fight." Her voice was calm as that of a person backing away from a riled bear as she made her way to the kitchen with the tattered bags of groceries. "Nobody was hit or hurt," she glanced at me, "and I guess it goes without saying she didn't swear or yell."

"Really, I wasn't asking you," my mother snapped.

"Fine. Izabella, was it a fight?" Remy called from the kitchen counter.

I shook my head.

"There you have it. It wasn't a fight." *Zing!* I fell in love with Remy in eight words flat, in love with the grace with which she could heave my mother straight off her pedestal in two sentences or less every time.

"Okay, Iz. Why don't you tell me why it is then that Mr. Herman wants to sue me because you smashed his window with a rock?" My mother flipped the page back of a legal pad she'd been using to keep notes and shoved my pen to the end of the table.

"Not so much smashed as sailed a rock through it. It's just a small hole," Remy began.

"Would you *please*!" My mother glared at her as she stuck the pen in my right hand.

*It isn't smashed*, I scribbled. *It's just a small hole.*

"I couldn't care less what it isn't; tell me why I am paying a hundred dollars to repair a broken window."

*They started it*, I wrote, hating the way it made me sound like a baby. *They were killing a seagull. I just threw the rock away.*

"Right through Mr. Herman's front window!"

"It was a hell of a shot. Would've clearly been a home run." Remy sauntered back into the room clutching the nearly empty bear-shaped jar of honey. "But you need more honey."

"Be . . . quiet!" My mother turned to Remy, her voice climbing three octaves and threatening to break some more glass. "And what's all over you?" She tugged the corner of my brand-new sweater. "What's all over her?" She looked at Remy.

"Oh, now I can speak?"

"What . . . is . . . it?" My mother pushed the words in her direction one at a time.

"Honey." She waved the bear in the air. "At least it's good for your skin." With my mother's face all clouded in anger, I couldn't tell who she hated more—me or Remy. "Moisturizing, you know, like lotion?"

"Remy . . . "

"Yes?"

"Go home."

*It isn't her fault*, I scribbled. *Leave her alone. She wasn't even there.*

"Are you kidding me?" My mother raised a brow at me. "You cost me a hundred dollars and now you're going to go and be mouthy?"

I should say right here, mouthing off is not an easy feat for a person without a voice.

"That's true." Remy pointed to the paper then snatched

an apple, which had fallen on the table from a grocery bag, and took a bite.

"Why"—my mother reeled around—"the hell are you still here? I'm talking to my daughter. Do you need something?"

"I need to drive her down to Herman's tomorrow to help clean up the mess. If Maynard doesn't get it fixed in time for the festival, he's threatening to file formal charges so his insurance will cover his loss of profits."

"Anything else?" The words were so controlled they threatened to die of strangulation in my mother's throat.

"Nope, that pretty well covers it." Remy pushed a wayward curl from her forehead with her free hand. "I'll be back in the morning." She yanked the front door open just as Grandma Jo was coming through it and the two women nearly collided on the front step.

"Did you find Kit's Cove okay, Josephine?"

"I did, thank you very much. It's perfect; not another soul in sight. One of the most peaceful spots I believe I've ever done yoga. My spirit is calm and right with the world."

"Well then, you may want to reconsider going in there." Remy stepped aside.

Grandma Jo leaned through the door, letting her eyes bob back and forth between my mother and me. Her long hair was swept into a loose bun and the tranquility of the beach seemed to have followed her home. After a moment, she patted Remy on the arm and walked into the room barefoot and sandy before closing the door behind her. As she stooped over to brush her feet clean, my mother plucked a second apple from the table and launched it at the door, sending it bouncing off the wood and across the floor.

"Arrrrrrrrrgh!"

"Ladies." Grandma Jo gazed from me to my mother. "What's all the ruckus?"

"Nothing," my mother snapped, rubbing her temples.

"Okay then, would you like to tell me what the door did to deserve being pelted with fruit?" She retrieved the apple from the floor and placed it back on the table.

Chewing my lower lip, I looked at my grandmother for help. She didn't look one bit shaken by the fact that I was standing there bathed in honey and, for the kazillionth time, I wished my mother had inherited her innate calm.

*I didn't do anything*, I wrote before handing the note to my mother.

"Right!" She steamed. "Other than throw a rock through a damn windowpane."

"All right." Grandma Jo's voice was hushed as she walked over to the sink and wet a towel. "I don't know what's going on here, and I don't care. There's no need for such high drama unless somebody's dead or in jail. And even that is debatable." She padded back into the dining room and pushed a waxy wad of honeyed hair behind my ear.

"It's only luck on both fucking counts!" My mother shook her head.

"Isn't it always a matter of luck?" My grandmother dabbed at my face.

"I'm telling you, Iz, I have reached my very last nerve with this."

Translation: with *you*.

"Zo . . . " Concentrating on wiping the sticky streaks from my cheeks, Grandma Jo didn't bother to look up. "Why don't you go back to work? I'll take care of this."

"Why don't you take care of the hundred-dollar bill while you're at it?" My mother stormed out of the room, slamming the door behind her.

Grandma Jo didn't question what happened even as she stepped back to examine me. "Are you okay?"

I nodded, even though I was so not okay that it would take me a solid year to tally the damage. It was the first time anyone had stopped to ask.

"Well, I suppose it's a good thing I know where to get more honey. And you were worried about the bees." She leaned back, letting her eyes drift over me to assess the damage. "Okay. You go upstairs and change your clothes. I'll go in there and change her attitude." She waved at the slammed door before tossing the towel into the sink with the same soft sigh I have heard my mother nearly deflate from a thousand times. I couldn't help wondering how three women who shared the same blood could all fall from God's hand and land on this world as different as snowflakes.

Grandma Jo was the only one who spoke at dinner that night, recounting stories from Israel and Africa over a pan of stir-fried vegetables and brown rice. About halfway through the meal she turned to stare at me.

"Do you remember this place at all, Izabella? I mean the island? The house? Anything?"

I looked at my mother, who was too busy glaring at Grandma Jo to notice me, and shrugged.

"Well, it will come back to you eventually. Don't you worry."

After the plates had been stacked in the sink, my grandmother folded herself cross-legged onto a sofa cushion she had thrown to the floor. My mother crumpled into the hole the missing cushion had left behind on the couch. Eight years of handling unspoken thoughts made me an expert at reading them, and something was pacing between them so forcefully it nearly took physical form.

"Homework, Iz," my mother said. "You need to finish reading the section on Robert Frost and then do your algebra."

I looked to Grandma Jo for assistance.

"'Some say the world will end in fire / Some say in ice. From what I've tasted of desire / I hold with those who favor fire . . . ,'" Grandma Jo warbled as lightly as a lark. "I love Frost. Can I see it when you're done?"

Same thing in disguise.

Letting my eyes volley between them several times

before pulling myself from the chair, I headed for the stairs. Luke, who had not left Grandma Jo's side since she arrived, flopped in front of her and angled his belly toward her fingers. I made my way to the top of the steps and slammed the door to my room convincingly before creeping back to the landing.

"What is it, Zorrie?"

"You cannot be here if you're going to do that." My mother's voice was choppy.

"Do what? The clothing and makeup? For goodness' sake, honey! I did the same for you when you turned fourteen." Grandma Jo sounded as though she were placating a jealous sibling.

"No, Mom. Not the makeup—and, by the way, no, you didn't. I'm trying to help her, not retraumatize her. You, and that whack job down the lane; you're all prodding her to remember. Stop it; just stop. She'll come to it on her own when she's ready. Don't you understand that?"

I rested my head on my knees, pulling them tight to me, and pinched my eyes closed. Was that true? That I could remember if I wanted to? That I had erased it all on purpose? I wasn't sure.

"No. I do not understand that. She was a young child. What do you remember from when you were six? Do you remember the time we went lobster trapping off the coast of Nova Scotia? Do you remember Mr. Dixon dressing up as Santa Claus and leaving little baby powder reindeer hoof prints on the carpet? Do you remember drinking lighter fluid in Mr. Tildridge's garage because you were thirsty, and me rushing you to the emergency room? We lose important things from our childhood just as quickly and easily as loose teeth, which I am willing to wager you also do not remember. Have you tried just sitting down and talking to her? Just tell her what happened."

"And risk her never speaking again—ever? Really, is that what you want? Don't you think I've tried to help her? She just walks away. She doesn't want to speak to me. I can't remember the last time she sat and just talked to me—even on paper—the way she does with you. She doesn't want anything to do with me."

"That is simply not true," Grandma Jo interjected.

"It is true. She hates me. Somewhere along the way, she came to believe it was my fault he walked out that night. She just loved him so much. It's like she can't breathe without him; like they were two halves of a whole. She blames me for what he did. How in the hell do I fight a phantom? I don't know how to move her forward. Half the time she just wants me to go away."

I heard a sob catch in my mother's throat, pinching me through with guilt. It was not true that I hated her, but the second half was true. It was not that my life wasn't complete without my father; it was that *I* was not complete without him. I still stared out my window at night listening for the Nikommo, begging them to lead me back to him. I didn't want to move forward. Didn't want to leave him behind.

"She doesn't hate you. She's scared of you, that you might confirm her worst fear—that this is all somehow her fault. The longer you let that fester, the worse it will be. Just say whatever needs saying, once and for all, and let the chips fall where they will."

"My God, she's lucky he didn't kill her, lucky he didn't take her with him like all the other times."

As if someone turned a fire hose on my gut, my stomach turned all watery and cold and for a minute I thought I might vomit. Burying my head in my knees, I squeezed my eyes tighter until a kaleidoscope of colors swam inside my lids. But the tears came anyway, stinging my throat and nose. In what universe was a thing like that lucky?

"Zorrie, he was a good man and he loved her beyond reason. He loved you. Don't let anger rob you of the good memories. The rest wasn't any more his fault than yours or Izabella's; you know that."

"Why don't you explain that to Remy or Thomas? Does it matter, really? It doesn't undo a goddamn thing."

I didn't know what that meant, but I did know Grandma Jo was right. Like fireworks inside my head, memories began exploding: good and bad, beautiful and ugly. The three of us hiking Stepstone Falls and my father running my mother piggyback up the peak to watch the sunset. Making popcorn over the fireplace and forgetting the top of the pan until we were chasing exploding kernels from one end of the living room to the other as if they were Mexican jumping beans. My mother slumped on the back step like a dropped rag crying when he disappeared for three days.

It was dizzying.

"Don't you think I know that?" my mother yelled. "Does one single person understand that I loved him, too? I loved him first. I love him still."

I tilted my head, taken aback by the deep ache swelling up in my chest. Wiping my nose with the corner of my shirt, I swallowed hard, trying to force my throat back open.

My mother sighed. "I don't even know how to start. I have no idea what she remembers, or if she's scared, or angry, or sad. I just don't want to push her, don't want to drive her to . . . That's why I got her that damn dog, so she would at least have something she could be close to. So she wouldn't be so—alone in there. She's so goddamn like him sometimes it hurts to look at her. I don't want . . . What if she . . . "

I did not pretend to understand my mother. But I did speak silence, and there was something about the way she couldn't force the words out that sent a storm of butterflies bouncing around inside me. *What if I what?* I didn't know what words, exactly, she was laboring to give birth to. But even with them all locked up in her voice box, I knew what they meant. What if one day I tilted my head into the sun and got the urge to fly? What if I listened to the wind just right on a summer night and heard the Nikommo singing? What if those embers she didn't know what to do with inside my father finally puffed to life inside me and set what was left of our world on fire?

"Zorrie, I am going to say this once, and I want you to hear me. . . . She is not Ansel. That is not what this is. She is not going to break down. She is not going to break, period. And she knows there is something here. She feels it. She thinks she's going crazy. Do you understand me? Your child thinks she is insane. . . ."

*What's the matter with her . . . she a retard or something? . . . Silent Sam plays with ants because nobody else w-ants to play with her. . . . Specialized programming . . . children with unique needs . . .* The words broke loose with such force I felt bruises forming from them bouncing off the corners of my brain. My stomach lurched again, sending bile biting and burning the back of my throat. The world spun all topsy-turvy. Luke oozed into my lap, licking my fingers as if spatters of pain could be mopped up in the same manner as a drippy ice cream cone.

"She thinks she's crazy, and she's *not*." Grandma Jo's voice was stern and soft all wrapped up together. "Is that better than a hefty dose of reality? She is half him, all the best parts. She feels the magic in this world the way he did. But she is half you, too—solid and strong and smart. I know it's scary—"

"Do you really, Mom? Do you know what it's like to watch your child disappear inside herself like she's slipping into a dark empty cave? To never, ever know what she's thinking or feeling? Never to hear her laugh or dream aloud? It's like watching her drown below an inch of water and her foot is stuck in the rocks and no matter how fucking hard I pull, I cannot get her to air. I'm her mother. I should be able to pull her out." I could not see her, but I could tell my mother was crying in earnest now, could hear her words catching on the sharp edges of what she said.

"Yes, I do know what that's like."

"It's not the same, Mother. You don't live with Iz day in and day out, watching her caught up in this hell."

"I'm not talking about Izabella." Grandma Jo's voice was soft, and level as a steel rod, and it was as if she'd hit my mother over the head with it, stunning her silent for a good long time. "She will be okay. The question is, will you?"

When my mother did speak again the tears were gone and anger filled her words. "I told you, I'm fine."

"Well, I happen to be a mother, too. And I am more worried about the other child in this house. You are thin as a blade of grass, angry as a wasp at this world, and burying yourself in a mausoleum of work. But if you prefer to speak about Izabella instead, Zorrie, fine. Give her some credit, will you? She's not as weak as you want to believe. How long do you intend to keep her in this bubble? That child needs to understand that she is a whole person with or without language, with or without her father. She needs to know she can take care of herself—without you choreographing each breath she takes. And frankly, I am not all that sure you want her to be able to. Is it possible somewhere deep inside you're trying to keep her dependent on you so she doesn't slip away completely?"

"Hey," I heard my mother's heel scuff the floor as she turned on Grandma Jo, "I am the one who brought her here, remember?"

I got to my feet, intending to go find a tissue and change, but my feet crept me down to the second-floor banister instead, peeking around the corner. For the first time in a long time, I felt the need to see my mother. I'd spent years looking at her as an empty shell, a robot that tallied up numbers and moved through the tasks of the day without feeling much about them. But she wasn't. She was cracked all over from the force of everything she'd stuffed inside herself, like me.

"And now you're frightened."

Silence.

"You think you may have pushed one notch too far. That she will not be able to handle this. Or worse, if she does, that somehow she's going to disappear on you like Ansel."

The world spun into slow motion then paused. When it kicked back into orbit, my mother crumpled to the stonework in front of the fire. She was crying, and Grandma Jo padded over to sit beside her, brushing the hair from my mother's face and tucking it behind her ear.

"Listen to me, Zo. You are doing the right thing. Trust that girl. She will not leave you, or hate you, or murder you in your sleep. She has carried this around for eight years. Enough. Let her get on with things."

My throat tightened; my stomach tumbled.

"Did you really think this would be more difficult for her than you? Coming back here, facing the other family, reliving what happened? Perhaps Izabella is an excuse to face this yourself?"

"Fuck," my mother said. Just like that. "Fuck, fuck, fuck! What did any of us do to deserve this? Why does he get the easy way out?"

Then my mother did something I have never seen her do before: she laid her head in Grandma Jo's lap and sobbed. They were speaking perfect English, and yet, it was more like trying to decode Gaelic, with too many pieces missing to make sense of it all. What did she mean by the easy way out? Because if there was one, I wanted to know where that door was. Living life with chunks of it shattered into little pieces that you cannot figure out how to put back together is a thing most people do not understand. I knew it was up to me to make sense of what happened, but the memories were broken beyond recognition.

Pulling Luke close, I buried my face in the soft folds of his neck and held him tight until the sick feeling in my stomach started to subside. When it was clear they were done talking, I got up and crept back up the stairs to my room with this last whisper from Grandma Jo caught in my ear: "She won't leave you."

And I knew that was true. After seeing my mother crumpled up like a fallen leaf, scared and sad, I didn't want to. I knew this, too: this place was deeply connected to me. It understood something about me that I did not

**Later that night,** I awoke to Luke whining beside me and pawing at the bedsheets. I pried one eye open to find a thunderstorm breaking over the island. Rain battered the windows in fat silver drops. Every few minutes, lightning cracked the darkness open like a dyed egg the day after Easter. When I was young, I'd thought that was precisely what was happening, that each bolt of lightning cracked open a little corner of heaven and sent bits of it flailing to earth. Luke shimmied closer, trying desperately to dig his way under my arm to escape the storm. Snuggling him under my chin, I covered him with the blanket, rubbing his belly and breathing in the scent of puppy. But all the petting was not enough to stop his shivering, and I felt the worry tickle up my throat and land beside his ear with a soft, "Shhh, shhh," until his breathing calmed to an even sigh.

# CHAPTER EIGHT

The next morning, I woke at dawn to John Denver crooning "Sunshine on My Shoulders" through my alarm clock, but it was not sunshine I felt. It was something wet and stiff pricking at my skin in the spots where my hair had slipped beneath my shirt. With one hand, I gave Luke a shove from where he'd settled himself in to lap the remnants of honey from my hair. While Remy might be right about the moisturizing benefits of honey, it is not an easy thing to rid yourself of. After spending a good hour scrubbing and shampooing the night before, the humidity was still setting my curls into sticky clumps around my cheekbones.

I freed a pair of jeans from the bed covers and headed for the shower, intent on sneaking out of the house before my mother woke up.

I slipped into the steam, letting the water pelt my face until it branded small red streaks into my skin, and then stuck my hair under the burning water. The sting ran down my spine in hot fingers, burning their way past my waist.

The thought of my mother all crumpled up the night before had kept me tossing and turning, with her words bouncing and echoing in my head. *She hates me. She wishes I would just go away.* I didn't know how I felt, but I knew that wasn't true. The very words sent shivers straight through me and I wanted to tell her they were wrong. I wanted to explain, but every time I felt the words creeping up my throat, the thought of my father walking out beat them to the starting line and the words fell back inside me like dead butterflies.

I picked up a cloth my mother had hung from the antique faucet, bit into it, and screamed and screamed until my voice had emptied itself into the fabric and washed away with the water. Even if I wanted to talk, wanted someone to take the secrets out of my hands and carry them away, I couldn't. I couldn't tell a soul—not ever. The idea of my mother thinking I blamed her set a flame of guilt burning inside me. She had no idea that it was my fault my father was gone. *I loved him first . . . I still love him.* I had done this to her, to all of us. And without even trying I was doing it again. She believed I wanted her to go. How many people can one girl send sailing off the planet? I didn't want to find out. I didn't want her to leave. . . . I wanted to disappear, wanted to follow my father into the wind and fly away. Taking the cloth from my mouth, I scrubbed angrily at my skin, trying to swab myself into nothingness.

A year ago, Tuckertown was awash in shock when the high school's lead cheerleader, Harriett Gleason, disappeared. Just like that. One minute she was eating fried chicken and clam chowder down at Captain Joe's with her parents, celebrating her acceptance into Tufts University, and the next she was gone. The following day, the truth of things began to unfold like the blocks of a Jacob's ladder. After her parents had smiled themselves into a deep sleep, she had slipped out her window, hitched a ride to the Newport Bridge, climbed her way to the top, and jumped right off the planet. They'd found what was left of her tangled in the dingy pilings underneath the bridge. Nobody knew why she did it, but some days I imagined that I did. She was holding tight to a secret so heavy it crashed her into the waves and drowned her with the weight of it.

After two more rounds between a bottle of Prell and the residual honey, I gave up. I shook out my hair before pulling on an old sweatshirt and opening a small pouch tucked inside a case of sketching pencils to check on my Yemaya Stone. I didn't know if my father had had his with him when he left or not, but I had scoured our house looking for it and come up empty. Pulling the tiny satin strings until the mouth of the satchel puckered closed, I tucked it deep into the corner of my back pocket before stuffing Grandma Jo's map on top.

In the dining room, I cocked my head, listening for any

signs of life. When I was sure my mother and Grandma Jo were still fast asleep, I rummaged in my mother's purse, slithered two Merits into the pouch of my sweatshirt, and crept into the morning with Luke at my side.

I was just stepping off the front drive when Remy bounced down the lane toward me in Mr. O'Malley's taxi, maneuvering it into puddles so that sprays of mud splashed every which way from under the Purple Monster. With each splash, Luke barked, scurried out of the way, and then dove back in to nip at the droplets. I could not help but admire the way Remy played with the world without caring one hoot if anyone was looking or not. When she saw me, she cranked down the window and leaned through it.

"So, you came through last night still attached to your head."

I nodded, giving her a shrug.

"Good, because I could really use you to help us get ready for the Yemaya Festival. There's a mountain of work left to do. That reminds me." Remy stuck her head into the backseat and rummaged around before popping back into the day. "Here." She stuck a folded flyer through the window. "The flyers came in for the festival. By the way, you're off the hook for cleaning up Herman's window today. Merchant's can't get the glass ready until the day after tomorrow, so Mr. Herman doesn't want to knock the pane out yet. Says the bugs will get through the boards." Remy laughed, shaking her head. "But since you've found yourself freed up for the day, maybe you have time to help me with apple pie baking later?"

I nodded again, sticking the flyer into my sweatshirt beside the cigarettes.

"It's sort of a family tradition. Right?" Remy glanced in the backseat as if speaking to someone. I ducked to glance in the back, too, but it was empty. "My mom and I have baked for the festival since I was toe high to a fiddler crab. Never missed a year yet."

Standing back up, I drew my eyes across the backseat of the car but still came up empty.

"Maybe your grandma would like to come along. I've got to head down to Salva's Market soon as they open on a butter run. They're a little pricier than Herman's, but what I spend in pennies I'll save in aspirin." I felt my cheeks warm with embarrassment. "Then I'll be back to drop that bike by."

I nodded with a wave, stepping back as she gunned the accelerator, taking aim at another large mud puddle and roared toward it, sending Luke into another yapping fit. When I could no longer hear the great Purple Monster's muffler, I ducked down the path leading to Witch's Peak. A hundred yards down the path the peak pulled into view and I headed toward it before tripping over an irrigation pipe that nearly sent me face-first into the dirt. Settling under an apple tree, I wiggled the flyer and a Merit free from my pocket.

That people would be surprised I smoked was the

very thing I liked most about it. Sometimes it even surprised me. And I liked that, too. The habit came on when
Libby and I were thirteen and got the idea to smoke our
first cigarette after sneaking the remnants of a bottle of
Smirnoff from the cabinet, intent on catching up with the
rest of Tuckertown in one fast night. The act was not one
of full-fledged rebellion, so much as a last-ditch effort not
to be left behind by the normal kids. Or maybe we just
wanted to feel normal for once. The alcohol didn't take,
but the dizzying rush of inhaling too fast and deep was
a feeling I'd warmed to. I drew hard on the filter, sending the cherry canoeing into the tobacco, and laid my
head against a knot in the tree's root before unfolding the
flyer from Remy. To my surprise, she'd used my sketch of
Yemaya for the cover.

> *The Yemayan legend honors the goddess as keeper
> of the secrets of the universe. In Yorubian culture,
> each star is believed to hold the luck of a newborn
> child. It is said that many years ago a great storm
> broke the sky in two, sending the stars tumbling to
> Earth as a million small stones until the children of
> the world were buried beneath them. For a hundred
> years, Yemaya walked the four corners of Earth,
> balancing on her hip a kelp basket and gathering
> them back up. The legend claims she then cast the
> stones into the valleys of the world, burying them
> in water, and watched over them until their luck*

*was restored. This gave her the titles of the Great*
*Mother and Mother of Seven Seas. To this very day,*
*the Yoruba believe every time a sea stone washes to*
*shore it is a gift of luck.*

Not always, I corrected. Looking up at Witch's Peak, I dug into my back pocket, emptying it of Grandma Jo's map and the small velvet blue satchel with my stone inside. For a long minute, I turned the items over in my hand one at a time, stacking them into a messy pile of paper, fabric, and rock. I knew beyond doubt that the path to finding my father was caught up in the heap somewhere, that if I could just choose the right item I could find my way back to him and make everything right again. The problem was this—it could have been one just as easily as the other. Picking up the Yemaya Stone, I turned it over and over, tumbling it lightly it in my fingers. I carried it with me everywhere. It had never really brought me luck, but I kept it with me just in case. Studying the waves rolling in over the reef, I folded the stone inside the flyer and set it beside me. The eight o'clock ferry was just pointing its nose for the break in the rocks that led to open water.

The night my father vanished, I remember thinking that I could not let him get back to the boat without me. After he'd left my mother and me upstairs with a bloody knee and a kicked-in door, I'd run down the hall leaving the floorboards whispering *hurry, hurry, hurry* with every step, and grabbed my pink ballerina backpack, the one Grandma Jo had given me the Christmas before. The fact that nothing had been in it except Berta Big Bear and a pair of Bugs Bunny pajamas hadn't mattered to me. I had to catch him before he left and I would walk out in my underpants if I had to.

I'd dragged it thumping down the steps toward the front door, but my puny six-year-old legs would not move fast enough and somehow the strap on my backpack had snaked around the banister. Every tug to free it tightened the knot. The door was open and my father was already halfway through it when I'd called out for him to wait. But it was as though I had already disappeared from his sight. Even then I knew what was happening—he was leaving me behind.

*Wait . . . wait . . . Take meee!* The scream had hit the air, chasing after him into the night until every last ounce of noise had run out of me, too.

The scream was loud; I know it was loud. My throat burned for weeks. But it was the soft *click* of the front door that had been deafening. The statement was poetic, almost, delivered without comma or exclamation point, just one big period chock-ful of silence. There was nothing more to say, and as things turned out it was a good thing, too. Because that was the precise moment my voice died—five years, eleven months, thirty days, and twenty-three hours after it was born, as if those tears had simply washed all my syllables away.

In the background, my birthday cake lay uncut on the dining room table, six small burned candles melted into ugly pink puddles around my name.

Taking a final drag from my cigarette, I crushed it into the dirt beneath the apple tree and shoved the memory back.

"What are you doing here?" The sound of another person on the ridge nearly caused me to leap clear out of my skin, only to find myself face-to-face with the boy who'd stood by and watched Mr. Herman nearly kill me.

*Here? On the island? Under the tree?* It was hard to tell what he meant, but his tone was sharp enough to have meant the universe altogether. To be fair, I had turned that very question over in my head myself more than once. Riley was standing close enough for me to smell the mustiness of him, a muddled-up mix of sweat, salt, grease, and grass.

"You're Izabella Haywood." He stated it as fact, leaving me wondering if I was supposed to answer.

I nodded.

"This isn't part of the Booth property." His words were desert dry. "This is my grandfather's field. Does he know you're out here?"

Clearly, a stupid question, since I did not even know who his grandfather was.

"Uhg . . . " An ugly grunting sound tumbled out of my mouth. Surprised, I jammed my lips together, watching him.

"I thought you couldn't talk." Riley flipped Luke's ear inside out, scruffing the soft underside just as Mr. O'Malley had. "You're not supposed to be up here." He glared. "This ridge winds in and out all the way along these parts. It's plain idiotic to come around if you don't know the way. More than one person's disappeared over it." There was a drawn-out pause and I swear I saw a flash spark in his eyes. "But I guess you already know that."

I looked at him, stunned, wondering if maybe he was crazy.

With his free hand, he pushed the shag of bangs straight back over his head then shook them loose again. The gesture trembled something inside my gut, but before I had a chance to decipher what it was, he pointed back to the path and the tremble faded to embarrassment at being ordered out of his company like a small child. Had he not been staring at me with the very definition of dislike, he would have been deeply handsome in a rough, farm boy sort of way.

Turning down the path, I hurried toward Knockberry Lane with Luke romping beside me, my mind racing to figure out what Riley's problem was. For no good reason he seemed to hate me.

"You shouldn't have come back here!" he called, leaving me with the feeling that he was not just talking about the field.

If anyone had grounds to be mad, I decided, it was me. After all, wasn't he the one who could talk, but had stood right there saying not one peep while Mr. Herman blamed me for the whole thing with the stupid rock? As curious as I was, I didn't want to be alone with him five thousand feet up a cliff.

Safely back on the lane, I looked behind me in time to see a gull dive from sight, leaving the *ffffrrrreeee fff-freeeee* of its screech caught on the wind. Moments later, it swept back up with a crab in its beak and lighted on Witch's Peak. I remembered the look in my father's eyes on Anawan Cliffs that day. *Someday we're going to fly like that.*

*Fffrreeee, fffrrreeee,* the gull screeched. Or maybe it was *ffflllleeee, flee.*

That is the problem with words.

# CHAPTER NINE

When I came in, my mother was standing in front of the French doors in the living room with both hands laid flat against the glass pane as she stared out at the sea. The sight of her there, searching a horizon filled to the brim with emptiness, tugged at something familiar and deep inside me. I knew what she was doing. I had done it a million times. I had just never seen her do it. She was wishing him back, bartering with the universe.

I'm embarrassed to say that in all the years since he left, I'd never really considered she might be aching, too. Maybe it was because she just seemed pissed off with the world and my father. And maybe she was, maybe she was pissed that he left her behind, too. I wanted to tell her that I knew that feeling. I wanted to grab her and tell her not to follow him, the way she'd told me, but I didn't. If I said I wasn't afraid of what I would find inside her eyes, wasn't scared to death of the truth hiding there, I would be lying plain as day. Letting that fear disappear into a foamy sea of distance was easier.

So I turned away to look for Grandma Jo to ask if she wanted to come bake pies. I went to the kitchen and, finding it empty of everything except a plate of untouched toast tossed in the sink, headed for her room, letting my eyes fall to the sharp points of my mother's shoulders beneath her blouse as I passed. Drawn tight with a belt, the fabric of her jeans bunched at the waist like a brown paper bag.

"Grandma Jo went down to the beach again to do yoga. She said she'd be back in an hour." My mother's voice was still. She didn't push Luke down from her knee when he trundled over to snuffle her pant leg.

Grabbing a banana, I headed toward the stairs behind her to put my hair up before going to Remy's.

"I know how much you loved him, Iz. I loved him, too." The statement seemed to tumble down to her feet and break into tiny bits.

I stopped and turned around, tracing her shoulder blades, following the thin rails of her arms out to her fingertips.

"Do you remember anything about the night he left?"

Roses. Fireflies. Praying. Stairs. The candles—*I hate you, hate you, hate you.*

I shook my head, but she never turned around; she wasn't really asking.

My stomach twisted into a knot as I wrestled the

memory back into its shackles. Luke must have sensed something come over me because he left my mother's side and was nudging at my ankle to be picked up. Holding him close, I let him lick my face until it was so wet I couldn't feel the tears running down my cheeks.

"I do. I remember everything. It was the grayest day I have ever seen. But it's funny, every time I think of that morning, I remember it as bright and sunny. It was the first chance we had to get away for a little while since I'd started school. With my schoolwork and his . . . traveling and writing, it was like we lost each other in the chaos, and man, did I miss him. I missed us, all of us. So that day felt like the brightest day ever when we got on the boat to come here even though the weather sucked. The rain wasn't falling, just hanging in the air like a veil. Like the universe knew something bad was about to happen.

"Anyway," she cleared her throat, "I thought you should know that. He was impossible, and impetuous, and moody, and he drove me crazy. But, I loved him despite all that or maybe because of all that. I was alive when I was with him. He taught me how to live. He gave me you. You probably don't get that, but . . . "

Time seemed to slow to a crawl, and I didn't quite know what to do, so I just stood there watching her tap the windowpane with her bandaged thumb, lost, in her own memories. The nails on her hands had been chewed low, leaving angry raw crescents of pink in their wake.

She was wearing my father's wedding band on her middle finger.

The memory of her leaning against my father's study door returned to me, his back turned to her. I saw the sadness and betrayal in her eyes, her finger brushing his cheek in their wedding picture as she climbed away from him to an empty bedroom.

Yes, I thought. I get that.

"When you were little, he used to drag you along on these adventures to get you out of Sunday school: to the cape, or the Thimble Islands, or Potter's Creek. Said Reverend Mitchell might be able to fill you with God," I heard her voice catch, "but it was a father's job to fill you with magic." My mother laughed, tilting her head. Still staring out the window, she tapped my father's wedding ring rhythmically to the pane of glass. *Tick, tick, tick* . . . like the hands of a clock struggling to move forward but finding itself stuck between moments.

I looked down at my hand, which had tightened instinctively around the banana, splitting the peel so that white goo oozed through my fingers.

"Do you remember?"

I did remember somewhere deep inside. My heart ached from all the remembering, actually ached, as though it, too, would split right down its seams like the banana, until I pushed the thoughts down to my toes to keep them away.

Just then, I remembered something else. I put Luke

down, shoving my one dry hand into my pocket, rooting around for my stone. It was gone; so were Grandma Jo's map and the flyer. The vague memory of setting them on the ground under the apple tree rushed back at me. My heart sank at the possibility of Riley snatching them. Clearly, he didn't like me, and there wasn't much chance of him dropping by to return them if he found them. He'd probably show them to his stupid friends, too. My mind was churning to put together a plan to zip back to the bluffs to get them when Remy Mandolin's voice barreled into the room, ending any chance of racing back to Witch's Peak.

"Ready to make pies?" she called.

My mother turned around, a confused look on her face. "Excuse me?"

"Pies," Remy repeated, grabbing a pear from the bowl on the dining room table. "You know, flaky round pastries you stuff with fruit and serve with vanilla ice cream."

"I know what a pie is." My mother sighed. "Why would I be making them?"

"You wouldn't," Remy quipped. "Not unless you were the award-winning pie baker of the Yemaya Festival four years running who didn't want to disappoint her public."

"Which I am not."

"Because I am." Remy bit into the pear and wiped its juice from her chin with her sleeve.

"Don't you ever eat at your own house?"

"I do. Pie. Which your daughter has kindly agreed to

help me bake. Right?" She looked at me for confirmation. I nodded, wishing I could make some excuse to rush back to Witch's Peak, but even if I had, the truth of the matter was that I was afraid Riley might still be lurking around. "Your grandma coming?"

"She's still out doing stretches, or meditating, or whatever it is yoga fanatics do to find peace in the universe," my mother gibed.

"Maybe you ought to try that," Remy suggested. "You know, rid yourself of all that stress."

"Ha!"

I walked behind Remy with the remains of the banana I'd mutilated, tossing it into the garbage and wiping my hand off before grabbing my jacket.

"By the way, I told Izabella I'd let her use that bike in your drive. It got me to thinking. You've got to pay Mr. Herman for damages, right?"

"Right," my mother answered coolly.

"With the taxi and ferry and trying to get ready for the Yemaya Festival, well, things are just a little crazy. I could use a spare set of hands. I thought maybe they could belong to Izabella. You know, when she's not working down at Herman's to clean up. And how long could that take? I could pay her three dollars an hour, and she could hand it over to you to help pay for the window. I know I don't have kids, but it's the sort of thing my mother used to do."

It was the third time I had heard Remy speak about

her mother and the mention rendered my mother surprisingly silent for a very long time. In fact, Remy seemed to throw her off kilter just by being in the same room. Even though my mother was snippy with her, her bitchiness lacked steam and I had noticed something else: underneath the sparring, there seemed to be some sort of connection between the two. Their eyes often held for just a second too long and a private unspoken conversation seemed to pass between them.

"Well, think about it and let me know. It would give her something to do, keep her out of trouble. With the bike, she would have a way to get to work. And, I've got to admit, I'm not half bad at history and math. She could bring along her books while we cart passengers and I'd quiz her. There's a solid two hours to kill on each ferry run."

"Okay." I don't know if it was the memory of my father, or if Remy had just worn her down, but my mother's tone had softened and she was looking right at Remy without any fire in her eyes.

"Okay?" Even Remy seemed surprised.

"Yes, okay. She's not a little girl anymore." My mother glanced at me as if seeing someone different than she had before. "It might be good for her. But today she's got to go to Herman's. And, for Christ's sake, keep her away from those girls."

"Tomorrow."

"What?"

"Tomorrow she has to go to Herman's. They couldn't

get the glass cut in time. I'll bring her down there bright and early, and when she's done there she can make the two o'clock run with me."

"Fine. But she takes her homework with her."

"Fine. Alrighty, then. Let's get to those pies. Tell Josephine she's welcome to join us." Remy made her way to the door, paused, and looked back at my mother. "You know how to bake a pie?"

"No, but thanks for the offer."

"Not an offer, just a question," Remy bit into the pear she was still holding. "But you can cut up the butter, if you want, as long as you don't let it soften."

"As fun as that sounds, I really—"

"Have to work. Uh huh, I know."


I was still considering how to get my Yemaya Stone back as Remy pulled a stack of pie pans from the pantry with a clatter.

"Pull up those three stools." She waved at a row of bar stools lined up against the wall and laid out three rolling pins in front of them. "Here's an apron." She tossed a neatly starched cloth at me, laying another stained apron in front of the third stool.

I tied the apron around my waist and climbed onto the far stool. Remy froze, holding a bag of apples an inch above the counter.

"Not there." Her voice wavered sharply. "There." She

pointed to the stool beside it. Setting a bowl of ice water and a mug of tea beside the vacant stool, Remy offered no further explanation.

"Ready? Okay, take your slab of butter and cut it into three cups of flour. Once you work it through, give it a pinch of salt and a tablespoon of that ice water."

Picking up a fork, I started chopping through the flour. The hard butter fought back, and by the time I'd worked it into some semblance of dough I had white clumps dappling my face and hair.

Glancing up from her stool where she was peeling the bag of apples, Remy let out a hearty laugh, plucking at my curls. "You've never done this before, have you?"

I shook my head.

We'd been at it for half an hour when Grandma Jo arrived carrying a casserole dish with her.

"Tofu macaroni and cheese." She lifted the dish proudly before setting it on the butcher's block in front of the empty seat.

"You shouldn't have," Remy said, snatching the casserole away from the empty stool and moving it over to the stovetop.

"It was my pleasure." Grandma Jo dismissed the comment with a wave of her hand. "I was making a batch for Izabella anyway."

"No," Remy crinkled up her nose at the casserole. "I mean you really shouldn't have."

There was something musical about Grandma Jo's laugh, like silver bells dropping to the floor. "Just try it."

"Bean curd." Remy shook her head in wonderment. "Who in the hell ever stopped what they were doing, looked at a bean, and said, 'I think I'll make curd out of that'? Do you like to bake, Josephine? I mean things other than curd from a bean?"

"I make a mean carrot cake and cheese biscuits that melt right over your tongue."

"Cheese or cheese curd?"

Grandma Jo laughed again, peeling off her cardigan and reaching for the third apron. Remy put a hand on top of it to stop her.

"That's my mother's. I've got another one right here." I looked around the empty cottage wondering if Mrs. O'Malley was running behind schedule while Remy dug free another apron. "Sit here." Remy pulled over the stool she'd been using for Grandma Jo, who was studying her thoughtfully. Remy glanced at her quickly and then turned her attention to me, laughing.

"You look a little like that picture of Yemaya you drew all covered in pearls." Plucking a floury glob from my hair, she popped it into her mouth then ran a chopping knife through the pile of apples until they were nothing more than small chunks. "Did you show your grandmother the cover of the flyer for the festival?"

I shook my head.

"Festival?" Grandma Jo spun an apple in her hand, peeling it with expertise.

"The Yemaya Festival is coming up." Remy snatched a copy of the flyer from the counter, setting it down beside my grandmother. "And your granddaughter is the artist gracing the cover with her illustration this year."

"Izabella Rae! You drew this? It's gorgeous." She picked the flyer up, examining it closer. "Izabella says you're somewhat of an expert when it comes to the Yemaya tradition."

I leaned into a slab of hard butter, splitting it into quarters and sending a puff of flour over the counter.

"I guess that just comes from growing up with her. I remember walking around these cliffs as a kid and seeing her around every corner." Remy tossed the apples in cinnamon and set them aside. "That reminds me . . ." She made her way around the butcher's block, knocking into the empty stool beside me. "Excuse me," she said, as though there were a person sitting there.

Mrs. O'Malley hadn't shown up yet, and Grandma Jo and I glanced awkwardly at one another.

Remy shoved a chair under a bookcase, set aside a copy of Erica Jong's *Fear of Flying*, and climbed up, removing a small wooden statue from the top shelf before clamoring back down to set it in front of me.

"Have you read that yet?" Grandma Jo nodded at the book. "It's fabulous. You'll never think of sex the same way again."

I looked up at her, wide-eyed.

"Not yet," Remy said, letting her eyes flick toward the book. "But I'm sure as hell going to now." She made her way back to the counter with the statue. "You know what this is?"

Grandma Jo glanced across the pile of apples.

Scraping the dough from my fingers first, I picked up the figurine, surprised that I did know what it was: a statue of Saint Agnes of Assisi. Back when my parents were doing all that fighting, and I was doing all that praying, I'd sent a million winged prayers to Saint Francis for the simple reason that Reverend Mitchell had once read us a story about God ordering Saint Francis to restore peace to God's House. I was so young I thought it was an actual house with a winding staircase and dirty living room, and that if Saint Francis could fix God's house, fixing mine should be a cinch. So when I was nine and we had to write an essay for Sunday school about a religious figure, I'd chosen him as my subject. In the essay, I'd copied a picture of him giving a habit to Saint Agnes, charging her to look over the poor.

That was a long time ago, though, and somewhere along the way, I'd grown tired of waiting for an answer and forgotten about him altogether.

"It's Saint Agnes," Remy said, taking a fork to the pie crust. "There's this religion, sort of, called Santeria that the slaves practiced. Slave owners and missionaries forced the slaves to worship the Christian saints and god. But the slaves already had gods of their own. Flip it over," she wagged her head at the statue, "go ahead." On the bottom of the statue was the figure of a small woman caught in a shell. Remy picked up the crust and flopped it into a pie pan, busying herself with pinching the edges. "It's Yemaya. The slaves didn't want to abandon their own gods, so they carved symbols and pictures of them into the bottom of these statues and worshipped them, instead, all the while. The whole time, the slave handlers thought they were praying to the saints. Cool, huh?"

"Very," Grandma Jo agreed.

I nodded, running a hand over the carved figure at the base of the statue.

"My mother got me those when I was around your age from an antiques store over on the mainland." Remy waved her hand at the empty stool.

I set the statue down, watching it while I measured out three more cups of flour, tossed it into the sifting can, and gave the crank a spin. The powder flitted through the screen with the grace of winter's first snow.

"If you really want to know about Yemaya, you should check out the library down on Chestnut Street. They had a bad fire a few years back—space heater on the second floor—but they've been able to save a lot of stuff and what they couldn't has mostly been replaced. They have a whole display set up for the walking tour. As a matter of fact, if you're interested you could drop a bundle of festival flyers off at the desk, and this." She crossed the room and pulled a book from the shelf. "It's overdue. Tell them I'll pay with pie at the festival." She laid the book beside me and opened the oven to peek inside.

It was seven o'clock when Remy finally set the last bowl in the sink. "Well, I guess that about does it for tonight."

The darkness beyond the kitchen window, and Grandma Jo at my side, erased any chance I might have had to sneak back up to Witch's Peak to look for my Yemaya Stone.

"I'll see you bright and early to bring you down to Herman's," Remy said.

I pushed the stool, which I had managed to cover with flour, under the butcher's block and began to shove in the one beside it when Remy stopped me. For a fleeting second, her eyes seemed to burn right through me, then the look was gone and the lilt returned to her voice, leaving me wondering if my mother was right about Remy being a raving lunatic.

"Here." She shoved three fives and five ones into my hand. "Give your mom fifteen dollars toward Mr. Herman's window."

I held up the five ones questioningly.

"Those are for you." She closed my fingers around the money, looking over at Grandma Jo. "Josephine, maybe you'd like to bake some of your biscuits for the festival? The ones without curds."

"It would be my honor. But only if you promise to try the macaroni and cheese I brought you."

Remy lifted an eyebrow then sighed. "Fine."

Tucking the money into two separate pockets, I picked up Remy's book and the stack of flyers, glancing once more at the stool Remy had nearly bit my head in two for touching, and walked out the door. By the time Grandma Jo and I made it to the Booth House, my mother was locked in her room, dictating prices into her handheld recorder:

"Bradley Museum Cavanaugh Collection. Oil-based, fair condition. Eighty-five hundred dollars.. Michael Scott Lasser sculpture, fifteen hundred dollars."

I laid the fifteen dollars on the counter and slipped upstairs to wash the dough from under my nails in the bathroom. Flicking on the light, I stared at the girl watching me in the mirror with an expression of curiosity on her face. The honey had mostly washed free of my dark strands, but the curls still spiraled down to my breasts in smooth loose springs that reminded me of coils of chocolate shaved from the brick. Maybe Remy was right, that honey was conditioning, or maybe it was the best hair spray in the universe.

Running the water until it warmed, I used one nail to scrape the piecrust paste from the other until tiny clumps littered the porcelain then splashed my face. It was almost as pale as the basin, as if God forgot to color it in altogether, then realizing his mistake, tossed a handful of freckles across my nose just to make sure people could see me. It would be easier, I often thought, if they could not—if I could just slip from shadow to shadow through the universe, unseen and unheard. Even my eyes were lacking real color. The dim tint of a perfect storm, that's what my father used to say. But, really, they were the pale gray of a day that a pending storm had snuffed all the light from.

For a splintered second, I couldn't tell if I was studying the girl in the mirror or if she was studying me, and I thought Grandma Jo might be wrong about me not being insane. Did I get the best of my father? I couldn't say. One minute the memory of him was sharp as a razor. The next it was all mushy around the edges and lacking form. Tipping my head upside down, I shook my hair to knock the flour from it and went back downstairs.

I found Grandma Jo in the kitchen making her famous tofu macaroni and cheese.

"Just in time," she chirped when I came back into the kitchen. "I was looking for a tester."

I took a bite and rolled my eyes heavenward. It was divine.

There is my mother's pasta, and then there is Grandma Jo's macaroni and cheese, made with Vermont Cheddar so sharp it stings your tongue. I did not even mind that it was whole wheat, or that she always snuck tofu crumbles into the pasta.

"Shoot!" Grandma Jo pulled her hand back from the

casserole, sucking on her finger. "That's hot." The memory of my mother shoving her bloody thumb in her mouth flitted back to me, and I couldn't help but notice how much they sometimes resembled one another.

"Can you put the wineglasses on the table for me?"

Pinching the rims together, I clinked my way to the table.

"Zo, dinner!"

"Busy," my mother called back from her room. "I'll eat later."

"You'll eat now, or Izabella and I will come in there with the food and eat on your bed." Grandma Jo's voice was warm but firm as concrete.

My mother shuffled into the room and began filling water glasses with ice. I followed behind her, setting the plates.

"Pie turn out okay?" She gazed up at me. Aside from my mother telling me she missed my father, too, we hadn't really spoken since the argument about Mr. Herman's window and I recognized the question for what it was: a white flag.

Laying a bread plate down, I nodded, trying to remember the last time we'd sat down to eat together. The scent of baking bread began to waft through the house.

"Maybe you and Grandma Jo can explore the island tomorrow night while I work."

"Maybe you can finish your work another time and we can go together," Grandma Jo offered as she pulled the bread from the oven, grated fresh Parmesan on top, and set it in a basket for me to take to the table. My mother sighed. I knew Grandma Jo drove her nuts, but I wondered, too, if she saw the way Grandma Jo prodded her back into herself. The cracks seemed to fill in when my grandmother was around, not perfectly, but noticeably.

Grandma Jo padded into the dining room barefoot carrying a candle and matches. She set a plate on the floor for Luke, who scampered up to sniff it. Maybe it was a result of what I had overheard the night before, or the way the puzzle pieces were shifting slowly into place. Maybe it was the smell of autumn roses in the air, or the flickering of fall's last fireflies in the yard. Whatever it was, I did not see it coming. Grandma Jo lit the candle. There was a burst of light, like a flashcube I had not closed my eyes to.

A cake. Six pink candles. *Let go . . . let go . . . let go.* And then the world went white.

"Izabella, honey!" I was surprised to find my body upright, my hands clutching the ladder-back chair with enough force to numb my fingertips. "Honey?" Grandma Jo's voice sifted through the white light from a distant land. "Here, sit down." Grandma Jo held me from the front while my mother tilted a glass of ice water to my lips. As I slowly touched down, their faces drew into focus, breaking through the blaze of white.

"Sip." My mother poured water down my throat.

"What is it?" Grandma Jo held my hand.

"Probably the heat from baking all afternoon. It's warm in here."

I nodded in agreement.

"Do you want to lie down?"

I shook my head, mopping the clamminess from my brow and getting to my feet.

"Better?"

I nodded, knowing for a fact that it wasn't true. Something in this place was sending all those memories I'd spent eight years burying bobbing to the surface inside me like land mines dislodged from the ocean floor. There was no avoiding them, no telling what might bump into one, setting it off.

# CHAPTER TEN

When I woke curled up on the couch the following morning, autumn had pounced on Tillings Island with both feet. Sometime in the night, my mother had come to cover me with a quilt and Luke had squirreled his way underneath, sticking a wet nose under my chin while he slept.

"Are you feeling well enough to go with Remy today?" My mother shuffled into the living room carting a clean load of laundry. The nod escaped before I thought better of it, remembering I was due at Herman's in half an hour.

"All right, then you'd better get yourself up and dressed before she comes blaring that godforsaken horn."

Untangling myself, I tossed the quilt aside, sending Luke flopping over with a sleepy snort, and went upstairs to throw on a clean shirt. I left on the old pair of jeans I'd slept in, since I was going to be painting anyway. A strapping frost the night before had left the leaves outside the window dipped in shades of molasses and cranberry red. Just looking at them made me hungry for a tall stack of Grandma Jo's flapjacks and homemade maple syrup, which I could smell cooking downstairs. Pulling on one of my father's old sweatshirts with a shiver and letting it hang clear down to my knees, I stuck my hair up in a curly mop and darted downstairs.

"I'm glad to see you're feeling better." Grandma Jo set a second pancake on my plate and patted my shoulder.

After wolfing it down, I tossed my plate in the sink and headed for the front door.

"Freeze." My mother came through the kitchen door clutching a mug of coffee. "Where in the world do you think you're going? Remy'll be here any minute to get you."

*Tell her to wait*, I scribbled on a brown paper bag from Salva's that was sitting on the table. *I'll be right back.* I'd just made it to the door when I remembered the strange way Remy had acted the day before and turned around, picking up the pencil again. *Do you know Mrs. O'Malley?*

"She used to drop preserves and biscuits by whenever we came," my mother answered after a calculated pause. "That sort of thing."

*Why hasn't she?* The lead on the pencil had worn below the crest of the wood and I was forced to scratch the last word into the smooth side of the bag. My mother leaned over, trying to decipher it, sloshing coffee on her chest as she did. For the craziest of seconds, it looked as though she'd done so on purpose. She leapt back belatedly.

"Shit!" she cussed, swiping at the stain with the bandage on her thumb. "That's hot. Do me a favor and leave the door unlocked in case Remy comes while I change. Okay?"

*I'll be right back*, I promised.

"You'd better be!" she called, bustling out of the room while holding her shirt away from her skin in a small stained tent. "I'm not going to sit here and listen to her go on while you lollygag about." Bolting out the door in a race to get back before Remy showed up, I barely noticed Luke scrambling out at my heels to make off after a rabbit in the side yard.

I ran down the lane as fast as my feet would move, and after making sure Remy wasn't coming down the road, cut into the path. Within three minutes, I was staring at Witch's Peak trying to remember where I'd set down the map and flyer and stone. Dropping to my knees, I raked my fingertips through the mud, letting the stones sift through my fingers until I hit the soggy edge of a folded piece of paper under a rotted apple core. Grandma Jo's map was dirty and wet, but at least it was whole. After ten more minutes of shuffling through the dirt I knew the Yemaya Stone was gone along with the flyer. Either they'd been brushed into the thickets by one of Mr. O'Malley's deer, probably the one who'd left the apple core rotting on my map, or Riley had taken them. Either way, I would never get them back.

Pulling myself to my feet, I adopted Remy's disdain for Mr. O'Malley's stupid salt licks and nursed my own for Riley. The stone was the one thing I had never lost from my father and a sick emptiness opened up inside me. I felt tears sting the corners of my eyes but pushed them away with the heels of my palms. Brushing the dirt off my knees, I walked back to the Booth House, miserable.

The Purple Monster was parked in the drive, and inside the house my mother was making a check out to Remy since Mr. Herman wouldn't take one from the mainland. Remy plucked it off the table and counted out five twenties from her own pocket, stuffing them in her shirt pocket to give to Mr. Herman before taking a plate of pancakes from Grandma Jo.

"Where were you?" she asked, shoving a bite in her mouth and glancing in my direction.

I grabbed the paper bag and wrote, *out.*

"I was just being polite." She gave me a sidelong look while she chewed. "I didn't really want to know anyway."

Still plotting the many ways I could torture Riley until he coughed up my belongings, I stared back at her with an empty face.

"Jeez, someone's in a tizzy this morning," she said, piling one more bite of pancake into her cheek before turning for the door. "Since you're already grouchy, let's go pay Mr. Herman his money and break up a window."

"Did you remember to pick me up flowers, Remy?" my mother interjected.

"No."

"But I asked you," she retorted. "Can you bring some back with you?"

"Let me see. While you were still sleeping, I hunted down goggles, gloves, and mallets to take care of knocking that window out. Now I'm going down to face off with an old grump who's already pissed as a grizzly about a broken window and help Izabella take care of the mess she left behind. Then I need to go scrub toilets on the ferry and make sure the deck's clear of puppy puke. After that, I'm steering a boat across the ocean to pick up a group of pushy tourists and coming back to cart those same tourists to every corner of this blessed island. In the ten minutes I may find for myself by midnight, I might, I don't know . . . pee or eat or something crazy like that. So, no."

"Well, I'm *so* sorry. But maybe if I had a car—"

"You don't need a car; you need a damn servant. Come on, Izabella, before Mr. Herman blows out an artery. Thanks for breakfast, Josephine."

I sighed, looking at my mother.

"Go on," she said, but there was a hint of gentleness in her voice that I wasn't used to. "Just stay in the car while Remy gives him the money. He'll be okay after that. And be sure to wear the goggles and gloves Remy brought."

Remy held the door wide, letting me stomp on by.

"And don't forget to do your social studies work. Remy has your book," she yelled after me.

Outside, I stood by the door waiting for Remy while my mother barked final instructions at her.

"Make sure he gives you a receipt. The last thing I want

is to be stuck on this island for eternity taking care of a lawsuit."

"Trust me," Remy lobbed back. "That's the last thing any of us wants."

"And make sure Iz stays in the car until he's paid so he doesn't yell at her all over again. For God's sake, don't let her anywhere near those girls."

"Anything else?" Remy asked. "Maybe she could just sit in the car and I could fix the window for her, too."

"You know what I mean. I just don't want—"

"Good God, give the girl a little credit. She's not built of sand," Remy said. "Now, if you're done, I've got one for you. Get your sorry ass out of this house. Take a walk, for Pete's pity! Lord knows you could use a little fresh air. You're starting to look like a vampire."

"The girl's got a point," I heard Grandma Jo yell from inside.

"And while you're out get your own damn flowers. There are about a thousand rosebushes on this property and a field of black-eyed Susans and daisies. Clippers are in the shed. Figure it out. I've got better things to do than run around trying to match petals to your sofa cushions." She came through the front door shooting me a quick wink, and when I looked over my shoulder, I was surprised to see the faintest glint of a smile turning up the corners of my mother's mouth before she spun around.

"Now," Remy glanced at me once we were in the car and she'd thrown it into drive, "you have your pen and pad?" I fished around inside the pocket of my father's sweatshirt and nodded. "Good. Then you want to tell me what storm cloud parked its rear end over your head this morning?"

I flipped my pad open and wrote, *nothing.*

"Right. And I'm gonna romp around this island to get your mum flowers tomorrow. Now that we're both done telling big fat lies . . . "

The back-and-forth between Remy and my mother was becoming my surest source of entertainment, better even than seeing how many of my mother's cigarettes I could steal before she thought she was losing her mind. But something had shifted between them. What began as sheer pissiness had softened into almost a sort of game.

**The Great Purple** Monster of Millbury skidded to a stop in front of Merchant's, nearly bumping the car in front of it in the process. I stared out the window praying hard that Mr. Herman would not choose this very moment to come sweep the front stoop. We sat there for the slowest minute in all of history before my eyes dragged away from the storefront to find that Remy had set the cash on my lap and was flipping through the *Mirabel*'s passenger list, pen in hand. Another minute crawled by with all the speed of a garden slug before she glanced up.

"You can't go until you actually open the door."

I stared at her wide-eyed, grasping at the frayed ends of the conversation between my mother and Remy not fifteen minutes earlier regarding my designated post as car ornament while Remy paid Mr. Herman and got a receipt. Her disobedience toward my mother quickly lost every ounce of entertainment value. I shook my head, shoving the money across the seat, only to have her stare at it blankly.

"Izabella, even if I wanted to—and let's be clear about this, I don't—I do not have time to sit here all day while you crawl under the front seat of this car and hide from a thousand-year-old grocer who hasn't strength or sense enough to knock a rat off a garbage tin. In four hours, Mr. O'Malley will be pulling the ferry up to the wharf, at which time we have thirty minutes to scrub down five restrooms and swab two decks before we turn the boat around to the mainland."

*I'm supposed to wait here until he's paid*, I scribbled. *Remember?*

"Trust me, Mr. Herman's not gonna run you to the hills when you're handing him cash. He's just an old man. It takes him forty-five minutes to hobble down Main Street to open the store. Go on."

*But you told my mother*

"I lied."

*But*

"Now listen here, Izabella, this is your debt, not mine, and you've got about two minutes to decide if you're going in there to settle it or not. Your mum may be worried about him raising his voice to you, but I'm not. You're not going to crumble to dust by someone being upset. Now, today was Mr. Herman's deadline. You choose. Fix it, or let him press charges. You want to call it off? I've got plenty of other things I could be doing other than smashing out a window."

*No!* I scribbled before tossing the pen across the seat and putting my notepad away to let her know I was serious about the issue.

"Have it your way," she said, firing up the taxi. "But I'm going to tell you right now . . . you can't have it both ways. If you want this world to take you seriously, you'd better stop hiding under your mum's skirt when things get hairy. You'd rather run off and sneak around than stand up and be counted for your choices. And that's just fine—if you plan on living in everyone else's shadows for the rest of your life."

Glaring at her, I snatched the money off the seat, opened the latch, and made my way into the store with my heart trying to thump its way free of my chest.

Mr. Herman was standing just inside as if he had been watching us argue the whole time. "I hope you've come through that door with my money."

I handed over the fold of money, feeling the slippery skin on the back of his fingers brush against my wrist as he plucked it from my hand. Mr. Herman tallied the bills as slowly as possible, counting them off in his most booming voice to be sure the whole store heard him.

"Forty . . . sixty . . . eighty . . . one hundred. Well,

at least it'll pay for a new glass. Probably not the same quality." He drew the moment into infinity to be certain every last customer noted the level of injustice I'd inflicted upon him.

When he was finished, I gave him a meek smile.

"Make sure you don't damage the wood when you're breaking out the old pane," he barked. "I need this storefront shipshape before the festival begins."

Outside, I found Remy already suited up with a pair of goggles and gloves reaching clear up to her biceps. One black rubber hand was holding out a set for me, too. While I pulled them on, she fetched two rubber mallets and a large roll of duct tape and marched over to the window.

"Here." She handed me the loose end of tape. "Start with this corner while we wait for Jim to bring his pry bar. We've got to pull these boards and finish taping it off before we can start hammering."

Busy taping, I did not notice the police cruiser pull up behind the Purple Monster until the sheriff sauntered over to us. Riley was at his side clutching a steel bar in his hand. My stomach teetered, sending a flush over my cheeks at the sight of him. I wondered if he realized I knew he'd stolen my Yemaya Stone. But the truth I refused to admit was that anger wasn't the only emotion kicking around in my gut.

"Morning." Remy brushed the sheriff's cheek with a kiss before patting Riley on the back. "Thanks for bringing the crowbar. I'm couldn't find mine anywhere."

"Not a problem. I think that one may be yours from

when I fixed my porch. I was bringing Riley down to the pier anyway."

"Can you pull those boards really quick, so I can tape behind them?" Remy tapped Riley on the shoulder, pointing.

Giving me a hard glance, Riley pushed past me and wiggled the teeth of the bar under the nails, pulling them free with a groan from the wood. Remy took the paper cup from the sheriff's hand and sipped at his coffee.

"That should do it," Riley said, stepping back so Remy could tape off the hole. When she turned, he gave the crowbar a toss, letting it fall at my feet.

"Did *I* break this window?" She shot a look over her shoulder. Snapping to, I realized I'd been staring at Riley. Blushing, I grabbed the tape and helped her finish it off.

"I'm gonna get a soda," Riley said, going into Herman's.

"Hurry up," the sheriff yelled after him. "I've got to get back to the station."

A few minutes later, Riley reappeared with a can of cola, heading for the cruiser. "I'm gonna drop him by the pier. You ladies have this under control?" the sheriff asked.

"It's as good as done," Remy puffed, handing the mallet to me.

As the police cruiser pulled away from the curb, I noticed two familiar figures standing across the street. Lindsey and Carly were sitting on a bike rack watching us. Our eyes met for only an instant, but it was long enough for Lindsey to toss her hair over one shoulder with a laugh.

"It's festival week," Remy explained, following my gaze. "No school. Sort of a fall break." She turned back toward the window. "Okay, goggles tight?"

I gave the band behind my head a tug and followed her back to the window.

"Okay, stand right here," Remy directed, pointing to the spot in front of her. "Before you swing I want you to look in that glass."

I stared at the spot where she had pointed. Through the hole, I saw Betsey ringing up a customer and gazing back at me, perplexed.

"Look again." Remy fiddled with a loose cuticle on her thumbnail.

It took a full minute before what she was looking at took shape and pulled into focus, and a grin worked over my lips. There in the reflection, I saw Lindsey and Carly perched like vultures on the metal rack behind me.

"Now go ahead and hit it like you damn well mean it."

Smashing at the window like it was Lindsey's skull, I did not stop until there was nothing left but small chunks, like bits of icicles, clinging to the edges.

"You should consider doing something about that habit," Remy said, standing back and checking my progress.

I looked at her inquisitively.

"You know, the urge you get to smash windows whenever those girls are around." She gazed across the street where the two girls were pretending not to watch. "At least this time your steam came in handy."

**Three hours later,** we'd carved loose the remaining shards of glass and Remy was driving in the last nail to board up the window until the new pane arrived. When she was done, Mr. Herman hobbled out to have a look.

"What about scraping the grooves?"

"Did it," Remy said, tossing the mallet into the trunk.

"There's still the matter of the chipped paint around the edges."

"Not today. I've got a ferry to run this afternoon. Besides, that can be taken care of once the new glass is set."

"Make sure it is," he grumbled. "And it'll need to be glazed, too."

"Right," Remy answered, opening the passenger door and cueing me to get in. "Ready?" She looked at me.

"I didn't hear an apology," Mr. Herman said.

I looked at Remy, wide-eyed.

"Well?"

"She doesn't speak, Maynard," Remy interjected. "I told you that the other day."

"That's not how I understand it. Word is she can speak when she wants."

I stared at Mr. Herman in disbelief. Through the open door, I saw a thin woman with a sharp nose gaze up from the box of cookies she was laying on the checkout belt.

"Well, you should know better than to believe the half-cocked gossip of a bunch of bored housewives. Now leave her alone."

"For your information, your nephew told me, not three

hours ago. Says he heard her for himself out on the bluff. And since she can talk when she chooses, I think I'm owed an apology."

"Then let *me* apologize," Remy chirped. "I'm sorry you're so bitter. I'm sure it's not entirely your fault you're a hostile old windbag." Mr. Herman looked like he'd been slapped as a cloud of anger swept over his face. I grabbed Remy's arm, trying to tug her out the door before things got any worse. "Oh, and the next time someone gets accosted outside your door by the riffraff on this island, I might have to start sending people to Salva's instead. You know, for their own safety."

Remy slammed the driver's door shut with more force than necessary and we drove the rest of the way to the pier in silence, with me trying to untangle what Mr. Herman had said. I hadn't spoken to a single soul on this island, and it wasn't until we skidded to a stop beside the Yemaya statue that I figured out what he was talking about. It was Riley who'd told Mr. Herman I could speak, which wasn't entirely factual since a gasp is not truly a word.

Sometimes, when I least expected it, tiny shreds of the knot in my throat broke free—not whole words but stray syllables. It had happened at my grandfather's funeral when they'd opened the casket and a small *oooowww,* as soft as a cat's meow, had popped into the air and gotten caught up in the groan of the coffin hinges. I remember how it felt, too, like a tiny chameleon skittling up my throat and hiccupping into the world, leaving a small empty pocket inside me and a dizzying whirl in my ears. But nobody else had ever heard. Until now.

Mr. O'Malley was just docking the boat when we arrived. A deck full of passengers shuffled toward the steps in a rush to be first off. Leading the pack, a woman with a toy poodle draped over one arm tottered forward in spiked fuchsia heels. The dog's fur had been tufted into a white fountain sprouting over a pink ribbon between its ears.

"Good Lord Almighty." Remy sighed, shaking her head at the woman. "Looks like Mr. O'Malley picked up a crew from Bloomingdale's Tacky Gear for the Fat and Wealthy department."

I tried to force a grin, fighting the sick feeling left behind by the sight of Riley grabbing the tie line on the ferry and wrapping it three times around a piling. *This property belongs to my grandfather,* I remembered him saying. He was Remy's nephew, Mr. O'Malley's grandson, which explained why every time I turned around he was standing there in the shadows. Then the kiss Remy had met the sheriff with pulled sharply into focus: he was not her boyfriend but her brother.

"Why the blazes do you people drag fleabags around with you everywhere you go?" Remy shook her head across the pier at the woman and her dog. "Though this time I've got to admit, I'm split right down the middle about which one's worse, the dog or the owner." She sighed. I did not point out that, for all her proclamation about disliking dogs, on more than one occasion I'd caught her sneaking Luke treats. "I'd better let her off and fast before the cream puff and her damn poodle get overexcited and pee the deck."

The white heads of ten-foot swells sloshed over the break wall, rolling inland in a foamy curl. The *Mirabel* teetered and tossed along with them, back and forth, bumping clumsily into place.

"Riley! Tie that off and come here."

He looked up, flipping the hair out of his eye. His expression darkened when he saw me.

"Let's go! We've got to get these people off and turn this boat around."

Riley gave the knot a yank and sauntered over to Remy. "Here's the log." He handed her a clipboard, which she propelled at me without hesitation before heading for the ramp.

"Izabella's going to guide people off." Her eyes bobbed between us. Though busying myself with the names on the clipboard, I caught the fringe of a look that passed between them. "Show her where to stand when you drop the ramp."

"I'm busy." He started to walk away. Remy caught him by the back of the shirt.

"Not as busy as me. Now show her."

"Why can't Grandpa show her?" He pointed at Mr. O'Malley, who was now sitting on a large reel of rope beside the ferry while Telly guided the cars out from the lower deck.

"Because Grandpa isn't feeling well. And I told you to do it, so go."

"Come on," Riley snapped, leading me over to the boat. "Just hand people a map and one of these when they get off the boat." He kicked a box of flyers for the Yemaya Festival set haphazardly on the wharf, sending three of them fluttering onto the boards like broken-winged moths.

"Steamship wharf is right here," he said, poking a finger at a red star on the map fixed to the clipboard. "Main Street's right there. If anyone asks you where something is just send them to Main Street, doesn't matter what it is. Unless it's a taxi. Anyone needs a taxi, just wave to Telly and he'll sign them up."

*What about my Yemaya Stone?* I thought, glancing at his pocket. *Is that on Main Street?*

Of all the people on Tillings, what were the chances that this one belonged to Remy? That Riley hated me was clear, even if the reason was not, but I wasn't too keen on him, either. Forget that he was cute, or had the greenest eyes in the whole wide world.

"Think you can manage that?"

Before I could answer, he'd hoisted himself up a side ladder on the boat and was pulling the pin free to drop the ramp.

The cream puff and her poodle pushed ahead of everyone else. Halfway down, the woman stalled—bringing the whole parade to a halt—and reached her free hand into her blouse between her breasts. Extracting a handkerchief, she dabbed the beads of sweat blooming over her brow and collarbone. When she was satisfied, she tucked the cloth back into her shirt, the corner sticking out of her collar, and marched straight for me. When at last they reached the bottom of the ramp, I handed the woman a map and flyer just like I'd been told.

"Can you please tell me where the Brass Lantern Inn is?"

I pointed to Main Street.

"Over there?" She smushed her nose up, squinting at the map. "Are you sure? Because they said take a left out of Steamship Wharf. That's not left." Turning the map sideways, she ran a finger along the names of hotels. I glanced down, pretending to look with her. "I don't see it on here anywhere."

I pointed to Main Street on the map while the poodle sniffed at my shoulder, leaving a wet spot.

"But they said left." Her voice raised a notch, causing several passengers to gaze back at us as they stepped off the ramp, and I felt my chest tighten. The palms of my hands grew clammy, making the clipboard difficult to grasp. Hanging off a rope above me as he wiped a splotch of ketchup from the side of the boat, I felt Riley watching.

"Ahh . . . " Barely audible, a second strangled hiss came out of my mouth.

"Are you okay?" The woman looked at me oddly.

"Go to Main Street and take your second left. The Brass Lantern's three blocks down on the right." Still in midair like a chimpanzee, Riley continued to scrub, never looking down at the woman.

"Second left," she repeated. "Maybe I should take a taxi. These legs aren't what they used to be. And Pixie doesn't really like to walk much anymore."

"Over there," Riley pointed at Telly, who was walking away. Thankfully, the only other passengers left were those waiting for a taxi, so they followed the cream puff and Pixie toward Telly in a small frenzied herd.

I found Remy and Mr. O'Malley bickering inside the ticket stand. I tapped on the window. Remy unlatched the door, clutching tight to a mop, and relieved me of my clipboard.

"Just look at the thermometer, you old polar bear. Forty-one degrees! Cold enough to preserve your frozen carcass for thirty days before rinsing it down the disposal," she scolded from behind a gray wool knit scarf, yanking a glove from each hand and waving her fingers in front of the small space heater. "Get your jacket from the car before Telly takes off with it."

"I'm not cold." Mr. O'Malley poked a mound of sweet sticky tobacco into his pipe, choking back a cough so determined it turned his face bright red and shuddered his whole body.

"Good Lord have mercy! There's your reason for feeling

no cold. Your body's so damn heated from trying to cough up a lung, you're generating enough electricity to warm half the island. I'm going to be stuck half way across this bay with you hacking up a vital organ. Are you looking at the thermometer? Put your glasses on, old man!"

"My eyes are good enough." Mr. O'Malley lit his pipe, fixing his gaze out the window while I pulled my sleeve over my knuckles.

"Then it's your mind that's going," she shot back. "It'll be twenty degrees cooler on the ocean. Not to mention that you've been under the weather all week. You'll freeze to death."

"I expect I'll be good," announced Mr. O'Malley.

"Mmm hmm. Good and dead from pneumonia."

"Then I guess I won't be cold."

"Get your damn jacket." Remy handed me the mop as Mr. O'Malley pushed his way out of the stand, leaving a puff of smoke sweetening the air behind him. As he passed, he tossed me a wink and I gave him a grin. In my mind, this is what my father and I would have been like if he hadn't gone—him barreling off across the waves with me chasing after him waving a life preserver in the air. Someone else might have heard the exchanges between Remy and Mr. O'Malley as bickering, but I knew the truth. This was their way of saying, "I love you more than all the stars in the galaxy." Even if the sentence did end in "you stubborn old goat."

"Bring Riley that mop. You can grab a bottle of Comet

and help me with the bathrooms on the ferry." The growl in Remy's voice said she'd gained some small satisfaction in being able to make somebody do what she wanted without argument.

I lugged the mop across the planks, looking for Riley and his bucket. When I found him, my heart jumped into my throat, and not because he was so handsome. He was hammering in a loose peg beside the ramp and Lindsey was standing shotgun chatting away. Her hands were folded across her chest and I could see the bright orange of her polish peeping out from where the fabric of her shirt bunched up. Remy must have read the hesitation in my step.

"I'm watching, there's nothing to worry about." Her voice was softer than the moment before. "Go on."

Taking a deep breath, I pushed the hair away from my eyes and tried to walk a little taller, telling myself I'd already stood up to Lindsey once, sort of—even if I was going to sweat my morning milk making up for it. Coming up alongside them, I tipped the handle of the mop at Riley, who ignored me flatly. Lindsey took one look at me and laughed.

"Oh my God! Riley, is this your new janitor?"

Riley glanced over at me, unamused, before driving another peg flush with the deck.

"What the hell was your aunt thinking?" Beneath Lindsey's snootiness, there was a flash of annoyance at my being there—something only another girl would have recognized. Wrestling the mop skyward, I shoved it at Riley, who continued to ignore me. I looked over my shoulder for Remy, who was standing beside the front of the ferry clutching a bottle of Comet and a toilet brush, watching.

"What's the matter?" Lindsey's words sang into the world all sugary sweet. "Cat got your tongue?"

After considering my options, I let my lips curl into a smile and brought the mop down hard against the bucket's edge. The force of it flipped the bucket cleanly on its side, splashing the soapy water from her shins up to her perfectly painted face until she looked like a melting Rocket Popsicle with one color dribbling down over the next.

"You little . . . " She kicked the pail and drew her arms back as though she might shove me.

"Knock it off!" Riley caught her midswipe, balling his fingers tightly around her arm, green eyes blazing.

Lindsey wrung her hands out in front of her, letting water drip from her polished nails. Suds had caught in her blond hair and her mascara had left raccoon rings around her blue eyes. More than once, I'd wished for corn silk hair and sapphire eyes like Lindsey's, to be one of those girls who shuffle their way through boys' hearts as quickly as a deck of cards and leave them pining into grandfatherhood. Girls like that don't have to speak a word for the whole wide world to fall in love with them; but they always do. They can twitter out a song strong and sweet as canaries in the morning sun.

But just then, for a moment, at least, Lindsey was as speechless as me.

"You're gonna pay for that," she whispered, collecting herself and pushing past me. I propped the mop handle against the boat beside Riley and marched back to Remy, trying to conceal the shock on my face from Riley defending me.

"Ha! Now *that* might have taught Miss Lindsey a thing or two," she snickered, handing over the Comet. "Let's go. That was a sound start, but we have more shit to clean off this boat before we go."

By the time we'd finished the bathrooms, a thick curtain of fog was rolling in. Remy squeezed the lever on the shortwave radio, informing a bodiless voice in the box that we were pulling out, when a lanky figure lumbered across the deck. My stomach tightened as I realized Riley was still aboard.

Ten minutes later, people going to the mainland shuffled up the ramp, weaving in and out of one another to claim a place beside the rail until they blended together like a hive of bees and one passenger did not stand out from another. Then one did, a tall brown-haired man wearing a striped sweater and jeans. Three paces behind him, a woman with long hair cascading across her shoulders like spilled ink fought the crowd to keep up.

Here's how it works in my fantasy: I am walking down

the beach among a thousand people. I trip over a tall lemonade someone left in my path, and when I scoop it up to hand it back, there is my father staring up at me with a huge dimpled smile asking what took me so long.

Somewhere in my heart, I knew it wasn't him. But fantasies are powerful beasts, and my stomach dropped straight out from under my ribs at the sight of the man leaning against the rail. Light-years away, Remy was yelling to Telly to draw up the ramp. Before I knew they were moving, my feet were heading down the steps two at a time toward the striped sweater until I found myself sneaking up behind the man. Had I been paying attention I would have noticed the woman with him returning from the snack bar with an open bottle of Coca-Cola. But I wasn't. I tumbled right over her leg, grabbing the man's arm as the circle of people surrounding him gasped, hopping back when fat splashes of cola flung toward them.

"What the . . . " the man shrieked. "Let go!" Those very words had repeated on me every minute of every single day since my father had plucked me off his leg like a diseased tick. The words that had long ago shriveled up inside me like winterberries crept up my throat: *I'm sorry . . . sorry . . . sorry.*

Recovering from the shock of me dousing him with a wayward bottle of cola, the man helped me back to my feet before peeling his sweater off over his head and dabbing at my sleeve.

"Sss – sss - orry." The word spit into the air between us on its own, and when I looked up to find Remy standing beside me holding Riley's mop, I saw the question move across her eyes.

"It's just cola." A silky softness settled into the man's voice, but it was all wrong. No lemonade or excited hug, no dimples, and when I blushed, turning my head away, the only thing left of the beach was a shrinking strip of sand.

When the mess was mopped clean, I followed Remy back to the control booth, passing Riley on the stairs.

"Told you," he whispered at Remy, who nudged him quiet.

I climbed back up the stairs and into the control room numb as a shot of Novocain and crumpled into the seat beside Remy. Every bit of me wanted to cry a thousand tears, drain out the embarrassment and hurt inside, but my throat was so tight it wouldn't come. I just sat, letting the cyclone inside me die down.

"Makes you wonder, doesn't it?" Remy took hold of a wayward sprig of hair, coiling it around her ear, and began flipping switches on the panel until a burst of static broke over the radio. "You dump a bucket a' water over Lindsey Stuart, and the world turns right around and soaks your butt right back! Damn karma. Gets me every time." She laughed lightly, as though there was something cosmically hilarious about the whole thing. "Either that girl's got one hell of a reach, or it's poetic justice. I wonder who that poor guy down there dumped on to deserve a good drenching!" She glanced down at the man, who'd been reduced to a T-shirt on the deck below. "He must've done something." She chuckled again.

When I didn't answer she added, "So I thought maybe we'd bring your mum her car this time. Then I thought, nah." She tossed me a wink, making no mention of the fact that she'd heard me speak, and I count this as the precise moment I knew for certain somehow she understood the storm blowing out of control inside me. "We need some sort of fun in our lives."

*Kch, chh*, the radio squawked. "Clear the docks," Remy ordered into the receiver. *Kch!* "*Mirabel* departing."

Then she pushed the black AV box and, as sweet as Grandma Jo's gooseberry pie, her voice came over the loudspeakers: "Ladies and gentlemen, we will be pulling into open water momentarily. Please make yourself comfortable. Our traveling time will be approximately one hour and ten minutes, give or take twenty-five hours for fog. Anybody out there have radar vision?" A soft rumble of laughter rose from the crowd.

"They think I'm joking." She laughed. Tossing the mouthpiece aside, she eased the ferry on course and leaned against the control panel, politely watching out the window as I blew my nose.

Neither of us moved again until we were a mile from land.

"I don't guess you want to tell me what bee buzzed your bonnet out there?" Remy asked, laying a sheet of paper and pen in front of me.

I looked at it but made no move to pick up the pen.

"Yeah, I didn't think so. Then I guess I'll tell you something instead." Leaning over the controls, she studied me with a cautious glance. "Nobody's legs are built to run forever, girl. One of these days they'll either drop right out from under you or run you right in a damn circle."

With that, she turned back to the windshield, and the *Mirabel* slipped through the narrow throat of the break wall toward Tillings's pier. I got to my feet and made my way onto the skinny deck outside the control room, breathing deeply. The houses on Tillings stood on tall weathered gray stilts just visible through the mist. A lone osprey sat on the break wall, nothing more than a crooked black shadow against the white rock watching us.

"Anybody up to walking into town?" It was the afternoon of my sixth birthday. Through the window the sun dipped low on the horizon preparing to dive beneath the waves. We'd only been at the Booth House for half an hour, but I could hear the excitement in my mother's voice even though it was muffled behind the bathroom door. On the other side, I was dancing around the hallway waiting for her to come out to save myself the sprint down to the first-floor powder room. What one single person could be doing in there for so long was a mystery. "Maybe we can stop and get ice cream."

"I've got to get some work done. Why don't you and Iz go ahead?" My father shuffled into view with a stack of papers, pausing to laugh at my frantic dance. "You'd better unlock that door and let this girl in or we'll be mopping up a puddle in the hall."

"Why don't you do your work after dinner?" The hammer clicked back on the lock and my mother slid into view.

For a full minute, I forgot I had to go to the bathroom at the sight of her. Dark hair floated down around her face, twirling into loose curls at the shoulder, making what had taken so long plain. Her eyes, which almost never saw makeup, were carefully lined with charcoal shadow, and a shimmer of gold brushed all the way to her brows. I couldn't yank my eyes off her. But my father didn't seem to notice. He turned away without a second glance, plodding down the steps; a thing I might have wondered more about had I not been frantically dashing for the toilet and barely six years old.

"Can't," I heard my father sigh, "I really have to get this done today. Maybe . . ." The front door thudding shut lopped off the rest of his thought. Through the bathroom window, I saw him cross the yard and flop into an old wooden Adirondack chair out back.

"Oh." My mother's whisper was barely audible, her feet statue still on the other side of the door.

When I finished, I scurried to the kitchen to find that my mother's feet had not only gotten going, but were pacing about sixty miles an hour from the counter to the refrigerator. She had a sort of lost look in her eyes, stopping only to chop the heads off three stalks of broccoli with unjustified force. When she ran out of broccoli stalks to behead, she spun on her heel, going after a head of cauliflower, then a bag of carrots, peppers, and snap peas until there was nothing left to attack with a knife that wouldn't buy her twenty-five years in the penitentiary. The notion struck me that if anyone got in her way, she would either march clear over the top of him, or freeze right up solid with no idea what to do.

Slipping through the front door, I followed my father outside, crawling up in the chair beside him. He laid his papers aside with a smile that poked the dimples in at his cheeks and made him the most handsome man alive. His fingers crept up to play with my hair, and over his shoulder I saw my mother in the kitchen window, watching us.

She looked at me and I saw it—the question brimming in her eyes that ached to ask by what magic I had persuaded my father to love me. In a matter of half seconds, it overflowed, quietly running down her cream cheeks in crooked, black smudges.

Even then I knew. I knew I had to hold tight to him

or he might flit away. With his deep dimples and shaggy brown hair, he looked like one person, but he wasn't. He could change in a single wink and he was always running toward you or away, depending on what corner of the earth the Nikommo were calling him to that day. If a person wasn't willing to run with him, she'd be left behind.

Back in the control room I slid the journal over the control panel and let it settle in front of Remy, who studied it as if it might be rabid and ready to pounce. *How did you know him?*

"Who?"

I yanked the paper back, scribbled hard, and shoved it back at her because I knew she knew. *My father.*

"I grew up here. He spent summers here. It's a small island."

Her response sounded rehearsed, like my mother's responses. I studied her carefully, reading her body.

Here is how you know if a person is fibbing or avoiding: it's in the distance. A person who really doesn't know, but wants to; they'll lean right into a question and dig. It's in our nature. A person who does know, but doesn't want to, will pull away and pretend to be ignorant and nonchalant about the facts in the way a person might slowly back away from a cougar ready to strike.

*How well did you know him?* I tapped the tip of my pen to the page.

"I don't know. He was the kid that lived down the lane. . . . Son of a green-nosed bastard! It's fucking pea soup out here." We had been sailing through dense fog the entire way to the mainland. Now Remy was squinting angrily through the white cloud wrapping itself around the *Mirabel* like an enormous scoop of melted marshmallow. "Seeing the damn wharf would be helpful in docking the ferry."

That the *Mirabel* bumped into the dock without sending anyone over the rail is a flat-out miracle, and when the worst of the pitching settled, Remy cut the engine, looking out at the crowd waiting onshore. The mainland wharf was a carnival of vendors selling crab cakes, deep-fried clams, crawfish boils, and popcorn shrimp. Some booths doubled as a mini-mart for beach wares and tanning lotion. An entire tunnel of boogie boards lined one side of the dock where a boy with yellow dreadlocks leaned easily against the rail chewing gum.

"Don't touch the controls." Remy wagged a finger my way and slipped onto deck. She wasn't going to answer me, not really. I could feel the truth tingling through me. She knew what had happened to my father. She was retreating and it was the first time I had seen her back away from anything. Watching her make her way toward the ramp from the window, I remembered what she had said about nobody's legs being built to run forever. I knew she was right about that.

# CHAPTER ELEVEN

When Remy finally dropped me back home exhausted and smelling of taxi fumes, Luke was not yapping to greet me. Inside, my mother's voice filtered toward the entryway.

"Okay, thank you. Please call us if you see him."

I stopped in the doorway feeling the hairs prickle up on my arms and the bottom give way in my stomach. Then a thought came back to me like a rush of water. That morning when I had run back to find my Yemaya Stone, Luke had been on my heels. I'd tripped right over him, but in my rush to the cliffs I hadn't even paid attention. I'd just kept running. How many hours had I been gone?

"Maybe Izabella took him with her," Grandma Jo said, her voice calm.

"No. She wouldn't have brought him down to Herman's with her. And they left straight from there for the ferry run. Remy wouldn't have let her take him back on the ferry. He threw up the entire way over here. The police haven't seen him. They said they'd keep an eye out, but . . . "

"It's going to be okay. Dogs run. It's in their nature. They can find their way home from a thousand miles away."

"He's not a dog; he's a puppy."

"Did you call the vet for the island?"

"Yes. He asked if Luke had tags and if he'd been vaccinated for rabies. It seems there are a lot of foxes on the island, and with Tom's salt licks drawing them in . . . " Worry filled my mother's voice. "What am I going to do, Mom? I don't even want to think about how Iz will handle another loss. Shit!"

"It'll be fine, Zo. Someone will find him."

"And what if they don't? The whole reason I got her that dog . . . What if . . . Any more loss and she's going to disappear inside herself forever."

"There are no other 'if's. They'll find him and Izabella will be fine."

I crept to the kitchen doorway in time to see Grandma Jo brushing back my mother's hair with her hand. My mother was sitting on the edge of the counter like a teenager holding the phone in one hand. For a fraction of a second, I thought she looked like me. Maybe it was the way her hair fell down to hang off her shoulders, or the fact that I sat on the counter like that. Or maybe it was the tremble of fear in her voice that I might disappear and leave her behind. And for the first time in a very long time, I believed that she didn't want me to. When she saw me, she slid down.

"Izabella! You didn't take Luke into town, did you?"

I shook my head, trying not to cry.

*Was he here this morning? After I left?* My hands were shaking so hard it was difficult to write. She must have noticed the tears biting the corners of my eyes and my hand trembling because she quickly started repeating what Grandma Jo had told her.

"I don't remember. I don't think so. Okay, don't panic. It's okay. Dogs run all the time. He couldn't have gone far; it's an island—a very small island. Why don't you go get Remy to pick us up in the taxi? Maybe he followed you to the pier. I'll walk around here and look for him." I glanced out the window at the darkening sky, remembering how scared he'd been during the storm. I'd made it across the bay twice without retching but now felt like I might throw up. I was like a giant walking eraser wandering through the world making the things I loved vanish one at a time. "Go!"

By the time Remy answered the door she'd already changed into her tattered terry-cloth robe, her red hair exploding around her face like licks of flame. I pulled out my pad.

*Luke's missing.*

She sighed heavily. "Do you know I haven't even sat down yet?"

I looked at her pleadingly.

"Fine," she huffed. "I knew that damnable animal would bring nothing but trouble from the moment he lost his lunch all over my boat." She tried her best to be annoyed, but I could read a trace of concern on her brow.

Grabbing her keys, she did not even bother to get dressed before starting up the taxi and unlocking the passenger door. "I suppose your mother wants to tag along, too. Get in!"

The Purple Monster roared down the lane, stopping at the Booth House only long enough for my mother to hop in.

"Grandma Jo is going to stay here in case he comes back on his own," she said, climbing in the backseat with a box of Milk Bones and rolling down the window.

"Who the hell are you," Remy snipped, "Hansel and Gretel leaving a trail of food home?"

"I don't know. Just in case he won't come to us."

"He's a dog. They come to dead carcasses, cat shit, and fire hydrants."

"Well, I didn't have any of those handy."

Remy shook her head, setting her hair dancing.

"I don't know where he would go." My mother stuck her head through the window. I bit my lip, studying the darkness beyond. "Luke . . . Come here, boy! *Luke!*" She shook the box out the window.

"Well, my car still stinks to high heaven of poodle from this afternoon. If he's any kind of dog at all he'll follow the scent," Remy said, barreling around the bend fast enough to send shells flying in every direction. "Besides, we're on an island. He can only go so far before reaching water."

I looked at Remy feeling my knees go weak. By 10:00 P.M., he'd already gone far enough that we could not find him, becoming the second member of my family to go missing from me on this island

When there were no other side roads to bounce down, Remy dropped us off, promising to check the cliffs and orchard once more and call around the island in the morning. I felt my mother's arm around my shoulders as she drove off.

"He'll come back, Iz. Don't worry. Dogs can travel thousands of miles to find their way home. It's in their nature."

I nodded, studying the moon overhead, fat and white as a winter frost, watching it shimmer and dance on the ocean below.

*Come on, Be. Come dance with the moon. . . .* I pinched my eyes closed, pushing the memory back.

From the front walk, I could hear Grandma Jo break out in song to Joan Baez on the radio: "May you build a ladder to the stars . . . and climb on every rung . . ."

My mother rested her head on mine, chuckling. "You realize she's probably dancing around naked in there." I couldn't remember the last time we'd stood so close. Usually one of us was pushing away from the other like a ship avoiding a reef.

"You made it to the mainland without throwing up?" my mother asked.

I nodded, lowering my eyes to trace the edges of the bushes for some sign of Luke, but they were still and dark.

"Telly still using the BMW as a lounge chair?"

I bit the inside of my cheek and nodded again.

On the edge of the cliff, Witch's Peak poked through the treetops like a cut of onyx in the moonlight, and I couldn't say that it wasn't a trick of light, but I swore I saw a shadow cross its tip, pause, and disappear.

"Let's go in." My mother turned for the door. "I'll leave the window open and sleep on the sofa. If he doesn't come back by morning, I'll go back out and look for him."

That night as I sat staring out the window, searching for Luke in the moonlight, an orange fox made her way toward Mr. O'Malley's salt licks with her kit so near their fur touched.

Something from earlier that day came back to me. As Lindsey had stormed away with suds in her hair, she'd told me I was going to pay for what I'd done. Now images of her throwing rocks at the seagull were haunting me, and I was pacing the floor, trying to convince myself that nobody could be that evil.

I walked across the room pulling free the small blue satchel and did something I had not in a very long time:

I prayed. I prayed to Yemaya, God, the Nikommo, and anyone else who would listen to keep Luke safe. A shadow on Witch's Peak shifted, looking back at me—or maybe it was just a cloud passing in front of the moon. From a place deep and unexpected, a small sob broke out of me.

# CHAPTER TWELVE

The next morning Luke was not back and my mother had just finished off a stack of posters that read, LOST SHAR-PEI PUPPY PLEASE CALL 335-9174. With Grandma Jo's interference, my mother agreed to let me ride Remy's bicycle into town to pass them out and look for him—though she would not have if she'd known where I was headed. It was already eight o'clock. In two hours, I was due to help Remy run a bake sale, so I needed to hurry if I was going to find Lindsey beforehand.

I straddled the candy-apple Schwinn, tottering back and forth and trying to recall the last time I'd been on a bike as I steered it out of the drive. At the end of the lane, I found Remy pinching back mums in her front garden. Mr. O'Malley was standing shotgun with a spade balanced in one hand, a pot in the other, and his pipe balanced between his teeth like the tin man in *The Wizard of Oz*. I pulled over to hand him a poster for the taxi stand, anxious to make it quick.

"Here's a helper," Mr. O'Malley murmured around the mouthpiece of the pipe, trying to hand over the pot before I'd even gotten my feet free of the pedals. I was just about to take it from him, only to be pulled up short by Remy.

"Don't you take that!" she snapped, nearly taking my head off in the process. "The moment he reclaims his hands, he intends to light that pipe full of hell grass. Do you suppose I've been kneeling here so long my knees are broken to bits for no good reason at all?"

Mr. O'Malley gave her a soft kick in the rear end as I handed him a poster.

"He'll be back, don't you worry," Mr. O'Malley assured me.

"Oh, Maynard Herman rang this morning, said the window will be ready this afternoon. Riley and his dad are going to set it, but he's expecting you tomorrow to paint the frame. Then I'll show you how to glaze it."

Mr. O'Malley started to say something but instead broke out in a series of choking coughs that rattled all six feet three inches of him.

"Dad?" Remy relieved him of his clay pot then reached for his empty hand. She held it gently a moment before pulling herself to her feet and digging into his shirt pocket to pull forth a crinkled sack of pipe tobacco. He didn't seem to notice as she pinched a wad between her fingers and tucked it neatly into the stack of his pipe.

"Dad," she repeated. "Here." She struck a match on the toe of her boot and touched it to the bowl of his pipe, puffing on it three times so that sweet smoke spiraled out before poking it between his lips.

"What?" he answered, a big old grizzly bear pulled too soon from hibernation.

"If you're not careful your lungs will clear. Then I will be stuck with you forever and never receive my rightful inheritance."

Straightening myself on the seat, I shook my head at the two of them and waved goodbye.

"You'll meet me at the bake sale by ten o'clock, right?" Remy glanced at me.

I nodded, making off down the lane.

It was early yet, but Remy had told me there was no school this week and I suspected if I found Riley I'd find Lindsey trailing him like a pesky burdock. He was probably already down at the docks.

The tires of the Schwinn made little trenches in the shell gravel, slowing me down until I hit the cobblestones of Main Street. Giving the handlebars a turn, I pulled down the rough planks of Steamship Wharf and finally leaned the bike against the wooden sea witch.

Telly was busy checking the roster inside the ticket booth, and I could see Riley on the upper deck fiddling with a loose rail, but Lindsey was nowhere to be seen. Snatching the bike upright, I walked it back down the pier past the Anchor Diner and headed for Merchant's

Hardware. I set it in the bike rack that Lindsey and Carly had been sitting on two days earlier and laughing at me as I worked at Mr. Herman's. It seemed to be their haunt.

But when fifteen minutes later there was no sign of them, I pushed the kickstand back up. I'd just swung one leg over the bar when the familiar pudge of Carly's butt backed out of the White Whale as she balanced an ice cream cone in one hand and a glass of water in the other. She tilted her head, nibbling at the bottom of the cone before sucking the ice cream through it as if it were a straw, when the door opened again and Lindsey came through it carrying a cup of water. Tossing the Schwinn to the cobblestones with a clatter, I marched across the street stopping both of them in their tracks. Maybe it was the look on my face, which said I'd just as soon clobber them as look at them, or maybe they were too busy eating, but neither one said a word until I was in arm's reach.

"Look, Carly," Lindsey sang. "It's the little janitor."

Glaring hard at her, I took the missing-dog poster I was holding and shoved it into her hand. She glanced down at it and I was surprised to see her actually reading the words on the page.

"Ohhh. What's the matter? Did you lose your puppy?" Lindsey dropped the poster, letting it flitter to the ground at her feet. Carly laughed, taking a bite of ice cream the size of my fist, which left a creamy smear of vanilla rimming her mouth. The fact that she was eating ice cream for breakfast said something about her, even if I didn't know exactly what.

I picked the poster back up, shoving it at Lindsey a second time.

"Get that out of my face!" Lindsey snipped, tossing my hand aside and starting to walk away. I grabbed her arm, pushing her hard enough to plant her back a step.

When she tried to push past me a second time, I caught her by the wrist and leaned my shoulder into her to hold her still.

"Whh—wh—where?" The words fell into the inch between our bodies as nothing more than a whisper, but they were there just the same. Taking two steps back, Carly watched me with eyes as round as Wiffle balls.

"I don't know," Lindsey said. I pushed harder with my shoulder. "I don't!" she snapped. "Jesus Christ, what do you think, I took him? I wouldn't do something like that!" Images of the wounded bird cowering away from flying stones scuttled to mind, and she must have seen that I didn't believe her because the sarcasm drained neatly out of her tone. "*I wouldn't!*"

She shoved me back a pace before throwing her full water into a trash barrel and storming away, abandoning a panic-stricken Carly for a moment before she regained her wits and scurried after her. Several people had stopped outside the White Whale, lingering to see if there would be any excitement. As Lindsey turned the corner, they decided there would be none and walked lazily down the street, leaving me to wonder over the hurt tone in Lindsey's voice.

Glancing at the big brass clock on the bell tower of the Congregational church, I trotted over to my bike. I had one more stop to make before meeting Remy at the bake sale.

The Tillings Free Library was a three-story Victorian converted into a public building. A small sign tacked beside the double door read, 1778 WILLIAM SAXTON HOMESTEAD. Tossing the bike onto the grass, I grabbed the flyers and bolted for the door before turning back to grab Remy's book.

The man behind the desk gazed up politely, taking the book from my hand. Flipping the back cover open, he tsked, wagging his head, and pulled the call card from his box. "Mmm hmm. Well, I guess it would be a miracle of unnatural sorts if Ms. Mandolin returned a book on time."

I grabbed a piece of scrap paper from a stack beside a cup of pencils fit for the fingers of elves and scribbled: *She says she'll pay the fine in pie at the festival.*

"Oh, she does, does she?"

I nodded.

"Well, you tell her they'd better be baked with golden apples," he warned playfully.

When he set the book aside, I handed over a stack of festival flyers and a poster about Luke.

"You ever consider a job with the postal service? People here usually take things out, not bring them in."

I wagged my head no.

"Uh oh. We've got a puppy on the loose? Sorry to hear he's missing, but I'm sure he'll come back."

A sharp pain worked its way up from my chest to the back of my throat.

*Could you hang it up?*

"I'll do you one better: I'll ask around and make copies to stick in the books people check out."

*Thank you.*

"You're taking that 'No Talking' sign a skoach seriously, aren't you?" he asked.

I rubbed my throat, an old trick I'd learned to make people believe I had laryngitis.

"I see. Then I guess you've come to the right place to recover. Anything else I can do for you?"

I shook my head, starting for the door. I was almost through it before I turned around and went back to the desk to grab another scrap of paper and a tiny pencil.

*Do you keep newspaper records?* I don't know what possessed me to ask or even what I thought I might find, but there was something in the way Riley seemed to hate me for no good reason that was eating at me. Something in the way people everywhere seemed to know who I was even though I hadn't set foot on this island since the day my father walked out. Their expressions changed when I was introduced.

Not that any of that would crop up in a news article.

"Of course. We keep them on microfiche upstairs in the reference section. But we lost a lot of the older films in a fire a few years back. We salvaged what we could, but I'm afraid they're in pretty rough shape. Anything in particular you're hunting for?"

*Yes,* I thought. *More than you could possibly fit on all the microfiche in the world.* I held the pencil over the paper for a second, not sure where to start.

*1966*

The man whistled.

"That's a ways back, but let's see what we can find." He came out from behind the desk and began climbing a narrow set of stairs to the second floor. We passed the display of Yemaya Remy had told me about. I paused to look at the array of cowry shells, pearls, books, and scrolls arranged neatly across the table. An oil-on-canvas nude of Yemaya took up the wall space behind it with golden drops of sun bouncing off her hair.

"Pretty, isn't she?"

I nodded, recalling that those were the exact words Remy had said about her mother.

"She's not truly a witch, but try telling that to folks around these parts! Ha! Still, it's true. She's an *orisha.*"

I nodded, biting my cheek. Grandma Jo was always right.

In the back of the second floor, he pulled out a chair at one of the microfiche readers.

"The films are over here, filed in chronological order. Here we go: nineteen sixty-six through seven." He set the film under the clamps. "You just turn that little knob to scroll through. Good luck. I'll be downstairs if you need anything else."

I sat down, peered through the lens, and began spinning through the articles. Most were melted and mutilated from the fire, but I slowed the film at October 1966, moving frame by frame until I got to October 4 and stopped. A gaping hole had been melted in the center of the article, but a corner of the accompanying image remained with a photograph of the sheriff holding his hat and wiping his forehead with the back of his wrist. A boy of seven or eight stood three paces behind him, staring straight ahead with an utterly lost expression on his face. What looked like the back corner of a fire engine was parked beside them, although it was hard to tell since that was where the hole in the film began. What was left of the caption read, SHERIFF JAMES O'MALLEY AND SON RILEY WERE AMONG THE FIRST ON SCENE.

I flipped through the next month, but most of the film had been burned away. Scrolling back to the picture, I studied the expression on Riley's face. His head was tilted, making it hard to tell if he was crying, but he was clearly distraught. The background of the photo was little more than a sea of shadows except for several flowers arcing up beside Riley on tall gangly stems. I let my eyes linger on them. Peonies . . .

The memory brushed against me with the sting of a paper cut and I closed my eyes, trying to push it back.

Not shadows. Darkness . . .


**Before I got** kicked out of school, my class had taken a field trip to the planetarium at Roger Williams Park. When the lights went out, there was nothing but a velvet dome of darkness with little holes punched through, sending pinpricks of light scattering overhead.

That's what it looked like that night, what was missing from the photograph. There must have been a million stars winking and blinking overhead and two had fallen to the field below in specks of red. They danced and dipped across the daises and black-eyed Susans like fairies, and I recall thinking it was the Nikommo. Stars. Taillights. *Take meee.* . . . There was a scream. No, there were two. One from me, one from the field, and I thought I'd heard them; I'd finally heard the Nikommo.

*Someday I am going to catch you a star.*

A screech. Brakes.

*Someday we are going to fly.*

Silence. Silence. Silence.


**Pushing away from** the microfiche reader I stood up gasping. My chest ached, wanting air. The memories were broken shards of mirror dipping in and out of my con-

sciousness, like the salmon of Potter's Creek stitching
their way upstream. I gazed at the film hanging out of the
reader. I knew that look on Riley's face, knew something
awful had not just happened; it had happened to *him*. October 4, 1966. I was here when it happened. But I'd only
been six; it couldn't possibly explain why he despised me.
Still, the lost look in his eyes tugged at something raw and
real inside of me.

Walking over to the cabinet the librarian had pulled
the films from, I took another film from a reel marked
1959 and stuck it into the empty canister for 1966. Once
I had returned it to the cabinet, I slipped the actual 1966
film into my back pocket. I didn't know what I would do
with it without a machine to read it, but it was at least one
real thing about the night my father disappeared. Somehow I felt like it belonged to me, not the world. Grabbing
my posters, I made my way downstairs more confused
than I'd been before I'd come in.

"Find what you were looking for?" the man asked from
behind his desk.

I shook my head with a wave and trotted outside
before hopping on my bike. For the next thirty minutes,
I handed out posters with Luke's information on them to
anyone who would take them and wove up and down the
small lanes lining the village square in case Luke really
had followed us to the wharf.

Running out of ideas and posters, I pulled into the
church parking lot just before ten o'clock, following the

bustle of trays and pans going in and out of the side entrance.

I was just crossing over to the stack of pies where Remy stood when I was stopped in my tracks by a woman's voice barking commands at the group of church ladies propping pastries into place.

"Yoo-hoo! Yoo-hoo! Over here with the scones. No, no, no—Bundt cakes go over there; cookies, bars, and brownies go here. Fruit pastries are beside the Yemaya—not that one, the pregnant one with crooked breasts! Buns!" squealed a fat woman wearing a paisley tent for a blouse. Brushed up into a beehive do, her hair was three shades of tangerine, making it look as though a fat marmalade cat might have crawled onto her head and died there. "Young la-dy. Yes, you. A little slow on the uptake, aren't we, dearie? That's okay; God loves all his children quick or slow."

I stared blankly at the perfectly round circles of red rouge drawn on her cheeks as if she were Bozo the Clown's sister. When I didn't answer, she tilted her head curiously. "You're not one of *those* children, are you? You know—touched?"

I shook my head.

"Oh!" She stepped back. "You're the Haywood child!"

I nodded clumsily, praying for Remy to come in and save me.

"I knew your grandmother. One heck of a pinochle player, she was. Your daddy, too. Used to sit right up at the table with the old ladies." She paused as though re-membering. "You're dumb, aren't you? Not the stupid sort, the quiet sort—like 'deaf and dumb'?"

I raised my eyebrows at her when she took hold of my wrist and began speaking very slowly, kicking the volume up three notches. Why people assumed my ears were at-tached to my vocal chords was a mystery, but it happened all the time.

"Why don't you go see Mrs. Trainor? She'll set you straight to work." The woman turned on her heel and marched back to her table, sending the fat of her fanny jiggling wildly. I wanted to tell her to fuck off, that I didn't have time to sell her stupid cookies, that Luke needed me and that he was more important. But I didn't, and the fact was I didn't know where else to look for him. I headed for a mousy-looking woman with tight aqua leggings and a sunny yellow sweater whom I guessed must be Mrs. Trainor.

"Well, aren't you sweet? What's your name?"

Remy sauntered up beside me quietly. I gave her a pleading look, waiting for her to jump in and answer for me. She did not. Mrs. Trainor bent a little lower, waiting, and I felt a warm flush redden my cheeks. I widened my eyes at Remy, who seemed to be staring right along with the woman waiting for an answer from me. I wanted to knock the plate from her hand.

"I guess she doesn't have one," Mrs. Trainor chirped, shuffling away.

"Guess not," Remy agreed, breaking the corner off a frosted brownie then pinching the side square to hide it. "Any luck finding muttley?"

I shook my head, biting my lip.

"He'll show up. Everyone on the island is keeping their eyes open for him and your mum's out searching. Probably has a lady friend somewhere."

"People! Peeeople!" the woman wearing a tent squealed again. "Let's focusss!"

"Priscilla, get yourself a cup of chamomile tea. Your blood pressure's so damn high your head's about to pop right off your shoulders like some sort of Japanese candle." Remy laughed aloud right to the woman's face. There was a muted giggle across the room.

"Let's not swear in God's house." The woman's voice tensed. "What are those?" She pointed to a box.

"Those are Grandma Jo's famous cheese biscuits."

"Who is Grandma Jo?" The woman eyed the biscuits suspiciously.

"They're cheese biscuits. Just chew one and stick a price tag on them."

"Why don't you make yourself useful and run the register, Remy?" she mumbled, reaching for a folded index card to price the biscuits.

"Not this year. I'm strictly a baker. Ask Izabella. She doesn't like to argue."

"Well, God's work isn't for every hand, I guess."

"Hey, Priscilla." Remy snagged a chocolate cookie from the plate of another woman passing by.

"Yes?"

"Bite me." Remy smiled sweetly, chewing the cookie. "This is the Yemaya Festival, not some freak festival of the Holy Cross." She patted the Yemaya bust on the shoulder in an animated act of sisterhood.

The woman glanced at Remy sternly then jiggled her way over to open the church doors to let the cookie buying commence.

"Don't you mind about Priscilla Peabody." Remy chuckled. "She thinks Christ came right down off the cross and hired her to coordinate the cookies of Christianity for him."

The fact of the matter is, I wasn't thinking about Pricilla Peabody or any other body. My mind was too crammed with thoughts about the burned picture in my pocket and running every horrific scenario I could conjure about Luke's whereabouts. The same *hurry, hurry* whispery feeling I had every time I went into the Pepto-Bismol-pink room echoed off the walls around me now.

I was still thinking about Luke when the first customer stood in front of me balancing a truckload of cookies, breads, and brownies, sounding annoyed. "Is anyone going to take my money?"

"I'll show you how to ring one," Remy said, coming over to stand at the register. "Then you take over."

When it was my turn, I tentatively began pushing down the buttons of the old Wood Grain Tin cash register.

"Little girl! Yoo-hoo, little Haywood girl." Mrs. Peabody leaned over her table of Bundt cakes waving frantically in my direction and puckering pouty orange lips at me like a fat goldfish glugging around its bowl. "Strudels are fifty cents, not thirty-five cents. Amanda, you owe the register fifteen cents for those. We may cheat our waistlines, but we don't want to cheat God!" I felt the heat move over my cheeks. "Chop chop!" Pricilla Peabody snapped her fingers at me.

"You can see from the girth of her hips, Priscilla has an eye for collecting the last crumb." Remy shook her head when the next customer had gone. "Do you know her husband disappeared three years ago without one trace? We can't prove it, but we think one day she just ate him."

I rolled my eyes at her, shutting the change drawer.

"It's true, I swear." She raised one hand in the air, laughing aloud.


*Kla ching,* sang the register four long hours later.

"Two o'clock, ladies! Time to clear out," shrilled Pricilla. "The pastor's got a wedding this evening. Nora Smith's girl is marrying that bloke from Boston at six. Let's move our withered derrieres and make way for young love."

Mrs. Peabody should have been a choreographer for the Boston Ballet, because fifteen church ladies rose from their seats in an act of synchronized standing, folded their chairs with fifteen pert *snaps*, and herded their way to the heavy double doors, discarding Styrofoam cups ringed with coffee in a large purple bin marked, REFUSE, along the way.

"Come on." Remy stood, snatching a few Boston teacakes. "Let's get you out of here to look for your motley mutt. Here." She handed two cakes to me. "There's a brick house just as you make the turn off Main onto Laurel Street. It'll be the only one with overgrown grass and a purple door. Mrs. Mulligan. She's a friend of my mother's. Loves sweets. Sweets and roses. And wind chimes. Drop this off to her on your way. The other one's for your house."

While Remy loaded up the taxi with empty baskets, I stood outside the front door balancing a large pottery platter and nibbling the corners off an oatmeal bar as I watched people pass on the other side of Main Street. Herman's was far enough down that I didn't need to worry about him seeing me when he came out to beat the sand from the storefront steps.

"I got a stack of posters from your mother," Remy called. "I'll bring them down to the pier."

I popped the remaining bar into my mouth and brought her the platter to put in the car. Climbing onto the Schwinn, I headed toward home, pausing to stick a poster in the window of Merchant's Hardware. It was purely by chance that my eyes slipped down the alleyway, catching on a white crumpled bag flitting in the breeze. Another few inches sharpened the corners of the image and pulled it into view with dizzying speed. Then my feet stopped pedaling altogether. What I'd thought to be a bag was really a tattered feather coat pulled into a tight ball—a weak attempt to fend off more stones.

The bird's neck was twisted unnaturally upward, and its black eyes, trailing past the mortar lines between the brickwork of Merchant's, stared sadly at the clouds as if the gull had spent its very last moment searching for God, wondering where the hell he'd gone when the bird needed him most.

*To Potter's Creek to watch the fish fly*, I wanted to tell him.

A fat blue fly circled once overhead before lighting down on the gull's left eyeball; when it didn't blink, I knew for sure it was dead. Sometimes it needs to be made just that clear. The fly stepped over the gull's eye, coming to rest on the yellow ridge of its lid where a brown stain like a tear ran down from the corner. My eyes settled on the stain, letting the *I'm sorry* sail silently through the air.

I rode away trying to decide if Lindsey was telling the truth about not hurting Luke.


With mint-green pillars and a front door painted the exact purple black of ripened Concord grapes, Mrs. Mulligan's place was impossible to miss. A bent woman with white hair spun up in pink rollers stood on the porch hanging wind chimes with mermaids on them from everything and anything she could find to slip a string around. She had managed to dangle five of them in the air, and a pile of about another fifty sat waiting to be hooked onto nails.

Kicking the stand in place on the Schwinn, I scooped up the teacake and pushed the front gate back with a screech. Mrs. Mulligan looked over her shoulder, eyeing the cake in my hands, and set down her chimes.

"Is that a genuine Gertrude O'Malley tea cake?" Her eyes were watery blue and ran slightly at the corners.

I nodded.

"God bless her soul! And aren't you sweet to drop it by. I'd walk a million miles to carry one of those home, but these bones are just plain old. They don't work well anymore and that's all there is to it. My son, Teddy, used to bring me to visit Gertrude every single week before he moved to Texas."

She looked at me, waiting for a reply. I rubbed my throat as if I had laryngitis.

"Oh, you poor thing! And look at me blathering on. Tea and honey, lots of tea and honey. Can I make you some?"

I shook my head thankfully, pointing to my bike to say I had to be on my way.

"Well, you make some straight away when you get home, you hear?"

I nodded, heading back to my bike. By the time I'd lifted the kickstand, Mrs. Mulligan had untangled another wind chime from her pile and was teetering on her tiptoes trying to lasso a plant hanger on her front porch. Thoughts of Remy fussing after Mr. O'Malley flittered through my mind and I wondered if Teddy had ever fussed over Mrs. Mulligan. I couldn't imagine Remy moving to Texas. I couldn't imagine leaving my own mother living all alone like that, breaking her neck just to hang a wind chime.

Shaking my head, I got back off the bike and made my way up the porch steps. I pulled a chair up beside her and took the chime from her hand, slipping it over the hook. Within three minutes, we were working in sync: me dragging the chair from spot to spot as she pointed to empty hooks, then handing the wind chimes up to me to hang. Thirty minutes later, her front porch looked like a steel jungle tinkling in the breeze.

"Well, I may not be able to make it down to the real festival, but you have brought the festival to me! Have you ever been before?"

I shook my head.

"Oh my, you're in for a treat. The African drums, curried chicken, people running around in masks, lanterns hanging from every tree. You can feel the magic spinning on the wind like it might pick you up and sweep you right away. Do you know, I met my husband there sixty-three years ago? Imagine that! We danced and held hands all night and then he kissed me right beside the statue of the sea witch. Before the festival ended that year, he bought me that wind chime right over there." She pointed to a string of shells strung through bamboo. "I've loved them ever since."

I touched the tips of the chime beside me softly.

"Well, that's enough of that. I've rambled on long enough. I'm sure you have better things to do than sit here growing cobwebs. Now don't forget what I told you, tea and lemon with a dollop of honey."

I didn't tell her I'd had about all the honey I could manage for the time being. When it was humid, my hair still stuck to my chin like a strip of fly tape.

Mrs. Mulligan watched me ride away, waving until I'd turned the bend and disappeared from view.

# CHAPTER THIRTEEN

My mother was in the garden when I rode up, seemingly oblivious to the crisp bite of the wind, wearing nothing but a T-shirt and jeans. I loved her in jeans. The frayed cuffs and worn knees meant, in this moment, she was just a regular person. She was sitting in a lawn chair staring at a thick pile of paper. I started inside with the teacake, but when I saw her pull a Kleenex from the fold of her sleeve, I stopped, crossing the yard instead. The manuscript she was holding was one of my father's stories, and she was looking at it with lost, red-rimmed eyes.

Setting the cake on her lap, I sat down on the arm of the chair, letting her fingers reach up to stroke my hair.

"Do you remember when he brought us into the forest hunting for puffballs? We hiked for hours and hours. He told us he knew exactly where he was going, but we both knew he didn't. I thought for sure eventually your little twig legs would give out and you would ask me to take you home. But, no. You just kept stumbling after him like a shadow chasing its body—you wouldn't give up until he did. Remember?"

I did remember. It was early fall and he had brought us to a place called Land and Sea, where thick woods crept right up against the ocean then broke into a mile of sand. I nodded, but she wasn't looking.

"And then he found that clearing in the woods and sure enough there they were, a big old circle of puff-balls. He called it a fairy ring, and I told him there was no such thing. He swore there was, that it was caused by the woodland fairies dancing, that every time something tried to grow their little feet stomped it out. He called them something, but I can't recall the name."

*The Nikommo*, I answered silently. He was talking about the Nikommo. Every time the moon was full, he said, the Nikommo came out to dance with the moon, who was their mother. They danced and danced until they had stomped a clearing for the light to shine through. And all the darkness that had crept into the world was erased by the moonlight. Staring out over the ocean, I could hear his voice. I didn't even know I was crying until my mother handed me a tissue from her sleeve.

" 'If you're ever lost.' he told us that afternoon, 'the fair-ies will lead you home.' I remember laughing at him, and then we realized we were lost."

It was true. My father had led us so far off the trail we had no idea how to get back. But he'd told me not to worry, because we were in a magical place and bad things didn't happen where magic lived. We followed him through thorny bushes and over fallen trees. I was scratched and scuffed from ear to toe, but it didn't matter to me—I would have followed him through the gates of hell and into the devil's bed. And then there was a break in the forest and a flood of sunlight and we were at the beach. *See?* he had said. *Never be afraid to trust the magic in the world.*

"My God, he was maddening. That night, when we finally made it home, he grabbed the Encyclopedia Britannica and handed it to me and there it was—fairy circles. He was right; they were real." My mother swiped the Kleenex across her eyes.

We sat there together for another few minutes, lost in our own thoughts, before my mother took a deep breath and shook the curls down her back as if shaking herself free of the sticky threads of the past. "We should go see what Grandma Jo is doing. Maybe someone called about Luke."

For a few moments, I had forgotten about everything but I followed her in with a nod. Nobody had called and dusk was creeping up on the island.

"You want to look for Luke before it gets dark?" My mother pulled a sweater on over her T-shirt, letting her black hair drape across her shoulders.

"I'll start dinner while you two are out," Grandma Jo said without looking up from the newspaper.

"Just cook for you and Iz. I'm not hungry yet. I'll grab something later." My mother had not lost the distant look in her eyes from earlier, and now she looked exhausted.

"You'll eat anyway," Grandma Jo said matter-of-factly.

"Really, I've—"

"Got work to do. Yeah, yeah, yeah. Your antiques have been there for two hundred years, and they'll be there when you're done eating. Probably be worth more, too."

My mother stopped, looking across the room to the armchair Grandma Jo was plopped sideways in, her toes playing with the fringe of a throw pillow.

"Good Lord! Did you see this?" My grandmother held the paper up in the air, pointing to a photograph of a street riot with a white teen throwing a bottle at a young black boy carrying an armful of books. "Riots in Boston over the busing program to desegregate the public schools. Boston, not Birmingham! They've lost their collective minds. What, do they think dark skin is contagious? There's a peace rally next week. Maybe I should go." She laid the paper back in her lap, shaking her head.

"No, you should *not* go. You'll end up in the hospital," answered my mother.

"Well, we should do something."

"There's stationery in the desk. Write a letter," My mother pulled a silk scarf around her neck, knotting it below the ear.

"Maybe. You better go if you're going to make it before dark," Grandma Jo said, flipping the page.

I followed my mother out the door, untangling Luke's leash as we walked down Knockberry Lane.

"Luke!" My mother's voice was getting raw from a day of calling into nothingness in hopes of an answer. We'd made it to the turn-off beyond the small cottage when we met Mr. O'Malley and Remy hiking in from the opposite direction.

"Ladies." Mr. O'Malley tilted his head.

"Good evening," my mother greeted them. "Out for a walk?"

"Yes," Remy answered a bit too quickly.

"Actually," Mr. O'Malley corrected, "she just doesn't want you to know we were taking one more look to see if that pup of yours got himself turned around by the orchard. This one was fretting over the weatherman calling for rain overnight." He swatted Remy gently.

"I was not fretting; it's a dog. I was just looking for an excuse to get this old goat to air his bones out for a bit. That's all," Remy grumbled. "And now that he has, I'll return him to his couch for the late news."

"No sign of him, huh?" my mother asked.

"Not a hair," Mr. O'Malley said. "But, like I told Remy, I wouldn't worry. Pups get the wanderlust. I once had a shepherd that was gone two whole weeks. By the time he came back, he'd been spotted from cove to cove of this place. A farmer kept him one night over in Mantuck. A boy played fetch with him down on the jetties. Ran over this whole blessed island having one ball of a time."

Remy looked at her father like he was crazy. "When? When did you ever have a dog in your whole blessed life?"

"I just did, that's all." Mr. O'Malley settled his eyes on me. "And he came back just as good as he left, 'cept spoiled and fatter. So many people around the island fed him their leftovers, he came back believing he'd like to have steak for his dinner instead of kibble. Other than that, though, he was just as shiny as new."

Remy rolled her eyes, tugging Mr. O'Malley's sleeve to get him moving again. They'd made it about ten yards before she turned back, yelling, "Don't forget about Herman's tomorrow. I'll meet you there at nine-thirty."


"Nothing?" Grandma Jo asked when we returned. Instead of setting the dining room table, she'd laid silverware and plates on the coffee table next to the fire, tossing three throw cushions from the sofa onto the floor for seats.

"Nothing." My mother sighed. "I'll get Remy to drive me around again tomorrow. Maybe we'll have better luck."

"I'll bet he's back by then," Grandma Jo crooned. "Silly pup."

"Let's hope so."

We finished dinner in silence, and Grandma Jo served Remy's teacake for dessert.

"Leave the dishes." She waved a hand at the sink dismissively. "I'll get them in the morning."

After dinner, Grandma Jo and my mother both disappeared behind their bedroom doors. I climbed the two sets of stairs to my room and turned the lights off, watching the wind pick up outside. Tiny droplets of water were already clinging to the window, and the sky said it wouldn't be long before it was raining in earnest. Witch's Peak towered in the distance.

Climbing under the covers, I had only just closed my eyes when a thought brought me upright in bed. I pulled on a dirty pair of jeans from the pile of clothes growing at the foot of my bed, fishing through the pockets until I found Luke's leash balled up inside and, carrying my shoes to keep from being heard, darted down the utility staircase. Grabbing a flashlight from the broom closet, I eased the door open, cringing as it squealed on its hinge, and slipped into the night

Trotting toward the path that wove to the ridge, I kept my eyes peeled for any trace of Mr. O'Malley before dipping into the shadows of the orchard and heading for the old apple tree in the middle. Once I was past it, I paused, making a whistling sound with my tongue and listening for an answer. Rain was starting to fall and the thrumming of it smattering against the rocks made me strain both ears to hear. I tried again. The muffled answer came in the way of a distant whine about three yards away. Another whistle. Another whine.

Getting on my hands and knees, I crawled along a trail of fallen rotting apples, stopping every few feet to whistle again and listen until I found myself crouched at the top of an irrigation pipe Two more whistles, followed by a bout of whimpering, and I was sure it was Luke.

Letting the leash slip from my hand and slither to the grass, I snaked my hand down the metal duct, brushing my fingertips against the wet fur at the scruff of Luke's neck. Rain was already pulsing down the pipe, creating a stream around him. He was jammed, the loose skin behind his ears slipping out of my grasp each time I got a hold of him. The panic in his whine rose with the water pouring in around him and the oncoming storm.

"Shh . . . shh . . . shh. I'm—I'm . . ." I pushed the words through the cracks of the vault I'd kept tightly sealed for eight years before I felt my throat harden to rock again. Luke barked and began to cry and I felt my heart begin to race. "I— I'm c-c-c . . . " I wiggled my hand deeper, getting hold of his paw. *Don't let go. . . . Don't let go. . . .* Luke scratched at my hand, desperately trying to wrench himself free and digging himself deeper into the mud. "I'm c-coming," I squeaked, beginning to cry like a baby. "Don—don't drown. P-p-please!" I needed him to know that I was there, that he hadn't been left behind. My father had vanished into the night before I could make things right, before I could tell him how much I wanted him to stay. I couldn't let that happen again.

With the rain starting to pound against my back, I knew I would never even make it to Remy's house in time to get help. The water was already to Luke's neck and he had dug himself into the mud so thoroughly his small body was acting like a drain plug. He whimpered, craning his neck into my fingers for help. "H-h-hold on!"

Other than a stray word or ugly hiss, I hadn't heard my own voice in eight years. With the rain barreling down and thunder rumbling, I could barely make out the words now—but they were there. I heard them. That was my voice, the one that had chased my father out of existence that night. I did not know if I could pull the right words free to save Luke, but I knew for sure he was going to die if I didn't try. Mr. O'Malley's cottage was the closest. I had to get him.

I stood up and bolted for the trail, the tears on my face washed clean by the rain. I'd made it less than ten yards when a hand grabbed my arm from behind, swinging me around in a 180-degree spin.

"What the fuck are you doing up here again!" Riley shook me as if he were scolding a three-year-old. For an instant, he looked like he might lunge for me, strangling me to death right there with the rising storm as his only witness. Still, even with him glaring at me through the night, he was the most welcome sight I'd ever seen. I grabbed his hand, pulling him with me. "Are you fucking crazy, too? Just like your stupid father. Let go of me!" The words rang through the orchard and the past eight years. But this time I refused to let go. I tugged at Riley's arm with both hands until he stumbled after me.

Back at the pipe, I dropped to my hands and knees and stuck my hand down, horrified that it plunged into water with only two inches of air on top. "L-L-Luke!" I gasped. "Help."

Riley didn't even seem to hear that I'd spoken, shoving me aside and looking around for something to pull Luke free with. Snatching up the leash, his fingers flew around the nylon, snapping it into a slipknot and guiding it into the pipe until he'd weaseled it around Luke's front legs. He tugged twice.

"Son of a bitch!" He pulled the line up empty of anything other than mud and a fistful of wet grass.

Two more tries and the leash tightened around Luke's legs. Riley tugged, edging him up an inch at a time until he was loose enough to scoop him out with his free hand. Luke whined, every inch of him muddied and shivering violently. Nevertheless, he was alive.

"Got him!" It was the first time I'd heard Riley's voice drained of rage. Standing up, he peeled off the flannel shirt he'd been wearing, wrapping it around the puppy and rubbing the mud and water from his nose. It was a full minute before he saw me sitting there with my face in my hands, wailing. I knew I looked dumb, the stupid kind not the quiet kind, but I couldn't stop. My entire body was heaving and shaking even though I knew Luke was alive. But suddenly, it wasn't about Luke. I wasn't fourteen. I was six and running, running, running. Everything was not okay. I wasn't fast enough. Time ran out.

"Come back," I whispered. The words were gathered up by the wind and kited away. "P-please come b-back."

Soaked through to my underwear, it took me a full two minutes to collect myself. I wiped my face, streaking mud from my sleeve across my cheek, and Riley yanked me to my feet before stuffing Luke in my arms like a swaddled baby.

"Go home," he said, looking at me uneasily for a moment before turning away and walking off to Witch's Peak to stand there in the storm. I saw him set something down on the rock and remembered what Mr. O'Malley had said the first day we'd gotten to the island about people leaving Yemaya offerings, laying their dreams and secrets at her feet. I wondered which he was doing out there in the pouring rain: trying to leave behind an offering or ridding himself of some horrible secret that he'd been carrying around just like me.

I did not believe the old sea witch paced the cliffs at night, not really, but a small part of me was willing to try handing my secret over to something bigger than myself, something with stronger arms to carry it. Maybe it was the way God had come up missing over the last year, or the way Yemaya had dragged Captain Booth's soggy body back home to safety even after he almost harpooned her that got to me. Or maybe I was just like my father and needed to believe there really was magic, something strong enough in the universe to pluck us out of our worlds and save us from ourselves.

Turning for home, I ran my hand over a gouge in Luke's paw from the edge of the pipe, glancing back at Riley. He was there, standing statue still in the pouring rain, staring into the distance as though searching for something he couldn't find—and then he was not. I only caught the tip of his head slipping below the edge of the bluff, but what I can say for certain is that the ground below my feet turned to quicksand. Maybe it is truer that the entire world turned to quicksand, sucking me into it with every step I took closer to the ridge.

The sensation started as a mere heaviness in my legs until the *shhh, shhh* of the waves breaking below filled them up with cold molasses and slowed me to a thin crawl. My fear of heights returned to me with drawn claws. Remy had told me the sand below Knockberry Ridge was the color of chestnut skins because it was sifted through with slivers of ships and wrecked lives. And who knew what else was down there. It sent a chill shaking straight through me at the thought. My throat clenched and a full thirty seconds ticked by before I realized I had stopped cold in my tracks with nothing but a bouquet of flowers staring back at me where Riley had been moments before.


*Take me. . . .* The red stars dipped and danced, danced and dipped through the daisies and black-eyed Susans, away from where I stood on the porch, with my mother clutching my shirt to hold me back. The Nikommo whispered and whisked them away and all I knew was that I had to get them back. A scream. A screech. The stars skipped into the night and toward the moon, skating across the ripples. Taking flight. And then they were gone. *Hurry . . . hurry . . . . hurry . . .*

**What had just** happened hung over me for a moment, settling on my brain one speck at a time until it punched through to my gut in a fit of blown-out panic. It is not every day a person witnesses someone tilting right off the edge of the earth and it is not a thing a person ever forgets—even if you spend a whole lifetime trying.

I didn't know what to do, so I did what had grown natural to me in times like these: I ran. Noise flooded my brain from every direction even though the world had gone magnificently quiet. If there was a sickening thud of Riley's body thumping over the rocks below, I did not hear it. The noise in my brain lifted to the high-pitched squeal of long fingernails running down the belly of a chalkboard or steel scraping endlessly over rock. Eight more legs seemed to sprout below me, each stumbling and tripping one over the next. No sooner would I get one foot planted beneath my weight than the other would skittle out from under it as I ran.

It was minutes, or maybe only seconds, before I landed on the front steps of Remy's cottage. The cold rain had turned my insides to sheer ice and knocking on the door threatened to snap my fingers clean off my hand. All the force I could muster produced an exasperatingly soft *rat-a-tat-tat* until Remy pulled open the door with a confused look on her face, eyes ping-ponging between me and the puppy in my arms.

"Je-sus fucking Christ!" She pulled me into the warmth of the kitchen and pushed me into a tattered Boston rocker beside the woodstove. "What demon of the night coughed you up? Where have you been? Does your mother know where you are?"

I shook my head numbly.

"Does she know you're gone?"

I shook my head again, but it was less pronounced as my whole body began to shiver from the heat of her fireplace mixing with the cold from my clothes.

Remy pulled Luke from my arms, setting him beside the fire, then yanked my shirt over my head before peeling my pants from my legs like well-pasted wallpaper. She slipped the terry-cloth robe from her own shoulders to wrap around me much the same way Riley had done for Luke. "Son of a bitch! Jesus, Mary, and Joseph, what are you trying to do, kill yourself?" She pulled the robe tight over my shoulders, standing before me in nothing but a pair of men's boxer shorts and a frayed long john shirt. From the television set behind her, light glowed and I could hear the theme song from *M\*A.\*S\*H*.

"R-R-R . . . " I pushed the sound with all my might through my shrinking throat. "R-R-R-i-i-i-ley!" His name choked out of me just before the opening in my esophagus closed completely at the memory of him teetering into the ocean from a 120-foot cliff, and the frustration of it was almost as overpowering as the fear. I folded myself in two under the warmth of the robe, rocking into the waves of silent heaving sobs that seemed to be flowing from whatever spring had been tapped earlier that day with my mother. Something was wiggling loose along with my voice, no matter how hard I tried to push it back. I couldn't pull it into focus or make the pieces fit, but I knew it hurt. It is an unnatural thing to sob noiselessly. Luke gave a concerned whimper, limping protectively over to my toes.

Remy knit her brow, going ashen at the mention of Riley's name. "What about Riley?"

"Ffff . . . ffff . . ."

She waited only a moment before realizing the floodgate had resealed itself and bolting into the kitchen. A split second later she reappeared waving an old receipt and an eyeliner pencil in the air.

"Write."

*The Ridge*

I had not finished the last two letters before Remy grabbed her two-way radio and ran into the night barefoot, wearing nothing but her boxers and long john shirt and screeching into it, "Jim! Jim! It's Remy. I think you'd better come over here." As she disappeared from view into the field that led to Witch's Peak, I snatched Luke up and held on tight, folding myself back into the rocking chair as I wondered why Riley would jump.

I hadn't even known Harriet Gleason, but that is who I thought of while I was sitting there. I imagined her standing on the football field cheering everyone else on and wondered if anyone had ever bounced up and down yelling her name. I pictured her opening her acceptance letter to college and wondered how many people in her life told her that the letter was nice, but they wanted her to stay. I wanted to believe that Yemaya had scooped up what was left of her and filled her back up with luck. Then I thought about Riley and the look on his face in the microfiche reader, like the world had just ended. He had never liked me, so I'm not sure why I cared, but I did.

I wanted to tell him it hadn't; the world hadn't ended—it had changed.

It was five minutes before the lights of the sheriff's cruiser pulled me back out of my thoughts. Remy was already trudging back across the field toward the cottage, looking wilted from the cold rain, but grounded. Through the window, I could see her lay an arm over her brother's shoulder and kiss him on the cheek. She spoke to him for a minute while he nodded slowly, glancing through the window at me. After a minute, he headed away at an easy walk toward Mr. O'Malley's yard.

Remy came back inside, letting the door slam with a sharp *slap* behind her. For a second, she stared at me as though she had something to say, then instead ducked into her bedroom and reappeared a moment later in a pair of men's sweatpants, an angler's sweater, and wool socks. Depositing a pair of folded sweatpants and a thermal shirt on the couch beside me without saying a word, she made her way into the kitchen. On the other side of the wall, I heard the gas stove pop to life and the tin bottom of the kettle scratch into place over the burner. While the kettle heated up, the *clickity, clickity, click* of her rotary phone made its way into the living room.

"Zorrie? It's Remy. I just wanted to let you know that Izabella's at my place. No, she's fine. I'll drop her back home once I get her dried up."

*Click.*

She came back into the room balancing a mug of tea in each hand and slipped one onto the floor in front of me.

"Riley's fine."

I felt my insides thaw for the first time all day and my stomach ached from being knotted up in a ball of fear. Setting Luke gently beside the mug, I grabbed the paper and liner. *But I saw him jump.*

"There's a side path that cuts down to the inlet by the peak. He was sitting down by the water. His dad's gone down to get him." She paused.

I leaned back in my chair and took a deep breath. My lungs felt starved for oxygen after holding my breath.

"But there is still the matter of you. What in the hell? Is there something you do not understand about me telling you to stay away from that ridge? Riley was born and raised on it. He knows every corner of this property and walks it almost every day. You, on the other hand, seem intent on killing yourself."

For what felt like eternity, we sat staring at one another in silence, Remy sipping at her tea, me rubbing Luke's belly. Finally, she set her own mug on the floor beside her rocking chair with a sigh.

"Riley told me he's heard you speak. I heard you on the boat. Does your mom know about your voice?"

I shook my head and stared into the flames lapping their way up the hearthstones. Her eyes followed as though she were turning the pieces of a jigsaw puzzle angle to angle, trying to make the picture fall into place.

After a time she said, "You know, when I was younger, while I was raising hell on the mainland, I got to visit this old Byzantine monastery. The monks take a vow of silence, creepy as holy hell; you could poke one right in the eye, and they wouldn't say 'boo.' They believe it lets them hear God speak and offers penance for any horrible sins they may have committed." She gave me a sidelong look.

"You know what I think? I think they're full of shit. *Holy* shit, but it stinks just the same. There is nothing in this whole world that cannot be forgiven. Even God fucks up, probably more than all the rest of us combined. When that happens, there's nothing to do but buck up and ask forgiveness for making a boneheaded mistake. And if we're big enough, we do it. We forgive." Picking up her mug, she downed the final drops before returning to the kitchen and setting it on the butcher's block.

"Throw those clothes on," she called. "I've got to bring you home before your mother makes her way over here and keeps my tired bones up for another damn hour."

**"You better get** some sleep," Remy ordered, stopping the car in front of the Booth House. "You've got a date with a paintbrush bright and early."

I scooped Luke up, and she scratched him between the ears and shook her head, sputtering something about a damnable dog. Grandma Jo and my mother were both up and waiting for me when I got in.

"I'm not going to tell you how incredibly irresponsible and downright stupid it was to go out in the middle of the night without telling someone." My mother gave me a stern glance so I thought better of pointing out that she just had. "And in return for the favor, you are never, ever going to do that again. If you need to go, you get me and give me a chance to go with you. You don't just leave, damn it." The words were dusty, like she'd had them packed away for a decade, waiting to set them free on someone, and I felt a sting in my chest, knowing exactly what she meant.

I thought about my father, and Riley, and Harriet, and Grandma Jo's map. For the very first time, I knew in my heart of hearts that there were some corners of the universe a person had to go to alone, but I didn't say so.

Grandma Jo shot my mother an approving look as she lifted Luke from my arms and fed him a peanut butter sandwich before plopping him in a sink full of suds.

"He's got a cut on his paw," she called through the door. "Someone grab me a bandage and some peroxide."

"Peroxide, Mom? Count yourself lucky that there's toilet paper," my mother answered.

"Come here, Izabella," Grandma Jo called back.

My mother gave me a final look that suggested she was serious about what she'd told me then tilted her head at me questioningly. "What are you grinning about? There is not one thing funny about this. I'm serious—you could have died. That isn't something to laugh about."

Making my way to the table for a scrap of paper I looked at her and scrawled across it then walked into the kitchen to help Grandma Jo. Behind me, I heard her shuffle across the room to pick it up.

"'You love me,'" she read aloud. "Well, of course I love you. What the hell is that supposed to mean? Why wouldn't I love you?" she sputtered like a crazy woman.

I glanced at Grandma Jo, who chuckled right out loud, handing Luke off to me while she went looking for something for his paw.

"That doesn't mean you aren't in trouble for sneaking out. How often do you do that, anyway?"

I glanced over my shoulder at her, nodding toward my hands, which were full of dog.

"Don't you think we aren't going to talk about this later,

young lady. I'm on to that whole 'I can't talk right now, my hands are busy' thing. You don't just go gallivanting into the damn night like some sort of gypsy."

She may have been ranting, but I knew what she was really saying, she was just saying it in Remy and Mr. O'Malley's language. She didn't want me to leave.

A few minutes later, Grandma Jo came back into the kitchen with a towel, a strip of fabric hanging over one arm, and two oregano leaves in her hand.

"This should do the trick!" She fanned them in the air. "See? There is use in spending time with a medicine man!"

"That's my good shirt!" My mother lifted the fabric off Grandma Jo's arm.

"*Was*, darling. That *was* your good shirt," Grandma Jo corrected, drying Luke with the towel. "Like all that old wood you spend your days around, sometimes a thing just wants to be put to good use." She lifted a corner of the fabric, shaking her head at the dull cotton button-down. "Or out of its misery. The nature of healing is all in letting go."

"Not for my shirt!" My mother's eyes widened.

"Well, healing the soul is a higher priority." My grandmother laughed, crushing the oregano leaves and packing them against the cut before wrapping Luke's paw in the remnants of my mother's shirt. "I'm sure your shirt is happy to die for a good cause."

"Okay, can we go to bed now?" My mother yawned.

I nodded.

"Do I need to put bells on the doors, or are you in for the night?"

I let a sparkle settle into my eyes, the way I'd seen Grandma Jo do a million times when my mother spun into orbit, and watched her go into her room without bothering to shut the door behind her. She was already out of sight when I realized both of my hands had settled onto the small shelves of my hips the way hers always did.

# CHAPTER FOURTEEN

"You missed a spot."

Wiping the sweat from my brow with the back of my forearm, I looked over my shoulder at Mr. Herman, who put on his spectacles to inspect the frame around the front window.

"Right here." He pointed to the spot where the two pieces of wood met at the corner. "You gonna get that?"

I nodded, pushing back my hair and leaving aqua streaks behind from the paint on my hand.

"See to it," he said, going back inside.

I'd already been working for two hours on a day unnaturally hot for October, and in that time, Mr. Herman had shuffled out to check on me on at least eight occasions. Half of those occasions were to make sure that I wasn't screwing anything up, but a few times I had the feeling he was looking for company. I know it sounds crazy, but I'd been watching him through the window for a while and all I ever saw him do was stand in the corner with his arms folded over his chest or sweep. It looked lonely, and in all the brushing back and forth to make sure I'd filled in the nail holes I started thinking about his crotchety tone. Remy had told me he didn't have family, and nobody seemed to really like him. This is what I came to: he'd barricaded himself behind a big wall of grump and grudge to keep people from getting in. He never said much—he just complained to push people away. His nastiness was his silence, his way of disappearing inside himself, where nobody could ever get in. That was a thing I understood. I had done the same thing; it's true. And so had my mother and father in their own ways.

I ran the paintbrush down the seam of the frame one more time. I had another hour before I had to go back to the pier to help Remy unload the passengers she was carting over from the mainland. She'd abandoned me earlier to help Mr. O'Malley, concerned that the ferry would be brimming to its masts with tourists making their way to Tillings for the festival.

I climbed down off the ladder and dipped the brush into the paint can before slathering the corner with aqua. After examining it from every angle humanly possible to be sure it was covered, I climbed back up to finish the top plank. Ten minutes later, I heard his voice again.

"You get that missed spot?"

I nodded, not bothering to look back at him. Satisfied that Mr. Herman would not find one speck of the wood's natural grain, I climbed down and was surprised to find a cold bottle of cola waiting for me beside the bottom rung. Picking it up, I looked through the front window to where Mr. Herman was bagging up groceries. When he glanced up, I smiled, and he gave me a sharp nod.

Across the street, the owner of a small boutique called Jasmine's stood staunchly at the door while a stream of tourists washed in, poked at the trinkets, and filtered back out onto the sidewalk. Around the corner, the high squeal of a child's laugh broke through the muffled murmur of voices of those sitting outside the White Whale. Electricity seemed to be pulsing across the island in anticipation of the festival. I recalled what Mrs. Mulligan had told me about the magic in the air, that it could pick you up and carry you away. I wondered if she would ever make it to the festival again, to the statue where her husband first kissed her. We had chosen to be alone: Mr. Herman, my mom, and me. Even my father had chosen it before he left with the *tap, tap, tap* of his typewriter and trips. But not everyone got to choose.

I packed up the paint, stuck my brush in a plastic container, and carried them in to Mr. Herman at 1:30 P.M.

"You'll be back to glaze it tomorrow?" he yelled after me.

I nodded before kicking the stand up on the Schwinn and walking it across the street to Jasmine's.

"Do you want it wrapped?" the woman at the register asked as I dug four of the five dollars Remy had given me from my pocket

I nodded, laying the bills neatly on the counter and admiring the hand-blown glass wind chime I'd asked the woman to retrieve from the window. Swirled through in blues and greens like a wave rolling onto the beach, it was stamped with cowry shells and had a silver sea star dangling in the center.

"There you are." She pushed the box toward me gently, tidying a pink bow about the package. Carrying the box outside to lay it carefully in the bike's basket, I headed for the wharf.

Telly was busy helping Riley move crates of supplies for the festival off the cargo deck with a forklift when I pulled up. Remy and Mr. O'Malley were still onboard. When the last crate had been set in line with the others, Riley hopped off the machine, tossed a replacement rope over his shoulder, and sauntered over to me with the clipboard.

"Remy'll be down in a minute. There's an extra run for the next seven days, so they're bleeding the fuel lines. Here." He handed me the clipboard. "If you get stuck I'll be in the ticket booth." He started to walk away but stopped, sticking his hand in his front pocket.

"This yours?" He stepped back in front of me holding out a folded flyer, crisp with hardened mud.

I stared, almost afraid to open it.

"Yes?"

I nodded, holding my hand out. Riley made a move to drop it in my hand, paused, and looked straight at me. The green T-shirt he was wearing picked up every green fleck in his eyes, which seemed to ignite when he looked at me.

"What does someone have to do to get you to talk? Stuff their head in a pipe and try to drown themselves?"

The comment caught me off guard and images of water creeping up, folding over a person until the life choked out of him, teetered the world around me before I pushed it back, back, back . . .

I stared right back at him and actually thought about trying to speak.

But before I could, he dropped the flyer in my hand and walked away. I watched him go, running my fingers over the hard bulge in the flyer's fold and knew without question that it contained my Yemaya Stone.


When the last passenger was off, I grabbed a can of Comet and started up the deck.

"We don't have time." Remy waved a hand. "We have to turn this boat around. If I don't see you tonight, make sure you meet me tomorrow morning before the eleven o'clock run. It should only take an hour to get that window glazed, and then we need to start setting up for the festival.

I waved back, stepping aside as Telly wrenched up the ramp, and watched as the *Mirabel* slid from view.

I took the long way home, passing my turn and swinging down Laurel Lane instead, stopping just beyond Mrs. Mulligan's house. I crept up the steps with the pretty package from Jasmine's in hand, thinking about the things Mrs. Mulligan had told me about meeting her husband at the festival. Sometimes, I could no longer pull my father's face fully into view, could no longer recall how far down his face the freckles cascaded or remember the scent of him. I barely knew her, but I didn't want that to happen to Mrs. Mulligan. Every time the taste of her first kiss faded and the memory got mushy as cornmeal, I wanted a soft breeze to surround her in the tinkling of chimes until it all came tumbling back to her. I wanted her to remember until the Nikommo called her back to her husband for real. I set the box with the pink ribbon on her mat, hopped back on my bike, and spun up the lane toward home.

Coming through the front door, I met Grandma Jo wearing her yoga leggings and carrying a sea grass mat.

"I'm off to the cove. Do you want to come along?" She waved the mat in the air. "I'll share."

Nodding, I ran to change out of my clothes, which were speckled as a robin's egg after a day of painting. Luke scampered along beside me.

"Izabella's coming with me!" Grandma Jo called.

"'kay," my mother's voice filtered in.

By the time I made it back downstairs, my mother had moved outside and was perched cross-legged on the porch with a sheet of paper and a collection of oil paints scattered around her. Biting a paintbrush in her teeth, she looked up at the sound of the door squealing open. I raised an eyebrow at the picture she was struggling over: a landscape of the cliffs with Witch's Peak looming in the right-hand corner.

"I'm not very good." She looked down at the paper. "It's just to relax, really. I found these in the basement." She tapped a tube of paint with the wooden end of her brush. "Then Grandma Jo showed me your sketch on the festival flyer, and after looking at a hundred paintings for the auction, I don't know, I guess I just needed something to do." I grinned, more at the child-like way she was defending her actions than the painting itself, which wasn't half bad. "Have fun with Grandma Jo," She called over her shoulder dipping the tip of her brush into the paint and scraping it deliberately against the edge to remove the excess.

Grandma Jo and I walked down a narrow path a half mile from the Booth House until it spit us out onto a small sandy cove. Every six or seven feet spiky clusters of dune reeds poked through the beach like lonely strands of hair. I laid the sea grass mat on the beach and turned around to find a pile of clothes beside the water and my grandmother swimming in the inlet. Unlike my mother, the fact that my grandmother was half nudist didn't bother me. It was just in her nature. I guess after years of wearing my silence, with shame crouching around every corner, I didn't have enough left over to be embarrassed by other people's choices.

Balancing on a string of boulders jutting out one side of the inlet, I walked alongside her, sticking my toes in the cold water every few rocks to see if it had warmed up any in two seconds. By the time I'd reached the end, my pockets were heavy with sea stones I'd gathered along the way. None of them looked like mine, but I liked the idea of gathering luck wherever you could find it.

"You want to come in?" Grandma Jo called out.

I shook my head as she swam closer to the rocks.

"Wow, look!" She reached down into the rocks and pulled up a bright orange starfish with a blue dot in the middle. I leaned over, letting her put it into my hand, and studied the tiny suction cups as they reached for solid ground against my fingers. "Isn't it lovely?"

Fifteen minutes later, Grandma Jo climbed to shore and, after wrapping a towel around herself, sat staring over the ocean. The sun had scooted behind a gray bank of cloud. I teetered back along the rocks to join her, watching the Moorhead lighthouse blink through the mist.

"This is one beautiful island. I'd forgotten how serene it is." She sighed. "Do you want to meditate with me? I always meditate before doing yoga. Touch your feet together sole to sole. Close your eyes. Ready?"

I nodded.

"Now, four cleansing breaths. One, two, three, four."

After a few minutes of relaxed silence, she opened her eyes. "Do you remember anything at all about coming here as a little girl?"

The fog light winked.

I started to shake my head, then looked at her and stopped. "Fireflies." It was more of a whisper than a word.

"In October?"

Staring at Grandma Jo for several seconds then letting my eyes skim over the ocean, I considered the fact that I'd never seen a firefly that late in the season before, or since, but I remembered them. If I closed my lids, letting myself fall through the years, I could pull them clearly into focus, twinkling and tumbling in my mind.

On the night of my sixth birthday, the last few fireflies of the season were skittling around the rosebushes outside my window screen, where an especially fat one had just come to rest. Another hung over the ocean flickering on, off, on. I'd studied it carefully, considering the world outside and the unfairness of being born just to spend your life being eaten, squashed, or shooed. I had decided we were in the same bucket together, bugs and me. We were the smallest things in the world. And while it's true I had been spared most of the eating and squashing, more and more often during that year when I walked into a room my parents fell into an awkward hush before shooing me back out with a distracted, "We'll be out in a minute, Iz.

We're having a grown-up talk right now," which even then I knew was code for "fight." "Please, you need to take your medication," I'd heard my mother tell my father. I knew, though, that was not true; he had told me so himself. With a tap of the screen, the fat firefly had zipped into the night, leaving me alone again.

If Grandma Jo was surprised to hear a word fall out of me and into the afternoon, she didn't let it register on her face. She turned back to study the shiver of ripples picking up speed until they rolled as a white tube against the shore and nodded without pressing the issue.

"Fireflies," she echoed. "That sounds like a good memory." She pulled herself to her feet and spent the next half hour stretching into odd shapes I could not even imagine my body assuming.

But she was wrong; it was not a good memory.

She didn't ask if there was more, and I didn't say because the memory had screwed the lid tight on my vocal chords like the rusted-up top of a mayonnaise jar.

So I grabbed my journal and sketched until Grandma Jo finished her yoga. When she looped a towel around her neck, plopping to the ground beside me, I slipped it onto her lap and watched her study the words quietly before staring across the sea as though searching for an answer.

*Was he crazy?*

# CHAPTER FIFTEEN

Grandma Jo never answered my question directly, though I had tossed and turned with her answer in my head well past midnight.

"You were the light of his life."

The statement shouldn't have vexed me beyond all reason, but it did, and all the tossing just jumbled it up more. My father had spent his entire life chasing after the light, and it never brought him home to me. It had never been enough, no matter how hard I tried to make it shine. I could not blot out the stars that led him away, could not compete with the pull of the moon.

I can't say exactly when I finally dozed off, but I was jolted to, still sleepy, by the bleeping of my alarm clock at seven.

I waited outside Herman's for Remy for a full half hour, holding a tube of glazing in my hand for the window with not one idea what to do with it. Just after ten, the Purple

Monster pulled up to the curb at breakneck speed and skidded to a stop. Riley got out of the driver's seat, shut the door with a thud, and sauntered over.

"Remy's tied up at the pier." He took the tube from my hand. "I've got to get back on down there to help out, but I'll get you started."

Pulling a penknife from his back pocket, he slit the tip from the tube and wriggled it into a metal contraption with a long trigger, giving it three solid pulls until a clear gluey strand eased out the tip.

"Here, hold the gun like this." He propped it in my hands and turned me toward the glass. The scent of sweet smoke and cloves filled my nose. I figured he'd probably been cleaning either the boat or the taxi stand with Mr. O'Malley, but it reminded me of what I had thought about Remy's cottage the first time I'd seen it—sugar cookies and warmth.

Placing both arms around me and guiding my hands, he squeezed the trigger slowly. "Now just pipe it out all the way around the edges."

I turned my head to brush a curl out of my face with my shoulder, glancing at him, then hurried to turn away when he glanced back. He was still talking, but I was busy picturing him racing down Remy's back hill on a toboggan and letting out a laugh. I had never seen him laugh.

"Once you're done, take this cloth and run it over the line to push it between the glass and wood. Got it?"

My heart was thrumming at the speed of light. I nodded, but the truth is I barely heard a word he said. I wanted to hate him; at least I had thought I wanted to. He had made it clear that he didn't like me. But every time he came close, my hands started to sweat and shake. I'd been carrying around the memory of his face in the picture from the library since I first saw it and, even though it didn't make sense, I felt connected to him in a way I couldn't shake. There was that. And there was this, too: he had the greenest eyes I had ever seen. They reminded me of stars in a pitch-black sky and there was a depth that said they understood the ways of the moon.

"Good. Remy says she'll pick you up at three o'clock to help set up the square."

As he climbed back into the driver's seat and spun off, I considered it a good thing that I didn't speak because whenever Riley was around my words jumbled up in my brain anyway.

"Don't forget the inside, too." I'd been working on glazing the window for forty-five minutes when Mr. Herman appeared at the bottom of my ladder carrying another cold soda. After handing it up to me, he pulled his spectacles from the breast pocket of his grocer's smock and hooked them over his ears, following the line of glaze from start to finish.

I sat on top of the ladder watching him until he'd checked every inch.

"I guess it'll do." Pulling the wire-rimmed glasses back

off, he hobbled inside, leaving me sitting on my perch, wondering. It was the kindest thing Mr. Herman had ever said to me and I was willing to bet it was the nicest thing he said to anybody that day.

Main Street was already brimming with tourists smushing their noses against windowpanes and wandering around with paper cups of frozen lemonade. A young girl skipped down the street past the White Whale with an ice cream cone in one hand and carrying a stuffed doll of Yemaya under her other arm. Finishing my soda, I picked up the glazing gun and went inside.

"Cedric," Mr. Herman said, wagging a finger at the boy bagging groceries. "Go get the ladder for her. It's heavy."

The boy stuck chips into the bag and disappeared, coming back with the ladder dragging behind him.

"Pick it up! You're going to scratch the floors," Mr. Herman snapped and sent the boy reeling under the weight of the unruly ladder, trying to accommodate his boss.

After another hour, Mr. Herman gave his final stamp of approval and I walked out of the market, giving the window one last glance before heading home.

"You want to ride along, Josephine?" Remy stood in the doorway waiting for me to pull on my shoes. The Purple Monster was parked out front, pulling a trailer chock-full of collapsible tables and chairs.

"I could use a little break," Grandma Jo said, walking straight out and climbing into the Purple Monster without bothering with shoes.

"Me, too," my mother said, setting a file down on the dining room table. She plucked a pear from the fruit bowl, tossing it to Remy as she passed.

Remy looked at her as though she'd sprouted green hair. "Really? You don't have to work? Are you feeling okay?"

"Just fine," my mother lobbed back sarcastically, following Grandma Jo out to the taxi. Remy bit the pear and watched her get in.


There was already a gaggle of people in the town square by the time Remy came to a stop, and I unfolded myself from the car. White tents lay on the grass waiting to be propped into the day.

"Okay, unload the tables first! It comes together like a jigsaw puzzle. Here's the diagram of what goes where. Once the tables are laid right, we'll stack the chairs beside them and throw a tarp over the whole shebang," Remy barked. "Izabella, grab the tablecloths."

Two dozen people hustled back and forth moving furniture, planters, and tents around the square. Grandma Jo and Mr. O'Malley busied themselves setting the poles for the tents while my mother handed chairs off the trailer two at a time. I don't know if it was the fact that she was relaxing or Grandma Jo's cooking, but the bones along her shoulders had softened and I had caught her smiling several times over the last day or two.

"Get outta the way or get smushed!" Remy called. "They're bringing in the statue. Dillon, Jim! Help unload it."

I stepped behind the sheriff to clear a path for the men to carry the statue of Yemaya into the center of the square.

"You hear the way she speaks to the law, Jim?" Officer Dillon lifted a brow at Remy, shaking his head woefully.

"She *is* the law. It's best just to accept the fact and move on." The sheriff landed a soft cuff on his deputy's arm.

"That means you can't give her a court order or something to make her go out with me?"

"Sorry, kid. You're on your own." The sheriff laughed.

"That's all right. I've dealt with hardened criminals. I'm not scared of her."

"Hardened criminals," Remy scoffed, putting her hand on her hip and crinkling up the diagram as she did so. "What hardened criminal have you dealt with, Dillon Baxter? You have lived on Tillings your whole blessed life, and there is not one hardened criminal on this island. Ha! Hardened criminals." She shook her head. "And let me tell you what: even if you had dealt with hardened criminals, they've got not one damn thing on me!"

"Told you," the sheriff whispered before heading for the center of the square, where Telly was coming in with the church's statue of Yemaya loaded on the front of the forklift. He drove to the center and climbed down to loosen the straps as five men scurried up to help.

"Riley, grab that table!" Remy hollered. "This one needs to go in front of the church. Izabella, get the other end. Then you two can set those stones into a ring for the fire dance right over there."

"Great," sputtered Riley, who had arrived with Telly. "Now Dillion's got my aunt all fired up and the rest of us are gonna pay for it." Riley followed me over to the table, lifting his end with ease. "Maybe you could teach him to shut up." He smirked and began moving the table, stringing me along on the other end.

From across the lawn, I saw Lindsey walking toward Remy with a large sandy-haired man. She looked at me, said something to the man, and started to turn the other way. The man grabbed her by the wrist, giving her a shake. His face was red, and for a minute, I thought he might slap her before he let her go with a shove and she slipped through a row of hedges on the opposite side of the square.

"Motherfucker."

I looked at Riley, who was watching the scene unfold, too, taken aback at the anger in his tone.

"Riley," Remy called. "This table needs to come off the one over there in an L shape." She pointed at another table.

"Come on," he grumbled.


By late evening the square was starting to take shape and Remy finally dropped my mother, Grandma Jo, and me back at the Booth House, smelly, tired, and hungry.

"I call the first shower." My mother tossed a green beach towel over her shoulder, leaving her sweater behind on the armchair, and climbed the back stairs.

Grandma Jo flopped down on the couch, kneading her bare feet, which had become blackened with mud. She patted the spot beside her with a smile.

"Tell me."

I looked at her with a degree of confusion.

"Who is he?" She handed me one of my mother's empty files and a pencil.

*Who?*

"The boy you were staring at all day. The one you were working with."

*Riley? He's just Remy's nephew.*

"Handsome nephew," she added, intrigued.

*He hates me.*

"I have seen a lot of hate in my day," Grandma Jo teased. "Trust me when I tell you it doesn't look anything like that. Tell me something else. How long ago did you start speaking again?" Her eyes were chicken soup warm, but the underbelly of her words said she really wanted to know. She could do that in a way my mother had never figured out, with a steely seriousness that had been drained clean of judgment.

I didn't answer her, not because I didn't want to, but because words falling out here and there isn't really speaking in the proper sense of things.

"I see." She laid a hand over my shoulder, leaning back

into the couch cushions. "You know, eventually you're going to tell your mother. And, eventually, she's going to understand. That's the nature of things between daughters and mothers."

I tried to count how many times those words had come out of my grandmother's mouth in my lifetime as I climbed to my Pepto-Bismol-pink bedroom. I still felt the room whispering to me as surely as it had the first day I'd stepped foot inside it, but I wasn't any closer to finding out what it was saying. The message was all jumbled around in my head, flashes of things from the past that didn't connect to anything else. One thing was always the same, though: every time I walked into the room, I felt I needed to hurry somewhere. The sensation was so potent I had to fight not to go running out again, since I did not have a single clue where I was supposed to hurry to.

I grabbed my journal and flopped down on the bed. The Yemaya Festival was only one day away and I played with the idea of writing a poem to go along with my sketch. After half an hour, the page was still blank. I set the journal aside, yanked my sneakers free, and switched the light off. Lifting Luke onto the bed, I began rubbing his bandage. His leg was still sore, but even my mother had to admit Grandma Jo's oregano leaves were working wonders. With a contented sigh, he tucked his nose in my armpit.

I was almost asleep when I heard Grandma Jo's voice flitting up the stairs.

"Zorrie, can I get you a cup of tea?" Everything about her was canary-like, especially her voice. If mine ever fully came back—and it did not sound like my father's—I hoped it would sound like hers.

"Hmm?" I heard my mom murmur, followed by, "Good God, Mother! Would you *please* put some clothes on?"

Chuckling, I pulled the covers to my chin and closed my eyes

"Why? What's wrong with my body? Freshen up, put clothes on . . . It's enough to make one self-conscious beyond repair."

"It's fifty degrees outside."

"I'm not outside."

"Mother!"

"Zorrrrieeeeeee . . . "

Grandma Jo pattered back down the hall. When she was gone, I heard my mother laugh right out loud.

Far off in the distance, the Moorhead lighthouse flickered like one of those summer fireflies, on . . . off . . .

I cannot say when the faces started to organize themselves into a dream, but this is the dream they made up. . . .

I was walking down Knockberry Lane to Remy's cottage in the middle of the afternoon. It was sitting ahead of me, but instead of moving toward it, I turned down Mr. O'Malley's drive toward Witch's Peak. A white thread was pacing back and forth on the ridge. I knew it was Riley, and for some reason I was happy about it. But the closer I got, the more I could make out that it wasn't Riley at all standing on the ledge with waves lapping hungrily below. The face belonged to my father and he was wearing the purple striped Father's Day sweater. He turned as though he were going to disappear over the ledge as Riley had done.

"Come on, Be," he urged, flashing his dimples. "Come dance with the moon. Come fly with me."

*Run. Hurry.*

I started to run to him, but Mr. O'Malley's salt licks kept tripping me up. When I finally made it to Witch's Peak, my father was gone and a woman with dark hair pulled back by cowry shells was staring at me with stormy gray eyes. She held out her hand without saying a word. She did not have to; I knew what she was waiting for. My hand moved on its own, digging until it found the stone, and handed it over to her. As she lifted it into the sky, I was being pulled back, back, back, even though my feet were not moving. The cliffs were shrinking until there was nothing but the stone flinging through the air, disappearing with the secret of my sixth birthday inside into the waves below.

# CHAPTER SIXTEEN

The morning of the festival arrived overcast and chilly. Since Remy was up to her ears in things to get done, Grandma Jo, my mother, and I walked the thirty minutes into town past the small tributaries that snaked in from the ocean and swamped over a series of salt marshes. The stagnant smell of dead fish, brine, and muck held tight to the damp air. Tall rangy swamp grass tangled at the feet of an egret poking for crabs.

"I'm just saying," my mother was grumbling to Grandma Jo, who proudly toted a box of her cheese biscuits, "I don't know why you had to paint her face with makeup. She's a teenager."

"Exactly." Grandma Jo patted my mother's arm.

"What's that supposed to mean?"

"Just that there may be someone other than you that she wants to look beautiful for."

"Someone? There's a *someone*?" My mother paused in

her tracks, looking back and forth between my grand-mother and me. "What someone?"

"I'm just saying . . . " Grandma Jo tugged my mother by the elbow to put her back in gear. "Doesn't she look beautiful?"

"She looks beautiful all the time." My mother's words hit the day with all the childishness of a pout. "She doesn't need goop all over her eyes to do it."

At this time of the year, when the blanket of reeds wove densely around itself, a person could walk right over the water of the salt marsh like Jesus without ever breaking through. Libby and I had done it all the time down beside the Tuckertown docks, bobbing along as though we were balancing across her mother's waterbed. Now my feet tingled with the urge to charge toward them and jump right on the surface.

"For goodness' sake, Mother, I can't believe you didn't bring shoes."

"They smother my feet." Grandma Jo wiggled her toes around in the dirt.

"Feet do not have lungs. We are going to walk the entire way there and they aren't going to let you in and we'll just have to turn right around and come back," my mother snapped, waving a hand at Grandma Jo's smudged toes.

"They would not dare lecture a sixty-year-old woman about how to dress."

"Yes, they would. Wearing clothing in public places is the rule, whether you are six or sixty." My mother's eyes flashed to the deep V of Grandma Jo's tunic. That she had left her brassiere at home beside her sandals was clear.

"Oh, for the love of Pete! Who made you so frightened of breaking a rule now and then? You would think you were raised by some hard-nosed son of Sigmund Freud instead of your father and me. They are *my* feet; I will tend my own calluses and pluck my own slivers, thank you very much. It might just do you a world of good to kick your own shoes off and run barefoot through the world screaming, 'you can't tell me what to do!'"

My mother laughed.

"Really, it's amazingly freeing. Try it."

"Okay, you can't tell me what to do!" She looked squarely at Grandma Jo as she said it.

"You see? I bet your blood pressure's down ten points already."

Main Street was a flurry of activity with a steady trail of people heading toward the square. On both sides of the street, shop owners busied themselves brushing leaves from their awnings and pounding dirt from their front mats. Those stores not selling Yemaya wares had closed for the day. At Merchant's Hardware a young boy fumbled with the lock on the front door then turned to his father for assistance. Mr. Herman sat on a step stool in front of his new window watching people pass, a cane propped beside him on one side and his broom on the other.

We could already see the frenzy of the square when I remembered what Remy had said about Mr. Herman taking forty-five minutes to hobble the short distance to work each day. I recalled the wistful look in Mrs. Mulligan's eyes when she'd talked about not being able to walk to the festival on her tired bones anymore. Mr. Herman's bones were old, too, and I wondered if he got to enjoy the festival or if he just watched everyone else enjoy it. Ever since I'd decided Mr. Herman's grouchiness was really loneliness, he seemed different to me. It was like Priscilla Peabody and the rest of the world ratcheting up the volume when they spoke to me—sometimes the world just decided a thing about a person that was all wrong. The thought of the bottle of soda at the bottom of my ladder came back to me.

Turning around, I grabbed Grandma Jo's arm, stealing a plate of cheese biscuits from her box. By the time I made it back to Mr. Herman, I was huffing and small beads of sweat dotted my forehead. I set the plate on the ground by the leg of his stool and ran to catch Grandma Jo and my mother. I'd only taken two steps before something hard tapped against my leg and I turned to find Mr. Herman bouncing his cane gently against my calf. He touched the plate with a wink and I gave him a smile then raced back the length of Main Street to where my mother and Grandma Jo stood waiting.

By the time we reached the village square, the smell of brine was fixed in my nose and most of the island was already there.

Mr. O'Malley was leaning against the hood of the Great Purple Monster, puffing his pipe and watching with interest. When he saw us coming down the walk, he stood upright, knocking the tobacco from his pipe with the heel of his boot.

"Mr. O'Malley," my mother said.

"Tom," Grandma Jo greeted him sweetly.

"Well, good day, Zorrie, Izabella, and the lovely Josephine. You've made it just in time to see the tribal dancers."

Mrs. Mulligan was right about the festival. The square had been transformed into a magical bubble of lanterns hanging from every branch. Artists' booths dotted the lawn like drops of dew, selling African wares—everything from woven baskets to clay-dyed clothing. String puppets of lions and sea witches dangled from dowels. A mud circle with a bonfire in the middle had been set up in the center of it all, and dancers dressed in kente cloth were painting their faces beside it. African music wove through the air like a needle stitching the fabric of the town together. The strong scent of ginger and curry burned from fire pits. In the center of it all, Yemaya seemed to be watching over the people of Tillings.

A young boy brushed between Grandma Jo and Mr. O'Malley carrying a cloth full of fresh herbs and fish bones.

"Offerings," Mr. O'Malley said.

Grandma Jo took Mr. O'Malley by the elbow, dragging

him along to the ring of fire. The image made me wonder about Mrs. O'Malley. I'd been waiting to meet her since we arrived. I looked around for her now and was wondering where she was when Riley walked into view carrying a stack of grape pies. He set them on a counter strewn with everything from Niagara grape kuchen to grape seed facial scrubs to apple butter. His eyes caught mine over the white cardboard boxes, sending butterflies flittering in my stomach, then he turned back to the woman behind the counter with a comment that made her laugh. I watched him walk away until my thoughts were cut through by the deep steely thrumming of African drums. Turning around, I made my way to the edge of the fire pit, next to my mother.

A man with black and red stripes painted across his face began to stomp a ring around the fire, speaking in a deep, melodic voice:

"Orphaned as a child, the Great Mother, Yemaya, wandered alone for many moons. As she grew into womanhood, she crafted a daughter from clay to keep her company and, on the sixth rise of the sun, breathed life into her, creating humankind. Through her belly were we all born, and in her hand do we live—great goddess of our dreams. She alone can reveal the secrets of the universe."

Holding on to Mr. O'Malley's elbow with one hand, Grandma Jo softly patted her feet in rhythm with the drums, which sent a grin skittling over my mother's face. My grandmother tilted her head to the sky, closing her eyes, and I knew while her body was right there in front of us, she was soaring away to someplace faraway. *Someday I'm going to fly like that . . .* , I heard my father whisper from some corner of the night. *Me, too,* I answered with a smile.

"In seven skirts of blue and white, she walks the shores wearing cowry shells in her hair and pearls around her neck as she watches over her children. Her voice sings out from the throat of every shell and she lies down every night on a bed of sea stones, unburdening her children of their secrets. Her breath is the storm raging over the ocean, guiding everything connected to the sea. Yemaya is the sea. . . . She sinks ships and carries sailors home. Ruler of all, mother of mothers."

Grandma Jo stomped a slow circle, ducking under Mr. O'Malley's arm.

"She is the tiger shark hungry for flesh, the seagull soaring on sturdy wings; she is the fish and the whales, the egrets and the oysters. We drink from her breast and offer her our precious gifts in return."

The man reached into a lambskin bag, pulling forth a fistful of fish bones and shells, and sprinkled them around the flames. The drums picked up velocity, sending his black feet into a frenzy, until the ground became a drum of its own and the red streaks on his face were a blur spinning around and around and around. Grandma Jo stomped the earth along with him, reaching her free hand out to call my mother in.

"Mom, no!"

Dragging Mr. O'Malley with her, she danced a circle around my mother, who had begun to laugh despite the blush moving over her nose. On the second round, my mother's feet started to stomp the ground, too, and before I could figure out what she was doing, she'd grabbed ahold of me and we were all spinning slowly in circles around one another, stamping the grass flat beneath our toes.

"We honor the Great Mother and wait for her to gather her children beside the sea to celebrate in preparation for the Great Feast."

The drumming stopped with the force of a head-on collision, dropping the man to the ground like a fallen marionette. When he rose to his feet, a thunder of applause surrounded us.

"I feel so . . . ," my mother puffed.

"Alive?" Grandma Jo asked.

" . . . okay." My mother laughed, as beautiful as she'd been the afternoon she'd come out of the bathroom on my sixth birthday and stolen my breath away.

"The legend says that all Yemaya's children will gather around her skirts and eat from her hand on the twenty-sixth day of October, and so in her honor we hold the Great Feast on that date each year," Mr. O'Malley explained. "Chief Tankin is the Yemayan storyteller here on Tillings. He works at the library." Mr. O'Malley nodded toward the man, who was wiping sweat from his brow.

"He's wonderful," my mother said to Mr. O'Malley.

"And look, he's not wearing any shoes!"

My mother shook her head at Grandma Jo. "You're impossible."

"Nothing's impossible, not even me." Grandma Jo winked at me before her eyes cascaded down my arm to the hand my mother was still holding.

Leaning against a table selling hot cider, Riley stood watching us and he didn't try to hide it when my eyes caught his.

Grandma Jo nudged my mother's arm. "Come on, Zorrie. Let's stroll over to the art exhibition. We can still see the dancers from there. Izabella doesn't need to be saddled with two old sea witches of her own."

"Excuse me?" My mother raised a brow in Grandma Jo's direction.

"Come to terms with it!" Grandma Jo laughed, pulling her toward the tent strewn with carvings, paintings, and weavings of sea witches. "We're aging gracefully, but aging nonetheless."

"I thought we came here for a big day of family togetherness." My mother studied me hesitantly for a moment, in my new tinted lip gloss and the stroke of mascara and blush that Grandma Jo had snuck on me that morning.

"Oh, Zorrie," Grandma Jo patted her hand, "that was just a ruse to get you out of the house. I thought you knew me better than that. Come on, now. Give her a little room to breathe; no kid wants her mother chasing up her heels. It's embarrassing."

"Tell me about it."

Feeling a tap on my right shoulder, I turned to find a man studying the festival map with a confounded look on his face. "Excuse me. Can you tell me where the art tent is?"

"She doesn't spea—" My mother started to intervene before Grandma Jo pulled her back around.

I gazed at his map and pointed across the fairway to the sailcloth set up a hundred yards behind the concession stand.

"Thank you." He waved, making his way through the crowd. Behind my mother's amazed face, Grandma Jo winked with a proud nod.

"Dance, Zorrie!" she sang out and began moving her feet. My mother looked as though she might lob one more objection, but the drums started up again, cutting her off. This time three dancers, all women, stomped into the circle, spinning in different directions, crisscrossing paths, then pushing violently away from one another as they went. I could not help but think that this was what it was like with the women in my family. We bounced off one another, passed by, then circled back around in a chaotic dance. At fourteen, I was only beginning to learn the steps.

Pulled in as an unwitting accomplice, Mr. O'Malley added, "I'm sure Remy could use some backup pawning her preserves and apple pies." He chuckled heartily. "And if she doesn't move at least half of 'em, I guess we'll know what everyone on Tillings Island is getting under their trees for the holidays."

I turned, searching for Remy's booth as Grandma Jo led my mother away. It wasn't long before I spied her behind a stack of jarred apple butter and made my way to the table.

"Are you here to work or scavenge? " Remy ran a knife through one of the pies and began plopping slices onto paper plates. I stuffed a wine biscuit in my mouth. "That's what I thought. Here." She shoved a piece of pie into my hand. "Watch the booth for me while I get more compote." I nodded and ducked under the counter to sit down in an empty chair. "That's Mrs. O'Malley's chair. Grab one of the folded seats over by Riley," she called, before jogging over to the taxi. Letting my eyes flick to the back corner where Riley was straightening a stack of empty white cardboard boxes, I snatched a chair and pried it open.

Beside the food tent, I saw Lindsey standing at arm's length from the man she'd been with the day we were setting up. He held a beer in one hand while she chatted with another girl.

When I had finished a half-hour shift with Remy, I dug fifty cents out of my pocket and nodded toward the A&W stand, boasting soda fountain drinks and root beer floats.

"Go on." She pulled fifty cents from her cash box. "Here, bring me a root beer." Then rethinking it, she dropped the quarters back into her box and grabbed a dollar bill, waving it in the air at Riley, who was pulling a vinyl flap in the back of the tent down over the post. "You go with her."

Riley blew air through a small hole in his lips with so much *umph* I could hear it beside the counter. Coming around the tent, he plucked the bill from between Remy's fingers. "Anything else?"

Remy tilted her head at him in an exaggerated challenge. "Please tell me that you are not sassing me."

"No, ma'am." Riley shook his head.

Officer Dillon passed us carrying a stack of boxes toward the wrong side of the tent. I trotted over and tugged his sleeve, pointing to the opposite counter where Remy had, in no uncertain terms, instructed us to pile them if we wished to live.

"Thanks," he muttered. "I sure don't want to get it from the boss!"

"I hope you're here to buy a pie." Riley and I watched Remy slap the lid of her cash box closed, eyeing Officer Dillon.

"Only if we can eat it together later."

"Don't you ever give up?" Remy shook her head, restacking the boxes once he'd set them down.

"Never, ever," he said and began helping her.

"Look, Dillon, it's nothing to do with you. I just don't go out, that's all."

"It's been a long time, Remy. Don't you think it's time you started again?" His voice had softened.

"Let's get out of here before she barks at us to do something else." Riley led the way across the square to the orange and brown A&W tent and leaned against the counter. Plucking three straws free from a box he waved the dollar bill at a woman stacking soda bottles.

*You want to go to the A&W?* my father's voice whistled back to me. We'd gone a hundred times, the two of us. To celebrate everything and to celebrate nothing at all. But that day, the one we'd spent at Potter's Creek, that was the last time he'd asked before he was swallowed by the night and disappeared forever. I could hear him asking, could trace the hope in his voice. He'd been trying to turn the ugliness from the day around, trying to apologize for the stupid dead salmon. What had Mr. Matteson said? Something about the world falling apart. But my father didn't care; he just wanted to make our tiny little universe right again. And I'd said no. I'd refused to let him.

Something inside me cracked. I felt it through my whole body. I don't know what it was, other than fragile and sharp and broken. I'd said no. For a moment I couldn't breathe. I tried to swallow, but my throat knotted up. *Why did I say no? Why the hell had I said no?* I wanted a do-over. I wanted to get in a time machine and zip back to that day. I wanted to take his hand and go to the A&W.

A universe away, I felt a tap on my arm. When I looked over the A&W counter a pretty blond woman with Dolly Parton makeup was waiting for me to do something and I could feel Riley's eyes on me.

"You want a regular root beer?" he nudged.

I nodded.

"We need three regulars." He reached around me,

laying the money on the counter, then sputtered, "I'm not gonna be the one who goes back without my aunt's drink. Maybe the sugar will sweeten her up."

The woman in Dolly Parton makeup slid three sodas onto the counter. She was wearing a white-and-red-striped apron that made her look like a piece of stick candy and I wanted to tell her it was all wrong. She needed black tuxedo pants with an orange stripe down the seam. But I didn't, and she swept the change into her hand, dropping it with a jingle into her pocket with a quick, "Thanks, darlin'."

Riley took one of the bottles from my hand, twisted the cap free, and handed it back. "You see the offering pile yet?"

I shook my head.

"You want to?"

I nodded.

When I stopped by Remy's booth to hand her the root beer, Officer Dillon was behind the counter wearing an apron and slicing pies.

"We're going over to the offering pile," Riley said.

Remy nodded, turning her attention back to Officer Dillon. "Where in the name of Jesus did you ever learn to cut a pie that way? Press, don't carve. It's not a Thanksgiving turkey."

"Yes, ma'am."

When I glanced back, I noticed Remy had her hand over Officer Dillon's, guiding the way he sliced her pies, but she was studying us as we walked away, her eyes all backlit with curiosity.

The offering pile was set up beside the statue of Yemaya, and people had left everything from fish bones and shells to potted herbs. I plucked a glass marble from the pile and let it roll back into the fish bones. Several lit candles glowed around the pile, with small bits of paper tucked beneath them.

Riley untied the shell choker from around his neck and dropped it on the pile. "What you offer depends on what you need," he said, leaving me to contemplate a half-eaten burger on the edge of the pile. "Some people leave prayers for people who are sick, other people ask for a good fishing season. The offering pile used to be for families of sailors. They used to leave gifts asking Yemaya to bring them back home safely." I let my eyes drag across the rooftops where widow's walks still adorned the tops of homes, then dropped them back to the pile, feeling empty inside.

"You want to see the art tent?"

I nodded and turned to follow him along a hedge of beach roses that ran the entire length of the square. The bushes were exploding with fall blooms, the precise color of ripened watermelon, and sending their faint perfume into the evening air. I plucked one free just below the blossom so as not to prick myself and twirled it between my fingers.

We'd only made it a couple of steps in the direction

of the art tent when I heard someone stumble behind the roses and then break through the hedge, swearing. I recognized the man as the one Lindsey had been with earlier. He had obviously finished his first beer and cracked open another. His skin was tan and wrinkled, with deep webbed creases that gave his forehead the appearance of crab apple bark. The closer he stepped, the fouler he smelled, filling the air with stale sweat, cheap cologne, cheap beer, and cheap cigars. The truth was, he was having trouble stepping at all, tripping around like the teenage boys who hid under the docks of Tuckertown and fumbled back into the day in a cloud of sweet dopey smoke.

Lindsey scurried up behind him, grabbing his arm to steady him. "Come on, Daddy. Let's go home." Her voice was a whisper.

"I'm fine," he mumbled, getting his legs back under him.

"No, you're not. Come on." Lindsey's face was red, but not so red a person couldn't tell she'd been down this road before. She pulled his arm again, sending him stumbling off balance and kicking over the offering pile.

"I ss-said I'mmmm finne." He stood upright once more, shaking her arm off and giving her a shove that sat her right down on the half-eaten burger. "Leggo a' me!"

When he saw her on the ground, Lindsey's father stepped toward her, raising his hand like he intended to slap her.

Before I knew what I was doing, I moved in front of

her to block him, planting my feet firmly in the space between us. All the feelings of the day my father had sent me sailing through the air and crashing into the closet like a broken doll rushed in, building a wall to protect her, and I wondered if that was how my mother had felt. Lindsey's dad put a hand on my waist, trying to move me aside, but I pushed his hand away and backed closer to Lindsey, so he would be forced to go through me to reach her. The man lurched forward, knocking my shoulder in the process, before teetering in place as he tried to regain his balance.

"Stay the fuck away from her, Mr. Stuart." Riley stepped up beside me, shoving the man back. In his state a steady wind would have been enough to topple him. He went reeling backward, bouncing off the statue of Yemaya, and landed sideways on the ground.

I looked at the man and then at Lindsey, who was fighting back tears. She hadn't moved an inch to stop her father from striking her, and what she'd said as she chucked rocks at the seagull that day came back to me: *Damn bird's too stupid to fly away.* But she was wrong. It wasn't stupid; it was wishing. It never worked, but we all did it anyway. Wishing the craziness to stop. Wishing the world as we dream it into existence.

Without thinking, I helped her to her feet and swiped the remnants of a hamburger bun from her back before knotting my sweater around her waist to hide the stain on her jeans.

"What the . . . ," the man sputtered, rolling onto his hands and knees and struggling back to his feet. "Get your fucking hands off my daughter."

A crowd had started to form around us, with all eyes on Riley and Mr. Stuart.

I stepped back as Riley shoved him again, sending him tipping back right into Officer Dillon, who'd run up with the sheriff at his side.

"Okay, Bob. Time to go sleep it off." Officer Dillon took hold of the man with more gentleness than he deserved.

"That's my daughter. I can take care of her my own damned self." The sheriff had ahold of Lindsey's dad, but I remained in front of her, just in case.

"That's right," the sheriff agreed, patting him on the back while Officer Dillon led him away. "Just as soon as you've slept it off. Don't you worry, I'll keep watch over her till you're feeling better."

"You better. You better . . . ," he said, stumbling alongside Officer Dillon, who half-guided, half dropped him into the backseat of his cruiser.

"I will. Don't worry."

Ten feet away Lindsey stood motionless, as if she was trying to figure out what to do. Carly pushed her way through the crowd.

"You okay?" Riley asked.

"Fine," Lindsey said, turning away.

"Come on, Lins." Carly took her by the elbow and Lindsey looked grateful for it.

"Jesus, Mary, and fucking Joseph! What the hell happened here?" Remy trotted over and took hold of Riley protectively.

Mr. O'Malley followed, bringing my mother and Grandma Jo along with him.

"Bob Stuart."

"He half in the bag again?"

"So far in you could roll the top down and still not hit his head," Riley said.

"Are you all right?" my mother asked.

I nodded, thinking about Lindsey and remembering what Grandma Jo had said to my mother on the day she arrived: *Sometimes it is just in a thing's nature to burst into flames.* In the end, there is nothing anyone else can do about it but watch it burn.

# CHAPTER SEVENTEEN

Later that night I went out to walk Luke. He had not left my side since nearly drowning in the pipe, so I left his leash on the porch and let the night wrap around me.

Remy's lights were on, twinkling in the distance. I walked toward them slowly, kicking shells from my path as I went and sending Luke limping after them in his bandaged paw and oregano leaves. My mother had actually picked him up and snuggled him when he'd come up to her after the festival. "He smells like a jar of Ragu," she'd said, sniffing at his paw and setting him down. "Great, now I want pasta."

The memory sent a grin fluttering across my face. It was good that she was eating again, like an affirmation that she'd decided she wanted to live—even without my dad.

A silver sliver of moon no bigger than a bent pine needle floated over the horizon.

The soft crunch of shells followed me down the lane

to the bend by Mr. O'Malley's driveway, the closest point between the lane and the cliffs. I stopped for a second to study the black crags of Witch's Peak, listening to the *swish* of waves below. A quarter mile out, Morehead lighthouse pulsed soft halos over the water. The smell of fall roses tinged the air. I did not even feel my feet turn off the lane or step quietly into a small clearing in the meadow beside Mr. O'Malley's yard to take it all in. Remy said the deer had a habit of crushing a circle around Mr. O'Malley's salt licks. Fairy circles, my father would have said.

Out on the break wall, waves swished up one side and broke into a thousand pearls on the other. I remembered what Chief Tankin had said about Yemaya. I thought of Riley, his father, Mr. O'Malley, Remy, my mother, and Grandma Jo—*She will gather her children back together beside the sea*—and how and why we'd come to this place and time.

On . . . off . . . on . . .

The flashing from the Morehead lighthouse reminded me of my own memories, how I could catch the corners and angles of something but never saw the picture altogether. We had been here the night my father left, right here the night I had told him to go. But what had come next?

Sitting down, I studied the lighthouse and kicked my heels to the weeds. Now that I was listening, the world had stopped speaking to me. *Four cleansing breaths*. I could hear my grandmother's voice roll in from the day on the beach. Blink . . . one. Blink . . . two. For a long, long time, all I heard were waves crashing below and the high-pitched *peep, peep* of singing frogs. We called them pinkletinks in Tuckertown. They were no bigger than a silver dollar, but as soon as they started chirping, you knew winter was finally over. Occasionally a cricket sang in the thrush then fell quiet again.

Off . . . on . . . off . . .

With the black sea below and the darkening sky above, the lighthouse seemed to dangle as a thread of light between two worlds, just like the fish in Potter's Creek. I had blamed my mother for my father leaving. I'd blamed God. But most of all, I'd blamed myself. Sitting there now, looking out over the ocean, I knew I had been wrong about the whole thing all along.

Before everything went wrong and I'd told him to go, I had been in my room with the anger at my parents' fighting filling me up like a bubble. It was the darkest night of my life, so it was funny that I remembered it punched through with bursts of light. Slivers of light zipping across the meadow. A kazillion stars. *Someday, I'm going to catch you a star.* . . . Six pink candles bursting to life. Pinpricks of red darting toward the waves, disappearing over the cliff—disappearing over the cliff.

Off . . .

My insides sprung like a rubber band pulled past its breaking point. My forehead turned clammy, my body cold. I felt my breathing slow until I was dizzy and had to lie back on the cool ground, trying to force air into my chest. But my lungs would not let go of the air they had. A thousand bees swarmed into my brain, buzzing the world quiet. The smell of fall roses stuck in my nose.

Offshore, the bulb of the lighthouse flickered on top of a pillar of white like a birthday candle. I clenched my teeth, refusing to turn away from the memory this time. Fighting to hold my ground like I'd done with Lindsey's dad. Keys. There were keys. Car keys. The spit of shells. Taillights going down the lane. Taillights shrinking into tiny specks the size of a lit cigarette. A thud. Taillights disappearing over the black rocks. The screech of metal scraping over stone that seemed to go on forever before stopping with a sickening crunch.

Vomit was rising in my throat. I stumbled to my feet. *Let go, Be! Goddamn it, let go!*

*Thump.* The door shutting. *Thump, thump, thump.* My backpack bouncing down the stairs after him.

Somewhere far, far away I heard the heavy thud of a door closing, and it was not until I saw a huge lumbering frame walking across the lawn clutching a square of white that I realized it was not pounding out of my thoughts. The memory was flooding over me, and I thought I would drown inside it like a great wave when Mr. O'Malley stopped halfway across his yard to set the brick of salt in place for his deer. For a moment, I wondered if he had seen me sitting there. Then he teetered, bobbed, and fell into the weeds with a grunt. Another grunt, then a horrible gasping cough. Like the ones Remy fretted over all the time.

Luke hobbled to his feet with a yap and, forgetting all about his injured leg, bolted for the spot where Mr. O'Malley had crumpled. Halfway there, he stopped and ran back to me, yipping wildly and biting at my hand until I'd shaken the memory clean and fought my way to the surface. Stumbling to my feet, I ran after Luke.

Mr. O'Malley was lying there holding his left arm, and for a minute I thought maybe he'd hurt it in the fall. Then I saw his face: it was white as the salt lick that had fallen on its corner beside him. He squinted up at me. "Gert?" That was it. Then his head rolled unnaturally to one side, his eyes staring off into the weeds as blank as the dead seagull's beside Merchant's Hardware.

*Wait, Mr. O'Malley, wait. I am getting help.* The promise hung silently in the air, and all of a sudden, I knew—Mr. O'Malley was dying. He was dying and didn't even know I was there.

"W-wait." I did not know whether Mr. O'Malley was already dead, but I knew he was dying. "Wait, Mr. O'Malley! I'm getting help!"

The cottage was dark now. It was a good thing Remy was not a believer in locking doors, because I barreled right through hers without checking, although with the energy surging through me, I would have gone through it just the same. An old umbrella stand toppled to the floor, and Remy blasted into the room carrying a baseball bat, her long johns twisted up around her and red curls shooting out in every which way.

"What the . . . Jeeez-usss, Izabella! What in blazes? Are you gonna come storming through my door like this every damnable night just to see if I'll go completely fucking insane?" Remy hollered.

"M-M-M-Mr. O'Malley," I gasped. The words labored from my throat all forced and crinkled, but they were as determined as I had been to get to the other side of Remy's front door and were coming through one way or the other.

Remy froze up solid. To hear my voice garbling out Mr. O'Malley's name like a lunatic put her right into a state of hysteria.

"What? What about Mr. O'Malley?" I don't even think she realized that she'd grabbed me by both arms and was shaking me dizzy. "Izabella, what?!"

"He's in th-th-the yard. He needs h-h-h-help." My lungs were overblown balloons threatening to pop right there on the living room floor. But they had lasted long enough. Just as she'd done when Riley had disappeared over the rocks, Remy grabbed her two-way handset and bolted outside with Luke yapping, leading the way, and me at her heels.

The radio squelched alive in her hand as she ran.

"Jim! Jim! Son of a bitch! Fuck! Pick up the goddamn radio! Get me a fucking ambulance *now*!" she screamed, choking down panic.

*Erch.* The radio burped. "Remy! What the hell is going on?"

"Just get a fucking ambulance. Dad's," she howled.

"Oh, shit," said the voice in the beat-up black handset.

"Now!"

"They're on the way, baby. Sit tight. It's going to be okay. We're coming. It's okay. I'll meet you there."

I closed my eyes and felt my chest tighten, then explode. My mother's voice spun toward me. I could feel her holding me back, refusing to let go. *It's going to be okay, okay, okay. It's okay, Iz. He's just going home. We'll catch the ferry in the morning and meet him.*

But it wasn't okay. It would never be okay again.

I ran after Remy and caught up as she landed on top of Mr. O'Malley with two hands on his chest. She didn't even stop to see if he was breathing. I guess you just know, when you love someone that much.

"One, two, three . . . ," I heard her whisper as she pushed blood through his heart. Every time she hit ten, she lurched forward to puff into his mouth. "Goddamn it, Dad! Don't you dare! I am not doing this, not again. Don't you dare leave me!"

Behind us, the faint sound of sirens made their way closer and red lights cut through the night, flickering on and off like fireflies. Shell bits spat into the air as the first police cruiser skidded off the lane, spinning into a half doughnut in the field. Officer Dillon jumped out of the driver's seat before it had completely stopped moving. Three steps and he was on his knees beside Mr.

O'Malley, taking over the pumping while Remy focused on the puffing.

"Come on, Tom." *Pump.* "The ambulance is on its way." *Pump.* "Don't you let go. Come on!"

A minute later the sheriff pulled in, leading the way for an ambulance. Three men bounded from it, followed by Riley and his dad galloping toward Remy.

"Dad?" The sheriff knelt beside Mr. O'Malley, feeling for a pulse in his neck. "We're all right here. It's going to be okay."

Remy continued breathing for her father while the medics strapped him onto a gurney and loaded him into the ambulance.

They had just gotten him in when my mother ran panting into the yard. Grandma Jo galloped up behind her, pulling a sweater over her naked breasts and fighting with the knit of the fabric, which had tangled around her. My mother looked at Mr. O'Malley, covering a small whimper with one hand. One medic ran to the ambulance's driver's seat while another tried to pull Remy, who was turning blue breathing for two people, off Mr. O'Malley.

"Get your fucking hands off me!" she panted. "He's my father and I know how he likes to breathe!"

The medic looked thoroughly baffled but decided to take over the chest pumping instead of risking life and limb fighting Remy.

"His finger m-m-moved," I yelled. The world stopped, only for a second, but it most definitely stopped. Remy stopped puffing, the medic stopped pumping, the driver stopped turning his key, Riley and his dad stopped heading for the patrol car. Everyone stared at Mr. O'Malley's fingers wiggling, except my mother and Grandma Jo, who were staring straight at me.

They were still staring when the ambulance sped away, leaving us alone in the yard. The night had grown black as Yemaya's skin, but not so black that I could not see tears streaming down my mother's face. It took a minute for me to realize they were coming down mine, too—for Mr. O'Malley, for my father, for the voice I barely recognized.

The memories that had begun to wriggle loose in the field before Mr. O'Malley collapsed came back to me then, as complete pictures connecting one to the next with breathtaking speed. To let them in meant inviting the pain to come, too—and it did. But for the first time in eight years, I knew it could not destroy me. It wasn't in my nature to burst into flames. I cried as they came; I cried aloud until the tears would no longer come.

Grandma Jo slid her arms around me, guiding me to the ground. My mother sat on the other side, running her fingers through my hair like my dad once had. We sat staring into the darkness for forever that night, hip to hip, watching the lighthouse. I had always thought that my mother had my grandmother's nose. That I had my mother's hair. In this very moment, though, it was not the stubborn chain of DNA that glued us together, but the frailty of love for the same man—the persistent ache left by his leaving.

After all my mother's years of digging to free my voice, she now seemed content to sit in silence listening to the waves wash in beneath us. *Shhh,* they whispered. *Yemaya,* I thought, and I imagined her sweet voice lifting from the shells, her thin hand reaching from the waves, cupped and waiting. *Let go.*

Grandma Jo put a hand on my knee, giving it a squeeze.

My mother stared at the waves, biting her top lip. After a minute, she pulled a cigarette from her sweater and lit it. When the match finally took, I could see her lashes were wet and clumped together in the corners. I wondered whether she was crying over the sound of my voice or the lack of my father's. Maybe it was both.

"I wasn't fast enough," I whispered.

"Nobody was fast enough, Izabella. You were only six." I could not remember my mother ever calling me by my full name.

The tears renewed, and I didn't know where to start hurting first. There were taillights heading for the cliff. And then they were gone. A crash. The weight of my voice on top of it had kept the memories buried for eight years; now they heaved free, shaking my chest until it ached.

The secret tucked away for so very long burned in my throat. My mother turned to look at me and I could tell she saw him there—the spark in my eyes, the way I wore his freckles across my nose. "I told him to go."

There was silence. A long silence.

"I told him I hated him." I felt my throat buckle and forced it open. I could not carry the secret any longer. "It never would have happened if it weren't for me. He told me. He wanted to fly."

Grandma Jo sniffled, tightening her grip on me. My mother's eyes were round, horrified, soft—loving.

"My God, Izabella Rae, you were six, no more than a baby. He was sick; it wasn't you. He refused to take the medication the doctors gave him. He knew you loved him. And, my God, he loved you more than air. It was the only thing that grounded him to reality. And all children hate their parents sometimes."

"Some hate them most of the time." Grandma Jo chuckled. "Your mother is the only child on earth who loves her parent all of the time."

My mother rolled her eyes with a grin. "It wasn't your job to chase after him. It's a parent's job to stay, no matter what, whether you want them to or not." She glanced pointedly at Grandma Jo. "He didn't leave because of you, baby. He adored you, and he knew you adored him."

"I should have stopped him. If I'd gone with him, if I hadn't gotten my stupid bag—"

"You would be dead, too." My mother's voice was hollow.

I felt Grandma Jo reach around me, touching my mother's shoulder.

"You were six," she repeated. "He was wrestling demons that were deep and determined. You couldn't stop him. I couldn't stop him. The best doctors in the world couldn't stop him." She studied me very carefully, using the cherry of her cigarette to light another. Then she drew the smoke deep into her lungs and hesitated. "Do you remember anything else?"

I thought carefully, listening to the cliffs and the wind, but they were empty. I shook my head.

My mother sighed. "I don't know what he was doing, what he thought he was doing. Sometimes he thought he was being chased, other times he thought he was superhuman. It was dusk, and the deer were coming into the field to feed. Your dad was driving very, very fast—erratic. He swerved into the O'Malley's yard. Mr. O'Malley was away and Mrs. O'Malley was setting out salt licks." My mother stopped speaking. "I don't think he saw her; if he did it was already too late."

I felt the vomit rising in my throat again. That was it— that was why Riley had acted like he hated me. *More than one person's disappeared on this ridge.* His words from the first day I'd seen him on the cliffs whirled through me. *But I guess you already know that.* He'd killed her. Whether he'd meant to, or not, my father had killed her. And that was why Remy was so protective of Mr. O'Malley. He was the last parent she had left. I thought about the empty stool while we were making pies. *My mom and I have baked for the festival since I was toe high to a fiddler crab. Never missed a year yet.* That was probably why she'd been sticking around so close, too. We were the same—Remy and

I. Both of us had lost a parent that day; Mrs. O'Malley and my father left this world in the very same minute— together.

My mother just looked at me, then back at the blinking lighthouse.

My heart felt as though if it suffered any more, it would break into pieces so tiny it could never be glued back together again.

"He was trying to kill himself?"

Neither my mother or Grandma Jo answered, and that was answer enough. "I don't remember Mr. O'Malley or Remy."

"They weren't here when it happened. I think something happened between Remy and her husband, and Mr. O'Malley went to get her on the mainland."

The statement thrummed in my ear so loudly it knocked the air out of me. I rolled back onto the grass, closing my eyes. In one single sentence I knew what nobody else did about Remy. Mr. O'Malley leaving to get her was her "I hate you." We were walking through the world with the same guilt and it was too heavy to carry alone. If I hadn't had a baby tantrum and screamed, "I hate you" on that very night. If she hadn't asked Mr. O'Malley to come get her that particular weekend. We were both moving through the universe searching for an "I'm sorry" big enough to fix it. But there wasn't one. She knew it and so did I, but not one other person could understand.

"By the time they got back, Grandma Jo had come to bring you to her house while I worked out the details."

"Why wasn't there a funeral?"

"Your dad hadn't wanted that, Iz. And people were angry. They didn't know him. They didn't understand. Anyway, by the time the coast guard could recover the wreck, there wasn't anything left to bury. We had a small gathering at the beach in Tuckertown to say goodbye. You were just so distraught—you wouldn't talk, you wouldn't listen, you refused to cry. You wrote him a letter promising to wait on the step every night for him to come home, and for five months, you did. You refused to believe he was gone. You locked the memory away so deep even you couldn't get to it. Dissociative amnesia, that's what Dr. Boni called it, when a person isolates something so traumatic they can't live with the knowledge and barricades it away where the memory can't hurt them."

Grandma Jo was staring into the night with tears silently streaming down her face, the way I had cried for eight years. In a way, it must have been the worst for her, watching all of her children drowning in a sea of hurt with no basket like Yemaya's to collect the pain in and wash it away.

"Would you like to go to the hospital?"

"We don't have a car."

"Well," my mother sighed, "Remy hijacked my car; I don't see any good reason I cannot hijack hers. Maybe next time she'll bring me my own." She stood up, offering me a hand, and turned to stare at the Great Purple Monster of Millbury. Grandma Jo gave each of us one of her famous hugs. "Know where Remy keeps the keys, or shall I hot-wire the beast?" We all laughed, wiping our eyes. That my mother would be seen driving the Monster was solid proof that things would never be the same again. And that was a good thing.

I started to nod, but stopped and instead said, "Yes."

The word felt smooth and easy in my mouth.

# CHAPTER EIGHTEEN

This is what the *Oxford Dictionary* says about recollection. "*Recollection*: (1) the act or an instance of regaining memory; (2) a rejoining, or coming together of formally adhered units; (3) gathering that which has escaped or eluded us. *To collect*: (1) to bring together into one body or place."

This is what I say. Recollecting is picking up your empty basket and reclaiming the pieces that make you whole, and as Grandma Jo would say, "whether you want them or not." It is picking up your stories one at a time and lining them up until they make sense; letting them take up space in the universe with a strong steady voice of their own; and refusing to let so much of yourself fall away that you are reduced to the weakest form of "to be."

I spent the week after Mr. O'Malley's heart attack doing that—recollecting. I was surprised at the stories that cropped up, surprised to find there were not only stories about my father but even more about my mother. Her face, although not always smiling, was there as she drove me to Sunday school, braided my hair, running her fingers through it in a way I thought had belonged to my dad. And sometimes, it was smiling for no good reason at all.

I had come to accept the legend of Yemaya; that mothers are a story all their own. You may choose not to read them some days, but their ink never fades and their words have an eerie persistence to them.

I was coming to understand that my mother did not hate me, only that some days, she hated loving me. That was a thing I understood right down to my toes. She had stopped smoking and started eating, letting the fog lift. We all had. And what we found within was not the monsters we had been terrified of but each other—all scared into our very own silence.

Two days after his heart attack I was bringing Mr. O'Malley a Tab from the soda machine at the hospital when I found Lindsey sitting next to his bed chatting about a passenger who had forced Telly to carry a case of seashells onto the ferry so he could make his own statue of Yemaya back in Millsbury. When I came in, she stood up, straightening her pants.

"Hi." The word came out of her mouth wrinkled and awkward, and she seemed at a loss as to what to do with her hands.

"Hi," I said, handing Mr. O'Malley his drink.

"I brought you this." She leaned over and lifted my

sweater from the chair. It had been laundered and folded crisply into a neat square.

"Thanks," I said, tucking it under my arm.

"Well, I guess I'd better get going. Feel better, Mr. O'Malley."

"I'll be back before you realize I was gone."

Lindsey turned to leave but paused at the door, then turned back to me.

"Thanks," she said. "He's not a bad man, you know. Really, he isn't." She seemed desperate for me to believe her. "It's just, since my mom died . . . "

"Yeah, I know," I said.

"Yeah." She gazed down at her feet, then back up at me. "Well, I guess I'll see you around."

"If you ever need to talk or anything . . . " The words surprised me as they filled the room, surprised me all the more because I meant them. Riley told me it had only been two years since her mother died; I had miles on her and I knew how long those miles could be when you were walking them alone.

"Thanks." Lindsey gave me a final nod and made her way down the hall. I didn't want to think about where she was headed or if there would be anyone waiting for her when she got there.

**Remy caved first.** I guess she felt indebted after Mr. O'Malley's attack, or maybe she was just pissed that my mother had stolen the Purple Monster—not once, but twice—over the past couple days. But four days after he was hospitalized and right back to complaining about the no-smoking policy at the hospital, Remy took the afternoon run to the mainland and returned in the BMW spitting shells this way and that, pulling into a tight doughnut outside the Booth House. The gray sparkle of it had dimmed with sea salt to a dull steely color, but my mother was glad to have it since it looked like we would be staying awhile.

Sometimes it is the very place your world ended that you have to return to if you want to start living again. I had spent eight years searching for my father, and he was here. I guess we both decided that made this place home.

I would be starting school after the Christmas holiday with real teachers and real kids, including Lindsey and Carly. It was hard to guess how things might have changed between us, but every time I saw Lindsey around town, I was reminded of Mary's sad eyes staring down at me in the church back in Tuckertown. How nobody should have her mother yanked from her world midstream. How we all fall differently when the world drops out from under us. Anger is a silence all its own, and I knew a thing or two about that.

**October 26 was** cold; cold enough to cover the wheat tips with frost, making them look like tiny paintbrushes dipped in glitter. I pulled my sweatshirt tight and headed down the narrow path toward the ridge. I'd been spending a lot of time there catching up with my dad, and every once in a while I caught Riley there visiting his grandmother. I had pretty much gotten my father up to speed with my life—my first period, Remy and how good she was for my mom. I'd even confessed to smoking every now and then. Now we mostly sat listening to the gulls together in silence.

And since Riley had stopped diving over the edge when he saw me, sometimes we just sat together saying nothing. Sometimes I just sat and pretended not to notice him watching me. But today it wasn't Riley I was searching for; there was something else I had to do. The bulge in my pocket was forcing a chilly dent into my thigh.

It was the day of the Great Feast, so I knew every single person on Tillings would be going into the village. But I knew where to find Yemaya, knew she would want what I had more than any old fish bones. I stood there for a long time watching the break wall crush waves into a thousand pearls. It's funny how one thing can smash into another until it becomes something else altogether. Secrets are dark scary rooms, but sometimes that is just the type of place a person needs to hide.

And here is a truth: letting those secrets go can be scary, too. But, I knew that was what she was waiting for.

Some things just make sense, and that it was Remy who first interrupted my silence is one of them.

"You're not planning on jumping, are you? Because I have had about all the losses I am willing to tolerate from this damn ridge."

"Not today." I laughed.

"That's good. Then I guess I'll join you. My feet are swollen up into watermelons. Would you believe I'm wearing Mr. O'Malley's slippers?" She sat down next to me and stuck her feet into the air over the ledge. "All that running back and forth from the ferry to the hospital. Thank God that old goat's coming home today."

"He's going to be okay, isn't he?"

"Just as long as he doesn't ask me one time more for that hell pipe of his, giving me no option but to strangle him right there in his hospital bed. I have already told that man that I will not face the world as the only person with two parents fool enough to die hovering over salt licks. If he intends to die, he will not do so giving the deer of Tillings high blood pressure." Remy shook her head, letting her eyes drift for a moment to another place and time.

"Mr. O'Malley had a heart attack after my mother passed away, too. His doctor has been telling him to quit smoking ever since, but he won't. First damn time I ever knew a doctor to be right."

"I'm sorry about Mrs. O'Malley. Maybe—"

"Good Lord, child! Why don't you just jump off this cliff and save the world from yourself? Maybe if the fool of a man I'd married had not pushed me into a wall one night, Mr. O'Malley wouldn't have felt the need to come break his nose and move me home the night my mother died. Maybe a million things would have been different. But if you hadn't come back here, Mr. O'Malley would have died. And that's a fact."

I was still thinking about that when Grandma Jo came trundling down the path holding out a big white ball with great pride. My mother was behind her, looking tortured.

"Look! Look what I found! Puffballs, a whole bunch of them, enough for all of us." The three of us stared at the mushroom in her hand curling up our noses.

"Nonsense! They're delectable; just wait until you taste them with tofu and soy sauce. The first time I had puffballs I was—" She was brought up short by the sound of an engine purring up Knockberry Lane.

We all watched in silence as Riley and his father helped Mr. O'Malley out of the patrol car. There was a short bout of bickering that we could not hear before they walked him out to where we stood beside the ridge.

"What in blazes do you think you're doing?" Remy's eyes flashed at her brother, who shrugged helplessly, then at her father. "You can turn yourself right back around and get those tired lungs into bed just like the doctor ordered."

"Hush now." Mr. O'Malley swatted a hand softly at his daughter, then laid it on my back. "I've got a thank-you that needs saying." Riley's dad nodded over Mr. O'Malley's shoulder. Riley stood still as the break wall, but his emerald eyes had settled on me. I gave Mr. O'Malley a kiss on the cheek, then stepped back to stand beside Riley.

"There, it's been said. Now get your old bones straight into bed. I set up the spare so I can stay with you for a few days," Remy snapped.

"That's not what the doctor said," Mr. O'Malley corrected. "He said no stress, and right now you're stressing me." Remy hit Mr. O'Malley with the sleeve of her shirt. "Anyway, I brought a batch of maple leaves for your mum—all marbled up with orange and red just the way she likes 'em. I got them from the sugar maple beside the hospital—you know, sort of an 'I'm sorry' for making her wait for me again."

"Mom does not want you to die. You go rest; I'll throw them down for you." Remy reached for the leaves, but Mr. O'Malley pulled them away.

"Just like you used to do at Christmas? Putting your name on other people's gifts! Get your own darn leaves; these are from me to your mother."

"Fine. I'll walk with you, then." Remy seemed to have cooled down a notch and took Mr. O'Malley's arm.

"You want to come?" He looked at my mother and held out a leaf for her to take.

"Thank you, Tom." Her eyes were watery as she took hold of his other arm and they made their way to Witch's Peak.

"How come she gets a leaf?" Remy grumbled.

"Because she's nice to me." He tightened his grip on his daughter.

"Well, there you go." Riley chuckled. "Five crazy people standing on a cliff throwing dead leaves down to dead people. And all to apologize for not dying."

I laughed aloud and when I looked up, he was staring right at me with something deep and unspoken in his eyes.

"I guess that makes you the only smart lunatic in the family," I said. "I thought you were in a million pieces down there after you climbed down the edge."

"I don't know why you'd care about a thing like that," he said lightly.

"Well, I wouldn't, except who would boss me around on the ferry?" I teased.

"Remy." We laughed in unison.

"You ought to do that more often." He pushed the hair from my face and let his fingers brush down my cheek.

"What, wear my hair behind my ear?"

"Laugh." His eyes softened.

"Hey, are you guys coming?" Remy called from the ledge. Riley laid his hand on the small of my back and led me to where they were standing. It occurred to me that sometimes families are created by death just as surely as they are by birth, and I knew that was just what had happened with us.

One by one, we turned our eyes to the waves below,

crashing over a beach the hue of chestnut skins, the color of slivered ships and wrecked lives. It was an eighty-foot drop down a sheer face of granite. I remembered the day my father had watched the gull diving and climbing off the cliffs of Anawan. *Someday I'm going to fly like that.* This ridge had ripped each of us apart and then put us back together. I remembered, too, what Grandma Jo used to say: *Izabella Rae, every great story begins in its weakest form and builds upward from there.* It was a story we did not choose, but we were all a part of it.

In the end, that's all any of us are—just a great caboodle of stories. They start when you're born and tell the world you were here when you're gone. And those stories are the realest thing about any of us, the stiff ribs of the life we have lived. They were all a part of mine: Remy, Riley, Grandma Jo, my mother, Mr. O'Malley, Telly, Lindsey and Carly, Mr. Herman, Libby, the salmon, the seagulls—even Mrs. O'Malley, whom I'd never met.

The gentle *shush, shush* of waves below filled the air, and the smell of sea salt wrapped around all of us, holding us together somehow. Here is a final truth: in the end, we are left standing not with those we choose but those we need in our lives. It was October 26, the Great Feast in honor of Yemaya, and I remembered exactly what Chief Tankin had said about this day: *She will gather her children back together beside the sea.*

Mr. O'Malley mouthed something I couldn't make

out and tossed his fistful of leaves into the waves below, watching them churn in the froth.

"Do you want one?" My mother held a leaf out in my direction.

"No, thanks," I said, shaking my head. "I brought something else."

She looked at me with an air of curiosity but didn't ask what it was. When she turned to toss her leaves to the waves, I wriggled the small velvet satchel from my pocket, slipping the stone my father had given me that day at Potter's Creek free. Tucking it tightly in my palm the way my father had taught me to pitch a baseball, I walked out onto the overhang and threw it into the wind, watching it turn over and over, tumbling toward the sea. I let it fly with so much force that I could not even hear myself saying, "I'm sorry I told you to go. I never meant it, not for one second." But, I'm pretty sure he heard me.

For the first time in my life, I was standing on the edge of a cliff, standing on the edge of my life, completely unafraid of the fall. The stone disappeared with a soft *plop* into the water, sending up little frothy fingers to catch it, splashing a dozen creamy pearls skipping into the air, and I imagined Yemaya's hand reaching up to snatch it before diving into the depths of the sea and washing all the hurt clean, restoring it into a tiny pearl of luck in that way mothers do.

# ACKNOWLEDGMENTS

There are no adequate words to express thanks for those who helped encourage, shape, and refine this work. My deepest gratitude goes out to my family for their consistent support, love, and patience as I drifted in and out of long periods of writing and revising that stole me away from kicking soccer balls and play dates. I'd like to thank my children, Alexandra, Dante, and Kian, who inspire me every second of every day and remind me that a lifetime is that block of hours built for catching dreams by the tail and bringing them home to live. My undying gratitude goes out to my amazing husband, Jorge, who is the embodiment of patience, love, and persistence and has spent many days running interference to carve out space for me to work. Stories always crackle to life long before they take proper shape, and I want to thank my parents, Ron and Heather, for giving me the opportunity and courage to tell my own and for surrounding me with magic and stories my entire life. Finally, thanks to my closest confidant and partner in crime through the years, my sister, Laurie Van Hout whose sense of adventure and zest always result in mischief, memories, and material.

I have been blessed and humbled to have worked with a team of brilliance throughout this process, without whom this work would have disappeared into a dusty cabinet. Immeasurable thanks to my amazing agent, Jill Marsal, who has believed in my writing for nearly a decade and, as fate would have it, reentered my world years later to take charge of it with enormous tenacity and intelligence. Behind every strong book is the sharp savvy skill of an awesome editor with the inspiring ability to step inside the brain of an author and clearly see her vision. My endless appreciation goes out to the wonderful Chelsey Emmelhainz for her faith and steely determination to fully actualize the vision of this work and Karen Richardson for her razor sharp focus and attention to detail. I also want to thank Kristine Serio for her sharp eye and early enthusiasm for this story.

While there is neither enough space nor ink to list everyone in my life who has inspired, supported, or otherwise influenced my work, I am both thankful and privileged to be surrounded by amazing friends and storytellers from whom I learn something new every day.

## About the author

## About the Book

Insights,
Interviews
& More . . .

About the author

# Meet Tamara Valentine

TAMARA VALENTINE obtained an MA with distinction from Middlebury College's esteemed Bread Loaf School of English in 2000 and has spent the past fourteen years as a professor in the English Department at Johnson & Wales University. Presently, she lives in Kingston, Rhode Island, with her husband and three children. ᠌᠌

# Questions for Discussion

1. *What the Waves Know* is told from the first-person point of view of Izabella, who hasn't spoken in eight years. The concept of stories and secrets rests at the heart of this piece. How does Izabella become the keeper of both through her silence?

2. How does the title *What the Waves Know* represent these elements of the work?

3. In what ways do religion and mythology make sense of the world for Izabella? What myths, specifically, does she embrace? Are there similarities between them even though they are drawn from different cultures?

4. Do you think it is true that Izabella cannot speak initially, or is she choosing her own silence?

5. Izabella not only accompanies her father on his adventures, she follows him into the stories that slowly take over reality for him. Is there a point when she makes a conscious decision to stop? If so, when?

6. The characters all represent different interpretations of what defines mental illness, as well as dramatically different responses to trauma and loss. How do they each reframe their lives in the face of devastation? How does each hold on to the past and let go of it?

7. The title plays not only on the theme of mental illness, but a person's culpability, or lack of it, in the face of mental illness. In what passages do we see this?

8. Throughout the story, Izabella both wants to hear the Nikommo and is afraid of them. Why? How do they speak to the issues with her father? Why might it be important that they are tied to her father's heredity? Is this potentially defining to Izabella? ▶

## Questions for Discussion *(continued)*

9. Izabella is afraid that she is insane. Why? What does this reveal about her actual breadth of understanding about what happened with her father?

10. One of the elements of the story is that the past and present continuously weave and bob around one another. Why has the author created a storyline in which you are constantly being pulled from one point in time to another?

11. Not only is the reader being torn between the past and present, she is also being thrust in and out of stories and mythologies. Why? Is there a clear truth behind the fiction?

12. While in many ways Zorrie's character is struggling to get Izabella to fall into societal norms, Remy's character is intent on ignoring societal rules and norms. How are the two characters different? What role does Remy play in healing both Izabella and Zorrie?

13. Why does Remy become so entwined in Zorrie and Izabella's life? How do the different members of the O'Malley family respond to Zorrie and Izabella returning to Tillings Island? How do the vastly different reactions represent the human experience of loss and grief?

14. Both of Izabella's parents impart aspects of their philosophies about life to her, and both visions of the world become equally important in her recovery. What does each parent give Izabella and how does it become integral to her survival?

15. Competing images of light and darkness are used symbolically throughout the story. What do they represent in the struggle for Izabella to reclaim and make sense of what has happened? One of the issues central to her struggle is weighing what is real against what is fiction, from religion to perception. How does she resolve this?

16. Izabella says she first came to know what it meant to be God standing in the waters of Potter's Creek. What do you think she means by this and how does it become a critical framework for the story?

17. Although the impetus of the story revolves around Ansel Haywood's disappearance, the author has included repeating images and references to the Divine Feminine in Yemaya, the moon, the Virgin Mary, and Venus. Why does this become inherently important to the story?

18. In ancient times, the moon was the sign of the "Triple Goddess," representing maiden, mother, and crone. How is this interpretation realized in the text?

19. The salmon in Potter's Creek becomes an important symbol for Izabella's story. How does it foreshadow what is to come in the story?

20. In many ways, each of the characters has a separate understanding and interpretation of the past. How does this speak to the idea of stories defining our realities?

21. Does Izabella become the healed or the healer in the story?

22. Why might the author have chosen a stone to represent the process of carrying secrets? How does this come to represent both the interconnectivity and independence of our own existence and reality? ⌒

# The Story Behind the Story

WITHOUT A DOUBT the most common question I am asked when I write anything is, "What is the story about?" It seems like a simple question, but it is not. How do you compress a group of complex characters and situations down to a four- or five-sentence answer? *What the Waves Know* is a story about voice, and silence. Memory, and the lack of it. Destruction, and creation. Mistakes, and redemption. It is all of those things, but the soul of the story is about stories themselves, those that are real and the ones we tell ourselves—both individually and collectively.

We are storytellers, all of us, and that fact begs the question of whose story gets to dominate the narrative. The stories we pass forward and the ones we turn away from rest at the heart of every conflict, from families to entire societies—they also rest at the center of every resolution. We live by them and die for them. They cause pain and they heal. So, to me, it is no small wonder that a storyteller walking around with the truth in her pocket may be frightened by her own voice, by the transformative power of her tale. I believe Iz is correct: we are all just the caboodle of stories we leave behind. They shape us, and those around us, with enduring persistence.

I grew up deep in the northern woods of upstate New York, the daughter of a mother devoted to helping children find their own voices and a father who is a lot like Ansel Haywood. He did not wrestle with mental illness, but he saw magic in every corner of the world, despite the fact that he was a criminal defense attorney who spent his days surrounded by the utter destruction of the human spirit. It is a fact that I continue to live in awe of and strive toward. When I was a child, my father would stumble into our bedroom and wake my sister and me in the middle of the night to go on snipe hunts. The snipe, if you were not fortunate enough to be raised among them, is a real bird with a fictional narrative. The legend dictates that the snipe comes out by the light of a full moon. To catch a snipe, you must trek into the woods armed with your pillowcase and a shaker of salt. The process goes something like this: you sneak up behind the fat little bird, shake salt on its wings, and toss the pillowcase over it. *Voilà!*

As an adult, I moved to rural Rhode Island and somehow the topic of snipes arose with our neighbor. "So," I asked her, "snipes are indigenous here? Have you ever gone snipe hunting?" At which point, she tipped her head at me curiously and fell to the ground laughing. When she had worn herself out, she gazed up at me and said, "You do know that isn't real, don't you?" *No,* I thought, poking my father's number into the phone while wondering what other fictions about the world I was wandering through life with.

That is the power of stories. We all struggle to tell our own, and writers spend a great deal of time agonizing over getting it just right in neurotic fits of wording, organization, elimination, and posturing, but there is also a great deal of surrendering to the story in ways that I imagine are a hair's width from true mental illness. During a graduate seminar, I once had a classmate ask how I developed diametrically different voices in a work. "I hear them in my mind," I told him with complete honesty, and other heads around the table nodded earnestly in agreement.

As an adult, I have watched several people I love wrestle with the voices in their heads—voices bigger and stronger than their own. It is often painful for everyone living through the experience. But as is so often the case, there is also an inherent beauty in that destruction—the yin and yang, the counterbalance. The wind is meant for flying into, the moon is meant for dancing with. In a world filled with stark realities, there is true exquisiteness in seeing things in a different way. We may not always believe in magic and mysticism, but we all have moments when we yearn to believe. I am a writer, and a dreamer, and a perpetual seeker of magic, so I am always mesmerized by moments when the story wrestles reality to the ground. But not all stories get told.

When I first completed my undergraduate degree I worked with young adults diagnosed with autism, a condition that inherently silences the people struggling with it in a multitude of ways. There were several young people whose diagnosis was questionable, and one who was a victim of trauma and had stopped speaking directly following the event. That was years ago, and I still wonder. We can be scared silent by the world. It has happened to all of us, and certainly we all have heard our own voice say things we ache to recall and erase. Words are powerful things that breathe their own life once they are born into the universe, so I can imagine a situation where a person decides to lay down that authority.

Several years ago, when I decided to try to tell this story, I had someone say, "So, you want to write a story from the first-person point of view of a character who cannot speak. Good luck with that." While there is truth in that challenge, I cannot imagine a situation where a character would have more to say. We should all spend the time we are given finding our voice and teaching it to sing, because in the end those stories are our legacy and lesson to the world.  ◠

# A Conversation with Tamara Valentine

**Q: What the Waves Know** *takes place on an island. Does this have a specific symbolism within the story?*

**A:** The island of Tillings is fictional, although its mainland counterpart of Tuckertown is quite real, even though I have taken liberties with the actual population and setting. There is something poetic for me about Izabella, who is struggling to find her balance in a world beyond her control, coming of age on a small swath of land surrounded by the shifting power of the ocean. And there is also the fixed reality of an island, which demands that people deal with one another since there really is nowhere to escape the realities around you.

**Q:** *You draw on, and incorporate, deities and mythology from multiple cultures in the story. Is there significance to the cultural references?*

**A:** The significance is less in the cultural reference than in the fact that each culture has a canon of stories through which they make sense of the world and craft a quasi-universal reality. Many of these myths and references overlap except in name, and yet we fight to the death to preserve our own as though everything we understand to be true is attached to them. And often it is. The references I chose to incorporate are powerful symbols of the forces that direct our lives, or throw the direction of our lives off kilter. Yemaya is a deity that captured my imagination, in particular, as she was one of the primary figures prayed to in Santeria when slaves were forced to abandon their own gods and pray to Christian saints. For me, it represents both the force of our own personal stories and a profound act of trying to steal the stories of others. In contrast, Ansel's stories are not derived from an existing canon, but become just as important to

Izabella's understanding of the world—and certainly, they represent the reality playing out in his own mind.

**Q:** *Mental illness becomes an inescapable reality in the story, but there is little discussion about it from Izabella's perspective. Why?*

**A:** Izabella's father is clearly wrestling with alter-realities and a host of fictions. That is true. But, we all carry fictions with us and I don't see Ansel's as being any more, or less, acceptable. Our society often reduces a person with mental illness down to a diagnosis, and we have seen much fear and stigmatization about mental illness in recent history, as though there is a singular face of schizophrenia or bipolar disorder, or any other mental illness. Among the most intense struggles for a person who loves someone with mental illness is the profound fear of having that person disappear into the illness. That is Izabella's deepest anxiety, that her father will leave her behind. She is faced with the constant decision to enter into his world, often at the risk of her own life, or make the horrific choice to let him slip away from her. It's an impossible dilemma. The other weight that she is forced to carry is the dread that she, too, might be the inheritor of the mental illness her father was ultimately struck down by. To realize that a thing is beyond your control, and that you may very well be standing in its path, is an intense position to find yourself in. At the end of the day, that is precisely what the waves know. The moon is moving the currents in the ocean, and there is not a single thing the sea can do to stop it.

**Q:** *Zorrie's character comes off a bit aloof and cold. Was that intentional?*

**A:** Although Zorrie and Izabella appear to be very different, they are actually very much alike. Izabella has withdrawn entirely inside herself in an attempt to protect her from something she fears will destroy her, and Zorrie has chilled the world out to protect herself. Even though neither character can see herself in the other, Grandma Jo does.

**Q:** *What role does Grandma Jo's character serve in the story?*

**A:** Grandma Jo is nearly devoid of anyone's story but her own, and that is intentional. Her character doesn't engage in religion, or mythology, or stigma except in the purest academic pursuit. She is intent on connecting with the moment unfolding around her at any given time and is fully self-directed and nonjudgmental. In many ways she is a true foil to both Zorrie and Izabella. Grandma Jo is also one of the manifestations of the "Triple Goddess" and a symbol of divine motherhood in her own right.

**Q:** *Remy talks to her dead mother and bakes pies with her ghost. Is she also mentally ill?*

**A:** No, Remy isn't mentally ill. Her character is unapologetically brash and gutsy, but she is also wearing the scars from the night her mother was killed ▶

## A Conversation with Tamara Valentine
### *(continued)*

and shares many of Izabella's fears about losing the parent she has left, as well as guilt about the accident. While Izabella has largely abdicated control over her life out of fear of doing harm, Remy has gone decidedly the other direction and taken control over everything and everyone. But both are motivated by the same fear of loss. ⌒

Discover great authors, exclusive offers, and more at hc.com.